Sign up for our newsletter to hear
about new and upcoming releases.

www.ylva-publishing.com

Other books by Georgette Kaplan

Ex-Wives of Dracula

Scissor Link Series:
Scissor Link
Face It

Face It

A *SCISSOR LINK* NOVEL

GEORGETTE KAPLAN

Prologue

2007

MICHELLE HARLOW WAS STRAIGHT. STRAIGHT, straight, straight. Elizabeth kept telling herself that because she wasn't sure Michelle remembered.

Elizabeth had been studying. Easy to do, since her roommate had disappeared to a party she'd insisted on calling a "social mixer." Probably part of Michelle's drive to make everything boring, which she'd been doing since they'd first met and Michelle had invited her to LinkedIn. It was amazing she didn't call her precious *Star Wars* movies "Star Police Actions."

Elizabeth liked being friends with Michelle, even if she'd never admit it. Despite being Daddy's little girl (she had a Disney princess bedspread. Who did that? If anyone was going to be sleeping on Princess Jasmine, Elizabeth would've thought it'd be herself), she never judged Elizabeth, not even in a hippie-drippie "your self-expression is so lovely" way. After Michelle overheard a phone call about Elizabeth leaving her strap-on in someone's apartment, all she asked was if Elizabeth used protection. *Yes, it's called fucking a woman.*

Elizabeth wondered if she scared Michelle a little bit. If that weren't the case, she'd have loved to share the details, since Michelle was clearly interested in a little bit more than whatever she got up to with her boyfriends. Instead, she listened to stories like how Richard took Michelle to a vineyard and they got to stomp grapes, and wasn't that fun? Or the time she'd caught Bill chatting with some girl while standing too close to her and she didn't know if she even *could* forgive him. Not that Elizabeth cared or anything.

It was just polite. Like smiling at a baby or feeding a stray dog. Even if Michelle was more like a stray deer…or a baby tiger. Something.

Elizabeth's convictions had been firmly in place until the moment Michelle had flounced in, buzzed enough to trip where the hall's tile floor became the dorm room's carpet and sober enough to catch herself on the bunk bed instead of taking a header.

Elizabeth had looked up from her Introduction to Psychology text to find Michelle staring at her with a downright predatory intensity. "We're watching a *Star Wars*."

Michelle loved *Star Wars*. Elizabeth didn't. At least not the prequels, which Michelle was on like she'd get a free good movie for watching them. Five minutes in, and even Natalie Portman couldn't trick Elizabeth into thinking it wouldn't be painful in an entirely bad, nonsexual way.

Elizabeth was assertive. She could've shoved Michelle away and gone to do her homework in the quad. It wasn't like she hadn't done it before. But apparently a two-drink minimum made Michelle all…cuddly. She'd dragged Elizabeth to the bottom bunk and collapsed on her lap, actually rubbing a few not-gender-neutral places as she got them both crammed into the same tiny IKEA bed.

Not that Elizabeth had a thing for straight girls. It was just nice to see Michelle unwind for once, though it obviously wasn't just the drinks that had pulled the stick out. Maybe she'd broken up with Richard? Wait, but hadn't they had a big fight that'd metastasized into some sort of break? She supposed they could've hooked back up again, then broken up for good. Like the reunion special after a show was canceled, proving the dead horse wasn't just faking.

Why did Elizabeth think that'd be so awesome when clearly it would just mean she'd have to pick Michelle up from wherever crazed sorority girls went to get over men who still wore their high school letterman jackets?

"So this is the last one?" Elizabeth asked, wary of future appointments with Jedi and Sith.

"Yup," Michelle replied. "The saga comes full circle."

"Good. I don't think I could take any more of these."

Michelle squinted at her. "Oh, Elizabeth—"

"I'm not saying it's wrong for you to like them. I'm just glad that it's done with. We've seen the whole thing. It's over."

"Yeah," Michelle agreed after a pause. "The Rise and Fall of Anakin Skywalker has been fully told."

"Uh-huh."

"I mean, it'd be great if they made more, but they're probably not going to."

"Great?" Elizabeth asked. "What would they even do? Make a sequel to *Return of the Jedi* where the Empire comes to power again, the Jedi are wiped out again, and they build a new Death Star?"

"Maybe they could make one between the trilogies. Filling in the gaps."

"Like what? How Darth Vader goes to the bathroom? Why the Starfighters are called X-wings if they don't have the Latin alphabet?"

"They're smart. They can come up with something."

"Chewbecca gets cancer. The Academy Award-winning story," Elizabeth suggested, and even Michelle wasn't too nerdy to have a sense of humor about that.

They settled down and watched the special effects. Elizabeth tried to be wowed by them, as hard as it was when she knew someone had just gotten a bunch of computers and had them go for a long time. It just didn't seem hard to her.

"Elizabeth?" Michelle asked, in a quiet voice. Mostly sober, as opposed to the chipper tone she'd had as she'd cursed America for not getting the subtleties of George Lucas's genius while trying to get the DVD out of a snap case.

"What?" Elizabeth had been ignoring the movie to look at Michelle's hair. It was tumbling all over Elizabeth's legs and chest, exploded there from the impact of Michelle dropping her torso in Elizabeth's lap. She had an inexplicable urge to touch that little river of gold that flowed from Michelle's scalp. Did straight girls do that, or was it too gay? Elizabeth was gay and she never touched anyone's hair.

Michelle's eyes narrowed like she was contemplating something. "You're a good friend. If you don't want to watch this, you can put on something else."

"It's fine," Elizabeth said. "Really."

"You're a very good friend."

Saints wouldn't have replayed that peculiarly emphasized "very" in their heads so much. That's why Elizabeth wasn't a saint.

She reached down and touched Michelle's hair, sinking her fingers in to feel Michelle's scalp. There was a warmth coming off Michelle's head, not feverish but subdued, and it persisted all the way down to the back of Michelle's neck. Elizabeth kept petting her hair, seeing if it got any hotter.

Christ, she was in love with a straight girl. She didn't know when it had happened, what final ingredient had caused the alchemical change that made their relationship so much more and at the same time so much less, if she had changed or Michelle had changed or if they'd just pressed up against each other too long not to click into place. Maybe it really was love at first sight. But then, in all the time Elizabeth had known her, Michelle still hadn't gone gay.

"You're lucky, you know that, Liz? You're actually an interesting person," Michelle pontificated. "Which most hot chicks aren't."

"Says the hot chick."

"I'm not hot, I just have good salesmanship," she demurred. "It's like one of those RPGs Shane plays. You put your…dice into perfect hair and tits that actually need a bra, there's not much left for personality. You have extra dice."

"Not very feminist of you," Elizabeth said gently.

"It is!" Michelle sat up, rubbing at her face. "It is, because men are the ones whose fault it is. You get a hot chick—it's not her fault she's hot—but instantly, every guy starts acting like she's funny and smart and everything she does is cute, so she never actually has to *become* interesting. And you're not like those girls."

"You're not like those girls either," Elizabeth said mollifyingly, rubbing Michelle's shoulder. "Or Bigfoot. Mothman…"

"I'm serious!" Michelle laid back down. "You probably know more women than me—aren't the hot ones all about make-up and clothes and guys, or girls? Y'know, even in your neck of the woods?"

"What I think," Elizabeth said, "is that everyone's *interesting* in some way. Just not to everyone else. I mean, some people are really into serial killers. Me, it's like, okay, I get it, you had a bad childhood, stop wearing people's faces… Right?"

"No wearing faces," Michelle agreed boozily. Then something sparked inside her and propelled her head backwards, to look up at Elizabeth. "Singers, now, singers totally prove my point. All singers do now is lip-sync and a little dance. No one writes their own music or anything. The moment people started spending two hundred dollars a seat to watch Britney Spears do karaoke, pop music *died*. And that's what my sister wants to be. She's in high school now, going out with all the boys, probably going to be married before me. Because if she shows *everyone* her belly button, her future husband is bound to see it..."

"Well, maybe you'll get lucky and someone will throw lightning bolts in her face." Elizabeth squinted at the screen. "Is that really what was up with the guy in the last one? I thought he was just really old. And not taking care of himself right."

Michelle stared straight ahead, coincidentally in the direction of the screen. "When I said your neck of the woods, I didn't mean about a literal woods."

"It's okay, I do own some flannel."

"Yeah, you're, like, a lesbian, right?"

That struck Elizabeth as a very odd thing to hear from a girl in your lap, whose hair you were petting, who you were watching *Star Wars* with. "Bisexual, actually."

Michelle got up, but it was just to plant her head more comfortably on Elizabeth's ribs. They were oriented in mostly the same direction now, lying on the bed parallel to the TV, so they had to turn their heads to see Ewan McGregor. Which Elizabeth wasn't doing, even if he had a beard.

"But you prefer women?" Michelle asked once they got settled. "Why?"

Elizabeth wondered how to phrase her response. Then she figured that Michelle was probably too drunk to care. "Easier to bum perfume off them."

Michelle laughed. She didn't normally laugh. She had a way of smiling and ducking her head. But she had a good laugh, even if she didn't get much practice. "But what do lesbians do, exactly?" Michelle blinked a few times like she'd lost her train of thought. "In bed, I mean? Not for social gatherings or..."

Apparently, that was the end of that sentence. "It's mostly just whatever feels good. Everyone's different. And everyone wants to experiment, too, so...it's not like a salon appointment," she answered, feeling a little awkward.

Michelle laughed again.

Elizabeth could get used to it.

"Elizabeth, you wanna feel my breasts?" She looked up with a zealous expression that made Elizabeth laugh, it was just so—and this was all so… It was like she was the one who'd been drinking.

"What kind of party did you go to?" Elizabeth asked.

Michelle looked upset now. "I just mean that if you wanted to, you could touch my breasts. God." She turned her head decisively to her left, watching the movie now.

"I'm…sorry," Elizabeth said reluctantly. She hated apologizing, even if it did come easy with Michelle. The woman was a kicked puppy, even if she had been underfoot. "Do you want me to touch your…" It sounded damn awkward repeating that. "Do you want me to touch you?"

Michelle shrugged. "You can if you want to."

Michelle was wearing layers, blue sleeves shooting out of her jacket's white fleece. The jacket sleeves were rolled up because Michelle had bought the thing on sale and the sleeves were too short for it. Elizabeth reached down and took her hands, balled up in the sheets that had splayed around their legs in all the maneuvering. Her fingertips massaged the backs of Michelle's hands until, naturally, organically, they relaxed. Elizabeth eased her hands down and joined them with Michelle's, thumbs sliding around Elizabeth's wrists to rub at her pulse points.

With their arms together, Elizabeth could lift Michelle with her barely noticing, hitch her up so Elizabeth could slide underneath and lower her back down so their faces were together, their cheeks rubbing as Michelle landed next to her on the pillow. "We don't just grope each other's breasts," Elizabeth said soothingly, her words soft since Michelle's ear was right there, begging to be bitten. "Us lesbians."

"Girl kissed me at the party," Michelle muttered. "Stuck her tongue down my throat. I kept thinking how nice it would've been if she hadn't tasted like Smirnoff Ice. I was walking and one of those campus carts asked me if I wanted a ride, and I thought I'd see you. I really wanted to see you." Michelle sighed longingly. She shifted, trying to get closer, and her hip banged against Elizabeth's lap, her crotch.

Elizabeth shuddered. It was a surprise how sensitive she was, how suddenly uncomfortable her tissue-thin panties and stiff jeans were. She wanted to be in something pretty, needed to be in something pretty to feel wanted, to be in control. But she could really enjoy being out of control.

Michelle seemed to echo her thoughts. She growled suddenly and flipped over, burying herself in Elizabeth. Elizabeth got a face full of hair as Michelle nipped at her neck, butterflying kisses from her shoulder to her ear. Only the thin straps of Elizabeth's tanktop stood in her way and Michelle pulled them aside, a gesture that sent ripples down Elizabeth's body until they centered on her cunt, wet and needful.

"You move fast..." Elizabeth exclaimed, breathless.

"No time like the present," Michelle moaned happily. Settling on top of Elizabeth, she linked their hands once more, pushing Elizabeth's up to the headboard. With a grin, she rubbed her thumbs across Elizabeth's wrists. Elizabeth dutifully moaned. Michelle smiled and leaned down to lick her way from the hollow of Elizabeth's throat to the point of her chin. "Still don't wanna touch my breasts?"

Elizabeth tried to answer, but Michelle was stronger than she looked—she held Elizabeth's hands just where they were. "No? Maybe if you saw them, you'd want to touch..." She swayed in to give Elizabeth a closer look, the zipper on her sweater jangling from its unacceptably high perch on Michelle's cleavage. Elizabeth reared up and bit down on it, letting Michelle's movements pull it down for her as she held the zipper in place.

Michelle was beautiful. Her breasts were perfect. Not too big, definitely not too small, and so perky it was like they had never even heard of gravity. Her nipples poked through the thin material of her top, demanding to be touched...pinched...twisted. Elizabeth actually felt her mouth water. *Please, God, let Michelle get off on that.*

"Turn off the TV," Michelle said, keeping those damned breasts just a little ways from Elizabeth's mouth where they needed to be. Her voice was lower and sultrier than Elizabeth had ever heard it.

"That's on my agenda," Elizabeth growled. She really had no wish to associate this memory with Jar-Jar in any way.

"Should *I* do it?" Michelle nodded toward the remote laying on the bunk-bed's ladder. Just that motion dipped her breasts a little closer, enough to make Elizabeth feel feverish.

"Turn. The TV. Off," she ordered.

Michelle complied happily, for a moment holding Elizabeth's wrists in only one hand. She was taken by surprise when Elizabeth didn't even wait for the screen to shrink to a dot to make her move. She wrapped her legs

7

around Michelle, snapping them shut like a steel trap, holding Michelle very still as she lifted her face to Michelle's cleavage.

"Oh!" Michelle said sharply, then, softer, "Oh…" as Elizabeth licked at the fabric over her nipple, giving her the barest hint of warmth and moisture. Her voice deepened, "Oh," as Elizabeth dotted the tip of her breast with small kisses, little more than invitations. She tried to shift over, but Elizabeth held her fast.

Michelle let go of Elizabeth's hands, buried her fists in Elizabeth's dark hair, and forced her lips elsewhere.

The moment she let go, Elizabeth rolled them over, off the bed, where they landed in a tangle of bedsheets and body parts and the pushed-up carpet Michelle had brought from home. Elizabeth laughed triumphantly as she mounted Michelle, pulling her tanktop aside, sinking her fingers into Michelle's incredible breasts and squeezing until Michelle cried out, from pain or pleasure or both.

"Lesbians…" Michelle gasped; Elizabeth couldn't blame her. She was rutting against her leg, clutching her breasts. "Lesbians use their tongues, right?"

Elizabeth paused, hair in front of her face, her knee poised at Michelle's wet center, her entire body vibrating like a plucked guitar string. "Yes."

"And fingers?" Michelle was out of breath. She had to swallow in air. "Not just…you know…rubber things?"

"Why?" Elizabeth asked, out of breath herself. "Would you like a rubber thing?"

"No." Michelle took a deep breath and said calmly, "I want your tongue."

A wide grin fixed, perhaps permanently, on Elizabeth's face.

The next time Elizabeth saw Michelle, it was in the quad, with students all around, tanning on the grass and taking advantage of one of the few places where free Wi-Fi didn't fall under the library's strict rules. She was on Richard's lap, laughing as he explained an old scar on his elbow to one of his football buddies.

Michelle spotted Elizabeth a second later and sped over to her as Elizabeth backed away. Elizabeth sat down a second before they collided, digging out her phone. Even as the LCD screen lit up, Michelle was sitting down on the bench beside her.

"Hey."

"Hey there," Elizabeth replied. She felt foolish. Useless.

"We're going to Buffalo Palace later. You want anything?"

"Huh?"

"Buffalo Palace," Michelle repeated. She really didn't have the face for duplicity. Everything came out perfectly sincere. "It's a new place on 122nd. All the guys are wild for it, but don't let that discourage you too much."

"What's Buffalo Palace have to do with last night?"

"What's last night have to do with right now?"

Elizabeth shut her eyes, trying to force down the blush rising to her cheeks. God, this was why she didn't date. Was everyone in the entire world so...frustrating? "You kissed me," she said, putting it simply.

"Yes, I know I did."

"I kissed you. I did *a lot* to you..."

"I know, I know...it happens a lot, really. A lot of people do that." Michelle squinted, like she was holding in whatever unknowable thoughts were contained behind her eyes. "They're just not all...like you..."

A doom-and-gloom thought hit Elizabeth. "What are you doing with Richard?" she asked, stricken.

"We're friends, Liz. Duh. Just because we broke up doesn't mean we hate each other all of a sudden."

"Friends like you and I are friends?"

"Of course not. I'm not friends with anyone like I'm friends with you." She took Elizabeth's hand. "You're my *best* friend."

Elizabeth wanted to rip her hand out of Michelle's. She wanted to pull away so hard that she took Michelle's arm off at the socket, like the default on some loan Michelle refused to pay.

She didn't, though. It felt too good, having Michelle's hand in hers.

Chapter 1

November, Present Day

JANET LACE SAT AT HER desk. Wendy Cedar sat *on* her desk, the tight pantyhose over her thighs straining as she crossed her legs under a crisp skirt. Sitting back in her office chair, idly eating from a container of chow mein, Janet managed to treat the sight of Wendy's thighs—and the woman attached to them—in an entirely blasé manner.

"I love the way you eat," Wendy said. She was leaning back, resting her hands almost on the edge of Janet's desk, and the position made her already short skirt ride up nearly to her panties. "Just...the way your lips open. I don't know how to explain it. It's like you *know* that whatever you put in your mouth is going to taste good and you're just determined to enjoy it."

"I sense a subtext to this conversation," Janet said, lips parting softly, chopsticks gently depositing a morsel of food inside her mouth, teeth working soundlessly behind wet lips.

"I can understand why you're hungry." Wendy toyed with the hem of her skirt, pinching one iota of the material and dragging it a little to the left, a little to the right, examining how it hung over her leg. "That was a long meeting. Were you thinking about eating the entire time? That must've been hard. Thinking about something and wanting something that whole time, but not being able to get it."

"You're really confusing me. I have *no* idea what you could be referring to. You're a closed book to me, Wendy. An enigma wrapped in a riddle that showed up on an episode of *Lost*."

"I'll give you a hint." Wendy teasingly jerked one side of her skirt up a little. She pinched the other side and pulled it upward as well, rising the skirt in fits and jerks until she'd pulled it over something long, black, and hard, protruding from her crotch with modest exuberance.

Janet gazed at it curiously, teasing Wendy right back by adjusting her glasses, knowing Wendy could read a world into the small gesture. "Did you have that on through the *entire* meeting, or did you put it on after?"

"Do I go big or go home? The whole damn time, Janet. It's great for the self-confidence. You could see why guys would think remaking anything from the eighties was a good idea."

Janet shrugged. "Takes balls."

"Actually, no, it's just the shaft. The balls cost extra."

Janet nodded. Then she took another bite of chow mein.

"Well?" Wendy asked.

"Well what?"

Wendy flattened her hands into two chopping implements, pointed squarely at her crotch. "*Well?*"

"Wendy, I'm eating."

"And I'm seducing you!"

"You can seduce me anytime. My food's warm now."

"*So am I,*" Wendy said sultrily, batting her eyelashes.

Janet had to admit, she was good at that. She wondered if Wendy had stolen some of her mascara.

Janet took another bite.

"Hand over the chow mein."

"You were the one who wanted me to relax my diet. Now we're back to me not eating glutens?" she teased.

"Give!"

Janet dutifully handed over the take-out carton, which Wendy stirred with the chopsticks. Then gave her strap-on a brisk tap, rocking it in front of Janet.

Janet gave it a long, hard look before glancing up at Wendy.

Wendy paused with a bite of chow mein halfway to her mouth.

Janet noted with a little satisfaction that her chopstick technique could use some work. She had one gripped in her fingers and was holding the other in her palm and just pinching the whole thing together in the chow mein to pull up whatever she could get—

"Do you like my strap-on, slave?" Wendy asked, interrupting Janet's mental note to send Wendy a Wikihow.

Janet's thighs clenched momentarily. It was almost frustrating, how Wendy could get her just by deepening her voice a little and looking her in the eye. As goofy and as silly as she could be, she could also be this—*goddess*. It was irritating as hell.

"It's beautiful, Mistress," Janet replied, meaning every word.

Wendy took a bite of chow mein. Janet stared at the dildo while she swallowed. "What do you want to do with it?"

Janet closed her eyes a moment. It felt like the air was going into her lungs hotter, scorching her throat and then coming out between her parted lips like liquid flame. "I want to kiss it. It's so big and beautiful and *yours*…"

"So kiss it."

Janet bent her head faithfully, turning to the side so Wendy could watch her lips as they parted, folded, forming a sucking seal on the head of the dildo, a quiet pucker as she kissed it, then pulled away, the contact just wet enough for her lips to pull at the silicone.

Wendy set the chow mein down and moved her free hand to rest almost affectionately on top of Janet's head. She pressed down.

Janet let herself be eased downward, her lips contacting the tip of the strap-on, closed but wet, smearing her own saliva around her mouth. "You're wet, mistress. I can smell you behind your cock…"

"*Open*," Wendy said, the slightest hint of force under her words. "Open your mouth."

Janet parted her lips slightly. She always resisted a little. Just to find out how much Wendy wanted it. It was petty, the kind of thing that would infuriate Janet if she was playing top, but she couldn't help it. The way Wendy reacted took her from cute all the way to… Janet didn't know what it was, but it was exactly her fetish.

Wendy pushed down again with a hint of firmness, and Janet obediently opened her mouth, feeling the dildo move between her teeth and across her tongue. Her throat, she knew now. Wendy wouldn't be satisfied until it was in her throat.

Just outside Janet's office, Elizabeth Smile sat at the secretarial desk, under strict orders that Janet and Wendy were not to be disturbed. She didn't know what they were doing, but she knew exactly what that meant.

12

She was watching cat videos on YouTube when Donnie Parsons made a break for the door, a binder clutched under his arm. *Project Old Spice*, as Elizabeth mentally referred to it.

"One moment please," she said to him, holding up a finger. The video continued playing out; the kitten fell behind the sofa. Elizabeth took off her headphones. "Yes?"

"Is Lace free?"

Elizabeth folded her hands together. "No, she's in a meeting."

The question had clearly been a formality. Donnie didn't seem to have a contingency plan for not going in. "This is important. It's the plans for our new system, a dual-roto—"

"Man, I just work here," Elizabeth interrupted.

His eyes narrowed. "It's important," he reiterated.

"So's her meeting. She's with the CEO's kid."

Donnie blinked. "The CEO?"

"Oh yeah. She's a majority shareholder. And she's letting Janet have it."

"She is?"

Elizabeth nodded. "She's had Janet bending over forward all morning."

"Bending over backwards."

"What?"

"The saying is 'bending over backwards.'"

Elizabeth inclined her head. "I bet you're right. If you'll just leave that with me, I'll get it to Janet as soon as she finishes."

Heaving a sigh, Donnie set the binder down on Elizabeth's desk. "It is urgent."

"Like I said, Janet will have it as soon as she's done being reamed out."

Wendy came out a few cat videos later, her brow sweaty, her hair a little messy, her clothes just finishing being straightened. She was quiet, but she had a way of walking that giggled, and she hummed with confidence as she leaned against Elizabeth's desk with a satisfied exhale.

"Don't look so smug," Elizabeth told her, reaching into the cooler in her filing cabinet and pulling out a Gatorade. "If I owned the company, I'd have sex on the desks, too."

Wendy took the Gatorade gratefully. "I don't own the company. Just one particular vice president."

Elizabeth rolled her eyes. "You need Jesus. Since I don't have that on me…" She picked up the binder and held it out. "Please don't spank anyone with this."

Wendy snatched it away from her and leafed through it. "Well now. I'll let Janet know."

"Again?" Elizabeth asked as Wendy started to turn the doorknob to Janet's office. "You're an animal."

"It was our lunch hour," Wendy said defensively. "And hey, are we still on for movie night?"

"Yes, yes, so by all means, get it out of your system before you have me over."

Owing to what Elizabeth could only think was Wendy's bad influence, Janet owned a home entertainment center that would've been the envy of any man-cave. Elizabeth almost felt bad about watching *Flight of the Phoenix* on it. Seemed like they should watch Ingmar Bergman or something.

"Babe, could you build an airplane out of another airplane?" Wendy asked Janet, sitting in her lap but otherwise keeping the private displays of affection to a minimum.

Elizabeth appreciated that.

"I absolutely could do that," Janet said, before demonstrating how a minimum wasn't zero.

"Dennis Quaid is really good in this," Elizabeth said. "But I haven't seen him in, like, any movies lately. It's too bad. He was great in *Innerspace*."

Wendy came up for air. "He's like a…not a poor man's Harrison Ford, but like not quite Harrison Ford. Like Harrison Ford has that certain something and Dennis Quaid has everything but the something, but he's still…"

Elizabeth nodded along. "The Zachary Quinto to Ford's Nimoy."

"Exactly."

Janet tightened the hand she had on Wendy's thigh. "I'm glad this is reminding you of ruggedly handsome character actors."

"Treat Williams!" Wendy cried. "Now *he's* a poor man's Harrison Ford."

"The Harrison Ford you would see in *Indiana Jones: The Series*," Elizabeth agreed.

"Yeah, on UPN."

"Syndicated on weekends."

"After *Charmed* or something."

"I liked *Charmed*."

Janet threw up her hands. "I would like to remind the jury that we watched *Moonlight* and it didn't provoke this much debate."

"We're calling *this* debate?" Wendy asked. She picked up one of the countless remotes that controlled the TV and its myriad of appliances and speakers, using this one to unerringly call up a music player and put on a light, airy Mediterranean beat. That done, she dropped the remote and stood, wiggling and swaying her hands in vague time to guitar strings being gently caressed.

"Actually," Elizabeth said, "my idea for *Indiana Jones and the Appropriation of Culture* would be that his long-lost brother shows up. Montana Jones. Maybe Nevada Jones."

"Let me guess," Janet said, "he's played by Dennis Quaid."

"Exactly."

Wendy was putting her hips into the music. "Is he an evil twin?"

"There are hints," Elizabeth said. "He's a bit of a rogue. You don't know which side he's on."

"So Indy can't trust him," Janet said.

"Exactly. But he wants to, 'cause it's his brother. But also there's a sibling rivalry thing."

"There is room on this floor for two dancers," Wendy said, "if you're done trying to fix *Kingdom of the Crystal Skull*."

"I didn't see it," Janet said. "The reviews were bad."

"You're a stronger woman than I," Elizabeth lamented.

"The name is trying too hard, though," Janet said. "He wouldn't have his own themed nickname. Wouldn't it make more sense for him to go by his normal name instead of a nickname, to show how different he is from Indy?"

"Yeah, that would be better," Wendy agreed. "But don't tell me you can't see Quaid in the role."

"He'd be good," Janet conceded. "As…John Jones."

"That's a comic book character," Elizabeth said. "Jack Jones?"

Janet clenched her fist loosely. "I hate it when heroes are named Jack; it's so uncreative."

"And John isn't?"

"John owns it, at least."

"What about Tom Jones?" Wendy suggested.

Both Elizabeth and Janet turned to look at her. "It's taken."

"By who?"

"Are you kidding me right now?"

"Janet," Wendy said seriously, extending her hand. "C'mon. Dance up on me."

Janet reluctantly got to her feet. "She's young," she said apologetically to Elizabeth.

"And what am I, Methuselah? If you don't dance with her, I just may. And who knows where that could end up?"

"We're not having a threesome," Janet said.

"Don't say that until your anniversary is coming up."

"I am very hard to shop for," Wendy admitted.

Janet went to her, letting Wendy teasingly brush up against her in invitation, then embraced Wendy, winding them around in a slow, loose circle. Wendy rested her chin on Janet's shoulder and sighed lovingly.

Elizabeth watched them, and she must've been doing it harder than she realized, because Janet looked up at her. "So Elizabeth, seeing anyone?"

"Always," Elizabeth replied, stretching out on the empty couch with her arms to either side and her feet up on the coffee table.

"A lot?"

"I do have two eyes."

"Oh!" Wendy realized. "Are you telling her about—"

"I was getting to it," Janet said.

"Getting to what?" Elizabeth asked suspiciously.

"Well, if you have any openings in your busy schedule," Janet said dryly, "we know a girl who would be just perfect for you…"

"Uh-huh. Is this like a relationship thing or are you pimping me out?"

"She got out of a pretty serious relationship about five months ago, she's ready to start dating again, she's been to dinner a few times but nothing's clicked…"

Wendy took over. "Why not see if you can find her click?"

"I'd rather you were pimping me out. The whole disgustingly-in-love thing, that's not for me."

"Oh, are we disgusting you?" Wendy asked, teasingly smacking her lips against Janet's cheek.

"Yes. You're so gay for each other it's making me homophobic. *Me*." Elizabeth stood. "I'm going to leave you to your dirty dancing. I have to go make passionate love to someone."

"Anyone in particular?" Wendy asked.

"What am I, psychic? The clubs aren't closed yet, and if I hurry—or if I don't—I can find some companionship for the night. Free-range, thank you very much."

"People really go to clubs in their thirties?" Wendy asked. "Janet, did you go to clubs in your thirties? That's crazy. We could've been like a weird college fling thing."

"I'm not *in* my thirties. I'm *thirty*," Elizabeth insisted. "There's a difference. And can the women who had a quickie on corporate property please not imply I'm too old for casual sex?"

"Not too old," Janet said quickly, breaking away from Wendy. "But as your twenties go on, it is somewhat natural to age out of the whole clubbing scene. You find someone, you make a serious go at it, maybe it works out, maybe it doesn't—if it doesn't, you try again..."

"If you had parents like mine, you'd know it's not that simple." Elizabeth shook her head. "No thanks. I plan on aging so well I'm still getting swiped-left-on at fifty."

Wendy shrugged. "Admittedly, it's not a bad plan."

"There, you see?" Elizabeth asked. "Out of the mouths of babes..."

"I think Janet's a babe, too," Wendy said.

"I'm outie," Elizabeth said.

"Go figure out if people still say 'I'm outie' in 2017!" Wendy called after her.

Wendy may have found most of the gay bars in town too loud, too physical, too obtuse, but Elizabeth loved the *life* of them. The music was always playing, people were always hooking up, dancing, talking so loud over the music that they had to shout. She loved how unapologetic it was. You stepped into a club like that and it was like no one was afraid.

She hadn't figured on how bad traffic would be and how long movie night would run—Wendy had successfully argued for them to watch both the original *and* the remake—so she went with a somewhat couture clubbing outfit. She'd removed her blouse and bra, put on her black leather jacket, and zipped it up over herself, but not so far that anyone couldn't tell what she was doing. It got her some appreciative looks, some modest interest, people intrigued enough to want to find out if she was a psycho or not. Her dancing did the rest.

Pretty soon, someone put out bait. A waiter stopped by with a vodka martini and directions to the table of who had sent it. Drink in hand, Elizabeth followed them.

The girl was beautiful. Not much on display, but a cute, studiously ripped blouse and riot grrrl skirt that were intriguing enough to promise more. A flannel jacket was wrapped around her waist. Black hair with a dyed lock of violet, a cutesy-goth skull tattooed over her collarbone, not twenty, not thirty, maybe twenty-five.

Elizabeth leaned against her table, toasting with the martini.

She said her name was Felicia. Felicia.

"Hi, Felicia, I'm Elizabeth. Just thought I'd let you know, we're going to be having sex tonight."

Elizabeth didn't have the connoisseur's love of the game, as she dubbed it, the fetish for painstaking seduction by degrees. The way she dressed, walked, talked—she knew she laid it all on the table. People had to either take her or leave her, and she was always impatient to know which was which.

Felicia's eyes widened with surprise, then shifted to amusement. She let out a charmed little giggle, and at that point, Elizabeth knew she wasn't going to be a liar.

"That's presumptuous," Felicia said, like someone laughing at a black joke while saying "that's so wrong." They just had to have an objection on the record.

"Well, then you're going to love this. I don't do relationships, and I'll probably be gone by the time you wake up."

Felicia twisted her own martini on the tabletop. "I'll try not to fall in love with you."

"I'll settle for perverse lust."

They talked, each taking the other's "Introduction to" course. Elizabeth paid attention, but the words weren't so important as the body language, Felicia picking up everything Elizabeth dropped. The way she watched as Elizabeth toyed with her olive on its toothpick, teasing biting into it before she finally did. Dipping the second olive into Felicia's drink and stirring it around. Watching the way Felicia drank after that, like she'd just come through a desert.

They talked more; they danced. There was no touching, then some touching, then one kiss, then more kisses. Elizabeth relished it, even if she knew she was asking a question that had been answered the moment Felicia laid eyes on her.

They went back to Felicia's apartment. Elizabeth remembered kissing her in the doorway, letting Felicia suck at her neck while she looked inside for any last-minute signs of crazy, then it was just a haze of pleasure, little moments standing out like jewels.

When she had her hand on Felicia's side and as her grip shifted with Felicia's heaving body, her thumb unexpectedly grazed the hardness of a rib in her soft belly.

The wicked little moment when an irritating strand of hair had fallen between their lips and Elizabeth had vexingly tugged at it before circling it back behind Felicia's ear and kissing her sorry.

The loose, downy ride of her fingers between Felicia's legs, all open and needing of her, then the pulse of Felicia clenching and knowing that she'd come—Felicia had come for her.

Then Elizabeth had guided her down to the mattress and surged up to straddle her face and Felicia had wound her hands over Elizabeth's hips, her buttocks, the small of her back, searching for a place to put them that was as perfect as her tongue in Elizabeth's cunt.

Elizabeth could tell she'd been wanting to do that since she'd bought the damn martini.

In the morning, Felicia woke up while Elizabeth was collecting her clothes. Freshly showered, Elizabeth wore her bra, her panties, and the warm water on her skin, and knew that to be such an overpowering combination that she struck a nice pose. "Did I wake you?" she asked, knowing she hadn't made a sound.

"You did a lot of things, but I hope you don't think I could've slept through any of them." Felicia sat up, noticing Elizabeth working herself into her pants. "Are you leaving?"

"Personal policy," Elizabeth explained. "I hate the whole 'hey, I slept over, now what, do we go again, do we get breakfast, do we hang out, do I have plans, do you have plans, do you wanna go bowling with me because it's league night?' So I always jet first thing in the morning. Nothing personal."

Felicia absorbed that a moment before laughing. "So I guess that officially makes me one of your conquests, then?"

"Don't worry about it." Elizabeth left the flaps over her panties unzipped as she rummaged for her top. She'd stuffed it into a pocket like a hanky, but it'd come out somewhere… "I'm like the British Empire. Everyone's been conquered by me at one point or another."

"The Empire has a sexier accent."

"You've got me there." Elizabeth began checking under the furniture. "I used your shower, by the way. You really have great shampoos. I only used a squirt, but I was wondering how come your skin was so soft and your hair had so much volume, all that girly stuff. I thought you bathed in Evian water or something. Turns out you just don't fuck around when it comes to body wash."

"Looking for this?" Felicia drew a thin top out from underneath her pillow. "You gagged me with it."

"You were very loud," Elizabeth said, coming over to take it.

Felicia didn't let go. "Thanks. For being so understanding."

"Understanding?" Elizabeth asked.

"Yeah. It's not like either of us were looking for the mother of our cat." Felicia let go of the shirt. "Besides, I have a girlfriend."

"Oh." Elizabeth danced between her jacket and her top to get both on. It worked about as well as it did at distracting herself. "That's some interesting pillow talk."

"It's not an exclusive relationship, obviously, but she wouldn't love it if some girl were texting me and hitting me up and everything. Much better to just have the stress relief and then get back to it, like any weekend thing."

"Yeah, yeah, exactly," Elizabeth agreed half-heartedly. With both her layers on, she fixed her hair. "So you and her, you're pretty serious?"

Felicia flopped down on her pillow. "God, yeah. Crazy serious. Pretty soon, we'll probably be trying the whole moving in together thing. She's getting her eggs frozen, so if you have any idea what *that* means—"

"Thankfully, no. Good that you have someone, I guess. On not just a daily basis, I mean."

"More like nightly." Felicia grinned. "Hey, do you know any good sales going on under the radar? Penn's birthday is coming up, so if something cute like those pumps is half off, I wanna know about it."

"These?" Elizabeth asked, looking down at her shoes.

"Yeah. Penn would look great in those."

"Her name is Penn?"

"Yes."

"First name?"

"What's wrong with that?"

"Nothing," Elizabeth said quickly. "Is it short for something?"

"No."

"Is she, like, Russian?"

"No."

"Okay, I'm just going to assume she's changed her name to avoid the Mob. Good luck with the shopping, and thank you for the lovely evening. I was terrific."

"You mean *I* was terrific?"

"Fishing for compliments?" Elizabeth asked. She backed toward the door with a smile she knew Felicia would find even more charming for how insolent it was. "You were great. We should do this again sometime, if you're still dating someone else. Next time, we can skip that whole confusing part where we want to have sex but I'm wearing pants."

The days had become short, overcast, shadows devouring all of the city that they could and touching all they couldn't. A cold snap had come in as well, driving rain from the gray skies. Just an insubstantial drizzle, which actually proved more annoying than the sleet it clearly wished to be. If Elizabeth were well and truly soaked, at least there'd be some consistency—it was the inconstant noncommittal that stung her.

Her phone rang and she ducked inside a bus shelter, the back advertising next year's summer blockbusters. Someone named "The Red Bee" glared dramatically at her and Elizabeth thought, *Oh, hell, they ran out of real superheroes to do.* She pulled her collar up to her cheeks, folded the hem of her coat over her legs, and when she looked at the screen of her phone it was like she couldn't figure out how that name and that face had gotten there. The phone rang and rang and almost went to voice-mail before she stopped trying to figure out how the past could dial her number. She answered.

"Elizabeth! Been a while!"

Michelle's voice was like light through parted clouds, the moon at mid-day. It was bright and friendly and full of cheer, like they were just their surfaces. The photos cheek to cheek, the texts with smiley faces, the hugs—Michelle's hand in hers, but she couldn't run her thumb along it, couldn't squeeze too tight, couldn't do anything or it would shatter.

She sounded like they had never been anything other than friends, but Elizabeth could remember the temperature of the skin under her bra and the taste of the sweat below her waist. It wasn't in Michelle's voice, not at all, but she could remember every detail. And that made the whole recollection feel stolen.

Which made Elizabeth feel guilty. "Michelle. Hi!" She cringed her way toward something to say and never got there. "Hi."

"I told you I might come to New York one of these days, remember? Well, a few dozen things all came together and I thought, maybe it's a sign from the universe, maybe I should just say to hell with it... Anyway, I'm coming in on the twelve o'clock flight."

"That's great!" Elizabeth enthused, although she couldn't quite specify *how.* "Need me to vouch for you so they let you in?"

"Not this time. Actually, I was just wondering if you could do me a big favor and pick me up? I'm probably going to spring for a rental car, but I just can't fuss with that now. You mind?"

"No, no, course not. In fact, I've had some plans fall through, so how about we make a day of it?" The lie felt like a tone-deaf note in a song that wasn't good to begin with, but Michelle forgave it.

"I'd love it! Just don't go to any trouble?"

"No trouble at all for a friend."

Michelle's voice was as sweet as unfamiliar candy on Halloween, the kind you got trick-or-treating, only once a year. "We're more than friends, Liz, we're sisters."

Chapter 2

ON THE RIDE OVER, THE shower stopped threatening and just came down, a pitter-patter of fattened droplets that egged the windshield before being swiped away. From the backseat, Elizabeth stared out the window, watching the hash that the watery splatter made out of the world as the wind massaged it across the glass. Everything was fuzzy, rising and falling along the streaks of the rain.

The one that got away. Didn't that used to have something to do with fishing? Really, Elizabeth felt more like some retired cop, too old for this shit, who was haunted by one unsolved case. A crate of evidence that should long since have fallen out of her purview, but that she still kept fastidiously arranged in some secret corner of herself, to be taken out and puzzled over when the night got too long and her mind got too comfortable.

What did Michelle feel for her after all this time, and in what possible world could anything come of it? Was there a world where she meant to Michelle what Michelle meant to her? And how could she get there, if the way hadn't already been blocked a hundred times over by her bullshit, Michelle's bullshit, other relationships, old foolishness, bad choices?

An unrequited love like that couldn't go bad, but after so long, it did sour. It could be more like an open wound sometimes. She'd been cut by the thought of them together and never been able to bandage it with reality. And so it just bled and bled. And like a cut on the inside of her mouth, a loose tooth, she couldn't stop tonguing it, no matter how it stung.

The rain stopped as they tucked into the airport, prowling the circulatory roadway that confused all invaders into submission. Her driver made three passes at the terminal, Elizabeth lowering her window to let in the drowsy din of the world after rainfall, the stop and go of traffic with pedestrians in badly choreographed dance, the smell of the rain and its taste of ozone. And the clouds finally parted and the sun came out and there was Michelle.

She had always been tall, always been slender—the years had hardly touched her, cocooned as she'd been in a good marriage, with a wealthy husband. She'd traded flats for heels, adopted a blonde-again hairstyle that suited a slightly narrower face—*a nosejob?* Elizabeth wondered. Couldn't be. For all her Irish pride, her face had trended toward the Nordic branch of her family tree: fine cheekbones, tiny nose, and a jaw that came to a petite point. Any freckles she'd once had must've given way like snow before ice.

The added height made her appear thinner, maybe more ephemeral, although that was countered by layers of fine clothing. A linen pantsuit, a glossy leather overcoat with frilly furred shoulders, a black-banded fedora with a razor of a brim, a ribbon of narrow scarf—they all wrapped around her like gauze. Her earrings even flashed like the sheen of some translucent shield around her. The ring on her finger was brighter even than the glow in her eyes.

They hugged, gave pleasantries back and forth, loaded luggage into the car's trunk, and then there was the jetlagged realization, as Michelle slammed the rear door shut, that she was looking at a shiny Lincoln badge.

"Oh my God, Elizabeth! You drive a town car?"

Elizabeth patted her arm. The touch was like a charge of static electricity, stinging and gratifying all at once. The hug, the pat—she never quite learned how warm Michelle was, and she kept chiding herself for wanting to know. "It's New York, hon. I don't *drive*. But my boss has a car service, and all the drivers are desperately in love with me, so they do me favors now and then."

Michelle gave her a square look. Looks like those always made Elizabeth worry that she knew—that she couldn't not *know*. "You big slut!"

"I slept with two of them," Elizabeth said defensively. "And they were both cute."

"The backseat's that big? This I have to see." Michelle came around to the driver's side.

Elizabeth forced herself to wait, to stay back until Michelle was settled before she climbed in after her.

The car whispered off, silent and smooth.

"You're one to talk," Elizabeth said. "You big gold digger. Don't tell me this is the first town car you've seen."

Michelle flexed her fist, as if testing the weight her wedding ring put on her fingers. "Hard to see the road from the kitchen. My husband, William, he has a very old-fashioned idea of marriage. Not only 'til death do you part,' but counting the seconds."

Part of Elizabeth refused to believe Michelle could make such a bad match. It tried to shout down the part that rejoiced at Michelle testing the resistance of her ring to moving up and down her finger. "He can't be all that bad—"

"No. Just bad for me." Michelle smiled and reached out, patting Elizabeth's shoulder, her touch warm, the ring cold. "I don't want to talk about it. It's private. Let's just—I know—let's go to Coney Island, like we used to. It hasn't sunk or anything, has it?"

"No, they voted against that."

"Good. That's excellent." Michelle shook her head. "Just like the good old days, huh? See what's still standing, make our way home on the Stillwell Avenue El."

Elizabeth smiled at the thought; the old cave had always struck her and Michelle as borderline depressing, but in a melancholy way fitting to ending a day in Wonderland. The rumbling train gave the perfect half-asleep haze to be picked up with, when they'd met their boyfriends for a car ride. Or, once, Elizabeth's girlfriend.

How were things supposed to stay the same from there?

"God." Elizabeth giggled; not too hysterical, she thought. "I don't even know if that…supervillain hideout is still standing!"

"One way to find out." Michelle hauled her phone from her pocket and Elizabeth had barely registered the threat of it before she was being pulled into half of a hug. "PS, selfie!"

She still didn't know how warm Michelle was, but she kept getting hints.

Being with Michelle felt like cheating on your diet, like one drink more than 'had enough,' like those hours awake snatched from the sleep you needed the day before something important. It was bad, but it was so good.

And at least Elizabeth remembered why she kept obsessing on every mile of the distance between her and Michelle.

Because it was worth knowing, by God.

For nostalgia's sake, Elizabeth had the driver let them off under the Brighton Street station, the El above casting circuit board patterns down out of the rails and ties. Elizabeth saw where Mrs. Stahl's had been, her knishes a reward for the long train ride there, the prospect making them hungry even if they'd eaten before riding—there was a pharmacy there now. She thought of pointing it out to Michelle, but she didn't.

"This is going to sound crazy," Michelle said as they walked south, through the brownstones that were jumbled every so often to a new community and now had Russians, with the next jumble looking to come up Central Asian; obi non and samsa joining borscht and blini. Of course, if Elizabeth was remembering her history, the borscht and blini had only gotten here in the seventies. Funny, how the things that were there when you were a kid seemed to be forever.

"I bet it's not," Elizabeth replied, passing a caged tree, autumn leaves flaring with color as they died. "Nothing you say could sound crazy if you tried. You make everything sound so reasonable."

Michelle briefly let a smile live before euthanizing it. "I will test that. These past few years, I've felt your presence—your energy, almost. Like you're with me, sometimes. Is that crazy?"

"Still not crazy," Elizabeth said. "We've known each other a long time. When you know someone a long time, they become a part of you."

"Mm," Michelle considered. "Maybe it's a psychic thing. I just felt you thinking of me, the way you can tell who's calling you before you pick up the phone."

"Oh, you have caller ID?"

Again, the smile and its half-life. "Have you been thinking of me?"

"I think about everything," Elizabeth demurred. "I take lots of baths."

She must've looked stricken enough for Michelle to be merciful, or twist the blade. Hard to tell sometimes. "Is that a personal question?" she asked.

They passed a group exchanging the throaty Klingon of Russian over chess. Elizabeth asked, "You think we should thank anyone here for electing Trump?"

Michelle was a drug that Elizabeth took every time she thought of her, every time she sucked at a memory like it was hard candy, every time she wondered what was lurking under those memories and what she had thoughtlessly painted over by never telling Michelle how she felt. And the drug only kicked in when she saw Michelle smile and didn't know how those lips could possibly have stopped kissing hers.

They passed the brownstones and the nursing homes and the old people who put themselves out in the sun while defending themselves against it, heavy clothes and umbrellas that wavered in the wind like party balloons. Stopped to eat at Cafe Tatiana, which sat on the Boardwalk and let the wind off the ocean get a clear shot at them. Michelle ordered what amounted to a very pretentious salad, while Elizabeth felt compelled to see what beef tongue tasted like.

The food arrived quickly and had that spice that only came from food served somewhere that seemed a little sketchy: paper plates, menus that weren't laminated, and napkins that were in plastic wrap instead of a dispenser. A waiter in a tuxedo slighty cheaper than that of a Chippendales dancer eyed them now and then, either to make sure they were eating or that they weren't stealing the napkins.

They were alone in the restaurant except for sets of domino players occupying the back tables, their moves sounding like an old-fashioned cash register, or a hip-hop song that never launched into verse.

"I was just thinking," Michelle said, a new smile just held in check by her moving lips, "that in the old days, you would've dared *me* to order beef tongue."

"What, and let you have it all to yourself?" Elizabeth took a bite. "I can't believe I'm at first base with a cow."

"Well, you did date Suzie Dinkins…"

"Hey, she was nice."

"Yeah, I'm a jerk."

Michelle looked out over the wood planks of the Boardwalk to the ocean, its blue sharpened by the cold until Elizabeth thought of the rime scent as the sea cutting all the way to them. Sunlight mixed like paint with the yellowing sand, making it an almost gray.

"I remember when you dared me to try Ukrainian borsht. *Ukrainian borsht*!"

"Sounds like the opposite of a porn name," Elizabeth commiserated, already smiling at the memory.

"I just wanted to get chicken noodles, because I knew I would like chicken noodles. You said no, this is Little Russia, we should try something—"

"A little Russian," Elizabeth recalled. "You liked it, too."

"I did! I ordered it ever since. Now look at me, I haven't had it in years..."

Elizabeth looked out to sea and watched the Polar Bear Club's diet suicide, daredevils plunging into the waves in swim trunks, seeing if the waters were cold enough to keep them. Elizabeth couldn't sympathize one bit, because she was feeling the exact opposite.

You know hypothermia feels warm, some scumbag voice inside her whispered.

"Of course, it's actually called Little Odessa," Elizabeth said, and let anything unpleasant in the conversation dissolve like salt into water.

Meal finished, check paid, and tip handed over, they walked the Riegelmann Boardwalk. Hurricane Sandy had delivered a finishing blow to the iconic wood, so the city had decided to let the future have its way. Concrete, plastic, and an insult of wood had replaced the famous planks. It looked less like the Boardwalk and more like a pattern of linoleum. Underneath, the "Hotel Underwood" where they'd changed clothes and fooled around with boys had been filled in, fenced off.

One step onto the new thing and Elizabeth could feel the difference. The old wood had had character. You got a literal spring in your step just walking on it. This new synthetic blend of low-fat, non-dairy, glucose-free Boardwalk was like walking through a foot of mud in comparison. Elizabeth and Michelle traded rueful chuckles as they tried to make the best of it, pretended their footsteps could ever sound the same as when they were long-legged girls in Keds.

"I guess I think about my youth more than you specifically," Elizabeth said, her voice going along with her footfalls and sounding tinny, unnatural. "What's still there, what's faded..."

"What has faded?" Michelle pressed.

"The things that aren't important."

"Me?" Oddly, Michelle was better able to smile now. It seemed like less of a distance for her lips to travel.

"Some of you," Elizabeth said noncommittally, wishing she could remember what Michelle had been to her and forget what she could've been.

"And is any of it coming back?"

"All of it." Elizabeth smiled slightly. "You never went home, when you could. You always came here, with me. I almost thought it was because of me."

Michelle squinted. "It was everything. It was you, it was the city."

"No, you just liked the city. Even then. You would've slept on the streets if they'd let you."

"It beat Ohio," Michelle said simply.

Out past the breakers, the workhorses of the sea went about their duties. Tankers, tugs, trawlers. Elizabeth remembered as a kid, she'd once sat on a bench and spent a whole hour watching a luxury liner sail out into the Atlantic. Lifestyles of the rich and famous. Now it seemed nobody was rich and everyone was famous.

In the shade of two monolithic condominiums that looked as if they'd been imported from the Soviet Union along with the immigrant population, they moved from Brighton Beach to Coney Island. There, the New York Aquarium waited for them where her parents had visited the burnt down Dreamland.

When Elizabeth first saw it, construction vehicles arranged like anti-feng-shui to the smoothly flowing lines of its buildings, she thought the whole place was being torn down. One more casualty in time's war on everything that didn't suck about the past. Then she realized the building they were hacking at in union slow-motion was being constructed, not demolished, and remembered that the place was having an exhibit added.

Not all bad, Smile. It's not all bad.

She and Michelle bought their tickets and went inside. They went through Glover's Reef and the Coral Triangle and the Great Lakes of Africa, with the lights down low and the water bright so it felt not like they were going from one fish tank to another, but like they were in a hall carved out of the sea.

Her memories of the fish had all run together, blurred with Animal Planet and the Discovery Channel, but she could still recall looking at Michelle and her wonder over all the different *kinds*. How impressed she was that it wasn't just the same species everywhere it was wet, but different ones in different parts of the ocean, different lakes, different rivers.

"Why are you staring at me?" Michelle asked, backlit by Brazil's Flooded Forests.

"Sorry." Elizabeth redirected her attention to the fish and their constant impromptu dance. "You just used to make the funniest faces, gawking at all the little fishies."

"I did?" Michelle looked at the aquarium, too, though she seemed more focused on her reflection in the glass. "I suppose I was a little obsessed. But…they're just fish."

"Yeah, not a lot of breakthroughs in the field recently." Elizabeth turned, leaning back against the railing and facing Michelle sidelong. "It's kinda funny. How we have these phases when we're young where something is our whole life, and then it just wears off. Now if I get interested in something, I'm actually into it. No more do-overs left, I guess."

Michelle drummed her hands on the railing. "Now I remember! You used to love volcanoes. Only thing we could agree on was those underwater volcanoes in Hawaii, with all the weird fish that lived around them—"

"Hydrothermal vents," Elizabeth remembered. "All those weird tube worms and the fish without eyes—or were those in caves?"

"I think caves."

"God, I barely remember any of that…" Elizabeth tightened one hand into a fist, palming it with her other hand repeatedly. "Three kinds of volcanoes. Shield volcano, which is just like a lava leak—that's the kind the guy hit with his plow. Then there's the cone volcano, which is just—"

"A volcano," Michelle supplied helpfully.

"And then there's the, uh, the Mount St. Helens one. All the pressure just builds up and builds up and then it blows all at once." Elizabeth's eyebrows wagged. She couldn't remember the name, but that'd been her favorite.

"We should've gone to a volcano museum," Michelle observed dryly.

"They don't have those in New York. Tectonics are more of a West Coast thing."

Michelle turned, leaning one side against the railing to face Elizabeth. "Well, since the only interest either of us has in fish is grilling them—"

"Which is frowned upon here."

"What do you say we move on?"

"Your wish is my command."

Out past the Wonder Wheel and Astroland, the Cyclone and the new Thunderbolt, none of them open, some of them dead. Steeplechase Pier waited for them, extending out for a thousand feet like it was trying to make an escape. They walked out over the crashing waves, safe from all but the mist that sprayed up to haze the air. Maybe Elizabeth was just tired from all the walking, but it seemed to pass some scent test for nostalgia. The fishermen trying their luck could've been there since her teens. The benches along the sides could've still been warm from her sitting down for a rest. The soulless plastic surgery of the Boardwalk to the east seemed to be holding off, letting the pier age gracefully. Or maybe she had just gotten used to it. You could get used to most anything.

They sat down on a bench and Elizabeth closed her eyes, feeling the wind off the ocean, the foam in the air, the smell of the sea. They could've been on the prow of a ship sailing for the horizon.

"Herring season," she said. "That's what this is. My dad used to fish all day while I ran up and down the Boardwalk. He'd probably get a social worker called on him these days. Not keeping me safe from all the rapists and terrorists and CHUDs…"

Elizabeth looked back toward land. The Parachute Jump stood watch, a towering array of steel that looked like a lighthouse's skeleton. It'd been closed even when she was a kid, though she'd heard a rumor that only adults were allowed to ride it. Now here she was, and it turned out no one could, not kid or big kid or grown-up.

"You know William Bridger, my husband?" Michelle was fiddling with her ring finger. She had on gloves, but Elizabeth guessed she could feel her ring through it. "I actually went after him, you know. Isn't that embarrassing? He loved these old, old bookstores, the ones you only see on Instagram—the one man in America without an Amazon account—so I asked to go with him. And we just browsed through the bookstore, talking and showing each other books and putting them in our little baskets. He got me this really nice hardcover of *One Thousand and One Nights*. Real expensive. That's how I knew it was a date. Our first date."

Elizabeth looked out at a herring gull, one of the few not huddled together for warmth, as it flew against the wind, gliding so steadily it was barely moving at all. "You're getting a divorce."

"Yeah," Michelle said. "How'd you know?"

"People don't sound that sad when they're talking about going out with their husband for the first time. Not if they're staying married."

"No," Michelle agreed.

Elizabeth had had so much planned. A walk past the Shorefront Jewish Geriatric Center, which had once been the Half-Moon Hotel—telling Michelle the story of how Abe Reyes, chief witness in the case against Murder Inc., had taken a header out the window in 1941, despite five of New York's Finest guarding him. Getting a pair of hot dogs from Nathan's Famous and seeing how much they cost now. Maybe sneak into the ruins of Childs' Restaurant, which had been a restaurant and then a candy factory and then nothing.

What are you trying to prove? she asked herself. A trip down memory lane was one thing, but she was pacing through it, back and forth, like she was measuring it for something. Bad mood or not, she had no call to make everything about their old relationship when it was so clearly about *this*.

"He's cheating on me." Michelle squinted as if she could see him doing it.

"He's crazy."

"Well, they're young and they dance and they have nice clothes. They're just not interesting." Michelle smiled, and Elizabeth could see why she hadn't before. It just looked like teeth—the grimace of a skull more than a curve of her lips. "So I guess he'd be crazy not to. How does it go? In an insane world, the insane man appears sane?"

"Well, you have a prenup, right? Some private eye with pictures of him in a motel?"

"I've got nothing, Liz. Nothing except you. Can we get out of here? It's cold. I wanna be somewhere warm."

"I know just the place."

Giving into the impossibility of continuing the hike, even in flats, they hailed a taxi and took it through the eyesore of Trump Village—the obnoxiousness of neon but in red-brick, though Elizabeth allowed that she was probably projecting. She watched to make sure the cabbie didn't take any shortcuts that would add a decimal place to the fare, but felt Michelle's eyes on her. They came to a stop at the Siren Lounge, close enough to the El for it to knock your hat off, and loud enough to make the El a whisper.

They approached the front door, Elizabeth surprised to find it closed instead of propped open and gushing out beats. She wasn't even able to check to see if it was locked before the owner, Mr. Diktovich, opened it up and told them it was closed. He had owned the place since before they could afford to eat there, and age had whitened his hair but not really changed his looks—he had always looked more hewn from wood than grown from an infant. He wore a baggy leather coat, leather holsters on his belt for every conceivable cargo right down to his keys, and a T-shirt that had faded so much it looked like it was something in a time-travel movie being erased from the continuum.

"C'mon, Mr. D, it's us! Lizzie and Mickey? You can't be closed, it's barely six o'clock."

"Six o'clock. Private function. We close early." Diktovich always spoke begrudgingly. He attended to everything as if it were a stubborn plumbing problem, even the club scene, which Elizabeth thought made the place tolerable. She'd dated enough club promoters to consider the very profession a warning sign in a relationship, like drinking before noon or pronouncing gif with a J.

"But we need to do some karaoke," Michelle pleaded. "*Need to!*"

"And I'm hungry," Elizabeth added with a small pout.

"I have leftover food to throw out. I was going to give it to the homeless, but if you want it…" Diktovich's words trailed off.

"Oh, yeah, definitely," Elizabeth answered.

The El came in overhead, dragging nails across a chalkboard as they ate. "I think I'd even like modern music better than that," Michelle said.

"What, you're telling me you don't like Maroon 5?" Elizabeth asked. "Philistine."

"Music was better when we were kids. It just was."

"'When we were kids?' You're thirty."

"Takes one to know one. Are there any other karaoke bars around here?"

"I'm shamed that you think I'm the kind of person that knows about more than one karaoke bar."

"All right then. We're doing guerrilla karaoke."

Michelle handed her take-out carton to Elizabeth, forcing her to look for somewhere to set it down where it'd be invulnerable to foot traffic. Michelle stood before her on the sidewalk.

"I will now," Michelle said, "perform every single word of Christina Aguilera's seminal 1999 hit, 'Genie in a Bottle.'"

"Wow, I had no idea it was eleven years old."

Michelle launched into the chorus like she was in an episode of Glee or something.

"Uh-uh, no fair starting with the chorus," Elizabeth interrupted her. "Also, you're embarrassing yourself."

"You live here, I'm embarrassing you," Michelle said in a quick aside, then kept going.

Elizabeth waited for some cop or someone to tell Michelle to knock it off; didn't you need a license to be a busker? The longer she waited, the harder it got not to think that this was the girl she'd fallen in love with ten years ago. And that it had been love.

Michelle sang in the shower. Not that Elizabeth was really listening to her. Wrong sense.

A gentle rain of water on bare flesh, pattering off the creamy skin it met to become a mist that was half-steam, half-aura. The roving cascade of the water down perfectly formed curves, catching the overhead light of the shower stall and reflecting it in a shining tattoo that pulled the eye in. Even the shower door was an erotic taboo, smeared with a glossy patina of condensation, one last layer between her and Michelle, penetrated only by the outline of Michelle's shapely body and her eyes, cool and receptive, with an underlying excitement, welcoming and daring Elizabeth to throw open the door that muted everything, the sound of the shower and the sight of Michelle and most especially her feel, and then, with it out of the way...

You are such a creeper, Smile, Elizabeth thought, trying to shake the image from her head. You'd think it'd be easy to do, since it was all in her imagination. Well, there *was* a very naked, very musical Michelle one room over, but that might as well have been a million miles away.

Who thinks about their friends naked? Creepers, that's who. You shouldn't think about anyone naked. Okay, that's unreasonable, but who thinks about someone they know naked? No one. You don't think about anyone you're even friends with on Facebook; you just think about Jessica Alba. Unless you meet Jessica Alba and get to know her and she asks to use your shower because she's staying in your apartment and it's New York just before Thanksgiving and even Jesus's manger has probably been auctioned off on Airbnb.

"You're thinking too much," Elizabeth told herself, pulling out her phone in the famed twenty-first-century answer to all existential dilemmas. "Next thing you know, I'll be turning into Wendy, asking someone to spank me—"

"What was that?" Michelle asked, coming out of the bathroom.

Elizabeth knew her fantasy life was getting too rich when she could do an imagine spot right through Michelle turning off the shower, drying herself, and dressing—even if she hadn't dressed much. A T-shirt. Panties. No bra. Not that Elizabeth noticed. That would be creepy. She just didn't *not* notice.

"Nothing!" Elizabeth said quickly.

"Because it sounded like you were asking someone to spank you." Michelle glanced at Elizabeth's phone. "Is there an app for that?"

"There *is*, but I'm not using it. And I'm just assuming it exists."

"Hey, no judging." Michelle sat down on the opposite side of the bed. Elizabeth could see her legs from the full, warm thighs that settled into the bedspread to the tapering sculptures that fell over the edge. "My husband wouldn't like it if he knew I was standing around in my panties with some strange guy."

"I'm not a guy," Elizabeth pointed out.

"You are an…interested party, though. Right?" Michelle opened her purse—she'd left it on the bed like some deliberate taunt—and took out a pocket comb to run through her hair.

"Well, I was straight, then I was gay, now I'm pan." Elizabeth winced. "Or, you know, a version of that that doesn't sound like I'm a Pokémon evolving or something."

"So you're bisexual, then."

"Pretty much," Elizabeth conceded. "But relax. I don't make passes at married women. Or married men. Fiancés in general…"

Michelle squinted at her. "Shouldn't you ask how married they are first?"

She was teasing. Elizabeth had the distinct, not comfortable but not unpleasant feeling of being teased. Flirted with. *Seduced.* But then, she'd had that feeling with Michelle before, and it hadn't panned out. "Panned out"—there was a phrase. Like panning for gold and only getting pyrite.

"How married are you?" Elizabeth asked.

"Just about as little as a woman can be with a ring on her finger." Michelle leaned across the bed to Elizabeth, resting her weight on an outstretched arm, her breasts falling against her tight shirt and her nipples denting the fabric, her hair wet and dark and curling like a crooking finger. "Does that matter to you? The ring on my finger?"

"Why should it matter to me if it doesn't matter to you?" Elizabeth asked. It was wrong; too-much-cotton-candy wrong, that oversweet taste that she knew would sicken her—but she could take being sick if it tasted this good first.

Michelle's voice dipped with her as she laid back, drowning in the mattress as it sucked her down into the covers an inch or so, like it was trying to digest her, squeeze her *under* the covers where she belonged, but she was caught between its teeth.

"I have a proposition for you," she said.

Elizabeth felt the muscles in her thighs twist and realized it was an urge to stand up, *not* to lie down beside Michelle, all panties and T-shirt and underneath—not to do what she'd just *done.* "I'm listening," she said, because she had been for what felt like her entire life.

Michelle turned onto her side, looming over Elizabeth, who was now flat on her back. "William's cheating on me. I can't prove it, but he is. We have a prenup. With a no-fault divorce, he gets half of everything, half of *my* everything. But if there's an incompatibility—something wrong from the get-go—then I can annul the marriage. He gets nothing."

Elizabeth was staring out the corner of her eye at Michelle, trying to think, which was easier when she just stared up at the ceiling. Michelle was in bed with her—why was that such a big deal? They were just lying there, for God's sake… "You mean if he were a bigamist or something."

36

"Yes. Or if there was a sexual incompatibility."

"Like he can only get it up if you dress like a sheep."

"Like he's a man...and I'm not into men."

Elizabeth raised her head. She looked at Michelle and watched the slow, sure smile on her face. "But you *are*... I mean, it's been a while since I checked, but you were leaning pretty hard the other direction."

"I'm not talking about reality; I'm talking about legality. Say now that William and I are separated, I start seeing another woman. We go on dates, we post things online, we move in together eventually. It's not like anyone's going to ask us to make a sex tape. It'd be just like we were roommates."

"And I'm the...beard?"

"You are out of the closet, if people still say that. If I go to one of my other friends, one of my straight friends, and ask her for this—and no one's single anymore, but even if someone was—well, it'd be far more convincing with you. You do get around, Elizabeth. I'm not judging, I'm just *saying*..."

Elizabeth sat up, hanging her head over her knees. Jesus, what was this? She put her head in her hands. What the hell *was this*? Some kinda fucked up monkey-paw wish?

"It would just be until the divorce goes through," Michelle said, putting a hand on Elizabeth's back. "Then we just wait a little while, we break up, and I give you ten percent of all that alimony I'm not paying. Plus, while we're living together, I could pay your rent. Get a few nice things around here to show you how much I appreciate—"

"Wait, just wait," Elizabeth insisted, part of her wanting to get up and pace—her legs were *throbbing*—but part of her wanting to stay there, connected to Michelle by that hand on her back. "So, what, you're just going to pretend to be a lesbian for the rest of your life? What happens when you meet some guy and—"

"Next year, my company's promoting me to their Bolivian division. I'll be down there for years. Assuming I meet someone—which I won't, because I'll be focusing on my career—who's going to care? What's William going to do, follow me to South America to make sure I'm only dating women? If I ever do come back, it'll be years from now, and he'll have moved on to bore some other woman to tears. Probably won't even remember me. I don't think he ever learned my middle name."

"This is insane," Elizabeth said, even with Michelle's hand on her back. "We're talking about—*you're* talking about pretending to be a lesbian. To get a good divorce settlement. People die for really being what you're going to pretend you are."

"I'll pay you twenty-five thousand dollars," Michelle said.

"I'll think about it."

Chapter 3

THE WINTER RAINS WERE TRYING again when she went to Wendy and Janet's, this time as sleet, putting down a snare drum beat along the roof and walls, jazzy and frisky, tingling along with Elizabeth. Her fingers were trembling as she buzzed Wendy and Janet, beating out a samba on the button. She tried to remind herself that this wasn't a real relationship—wasn't quite a real relationship—it was a mostly fake relationship with a real twenty-five thousand dollars, which was more than she'd gotten out of a lot of relationships.

Wendy picked up. "What the fuck do you want?" she demanded, practically barking through the speaker, and Elizabeth heard an almost subvocal squawk from further in the distance; she took it that was Janet. "Well, come on, they just—"

"It's me," Elizabeth said, already feeling herself coming to her senses, which was almost better than the infatuated euphoria of puzzling out her relationship with Michelle. Almost. "Is this a bad time?"

It took a moment for the line to open again, and then: "No, no," Wendy said, sounding rueful over her earlier rudeness. "Come on up."

When she went in, Wendy was wearing one of those pocketed white tees that came six for a dollar at Wal-Mart and a pair of frayed white denim shorts that cost two hundred dollars at Saks, guzzling from a blender bottle of filtered water and ice cubes.

The shower was running. That explained where Janet was.

"I've been thinking a lot about what you said," Wendy said, sprawling out on the couch in a way that made it impossible to drink more without spilling all over herself. She held the bottle out in a faintly ridiculous matter. "And I've come to a conclusion."

"Oh yeah?"

"Yeah." Wendy pressed the base of the blender bottle to her forehead, as if taking in its chill by osmosis. "If Indiana Jones is fighting Nazis, then Montana Jones can't be at all loyal to them."

Elizabeth saw her point. "Because they're Nazis."

"Yeah. It's like, you can choose between Harrison Ford and Nazis. Not really a hard choice."

"Depends if you're the American electorate or not."

Wendy shook the bottle at her. "Do you need something to cool off that hot take?"

"Personal question: is that dog collar a new look or…"

Wendy set the bottle down, almost spilling it, and quickly unlatched the collar.

"Thought so," Elizabeth said. "I probably should've called ahead."

"Probably. You big extrovert."

"I had a dog when I was a kid, and he *hated it* when I put my shoes on and he thought we were going for a walk, but really I was just going to Suzie Farrell's house…"

Elizabeth ducked as the collar flew overhead.

"Please be careful with that," Janet said as she came out of the bathroom, belting her robe. "It cost me fifty dollars. The workmanship isn't any less important just because it's invisible." She picked the collar up. "Real leather, you know."

Elizabeth balked. "You go on Etsy, you could find something just as good for ten bucks made out of pig fat, I guarantee you."

"I like to support local businesses."

"Nice to see someone looking out for the little guy running a sex shop."

"It was a transgender individual, actually, and they-singular offered a very confidently friendly customer service experience." Janet pulled the collar between her fingers. "It actually has Wendy's name very finely woven into the leather. Is that not worth a slight surcharge?"

Elizabeth shook her head. "You kinky types had *Fifty Shades of Grey* actually making people think you were cool and dangerous for about a hot minute, but you're really just nerds who are into black fashion accessories instead of Tolkien. Sad."

Janet tossed the collar—gently, underhanded—to Wendy. "What can we help you with, Elizabeth?"

"Well…" Elizabeth pointed at Janet. "Hey, you missed a spot."

"No, I did not. Please cease your tomfoolery and get on with what's bothering you."

"You'd make a great therapist."

"Well, I'm dating Wendy."

Wendy was checking out her name on the collar as if noticing it for the first time. "I think Janet would be one of those therapists who talks her patients into killing themselves so she can eat them. Like, evil, but kinda awesome still."

"While we're not on the subject," Elizabeth piped up, "sorry about… cock-blocking you? Clit-blocking you?"

"Cock-blocking is fairly appropriate," Janet said.

"Not touching that one."

"Neither did she," Wendy added quickly, snapping her fingers.

"Let me make it up to you," Elizabeth continued. "I'll order some delivery, pick up the bill."

"I'm not sure." Janet looked dolefully at the window. "It's coming down pretty hard. I hate to make anyone drive through that."

"I'll tip thirty percent," Elizabeth said.

"I'll kick in a fiver," Wendy added.

"And I'll see if we have any coupons," Janet acquiesced.

Wendy rolled her eyes. "Babe, she just said she was going to pay for it."

Janet was already getting up. "We still might as well use them. They're going to expire anyway."

"So they expire, woman!" Wendy called after her, but Janet was already in the kitchen, taking the lid off the coupon bowl.

"Why is it listening to this strikes me as more embarrassing than interrupting your coitus?" Elizabeth asked.

Elizabeth had laid out the whole situation by the time the Chinese got there, and hearing the buzzer gave them all time to ruminate on it, Elizabeth included. She was off in her own little world as Wendy collected the money.

"I just realized," she said, "we're three kinky gay women, one fresh out of the shower, and we're getting food delivered."

Janet saw where she was going with that. "We should've ordered a pizza with extra sausage."

"That's our problem. No respect for tradition." Wendy went to answer the door. "Hide the dog collar."

And as they ate, Elizabeth felt an acute pang, an almost tangible note of longing within her.

Wendy had thrown a flannel blanket over her lap, burritoing her legs in it to keep warm, while Janet had put on black Dior pants, a white D&G blouse, and a white Kmart sweater that was clearly Wendy's handiwork, but looked so fuzzily comfortable that Elizabeth wanted to pet it. And the two of them puddled together, play-fighting over the blanket, feeding each other—nothing overtly sexual, just a keen awareness of each other's bodies that was impossible to miss.

It reminded Elizabeth a bit of her own girls' nights in with Janet, just with a level of intimacy that was unsurprisingly greater. As close as they'd been, they'd never dated, never fallen into bed together. Janet had been married, and Elizabeth had rules about mixing business and pleasure, at least when it came to working on the same floor. No Garden of Eden was complete without one forbidden fruit, after all, and Elizabeth considered herself smarter than any given nudists.

It was almost enough to make her wish she had her own Wendy, or Janet, she supposed—someone to share a blanket with after the sex had been interrupted by a well-meaning but devastatingly sensual woman with a bad sense of timing. But the thing about relationships was that every single one before the current one had failed. Janet's marriage. Wendy's high school sweetheart. She hoped it would work out for them, but for her... well.

"So let me get this straight," Janet said.

"Like your girlfriend," Wendy interrupted.

Janet shot her a silencing look. "Your lost love—"

"She's not my lost love," Elizabeth interrupted, and was herself the recipient of a withering glare.

"Your...Michelle wants to fake being in a lesbian relationship with you for, frankly, unimportant reasons. You yourself want to fake *faking* being in a lesbian relationship with *her* so you can get some sort of closure on this Sapphic crush for her that you've nurtured since college."

Elizabeth was about to point out that that wasn't her *plan*, only somewhere along the line, she realized that asking them what she *should* do had turned into telling them what she *would* do. The change had been almost imperceptible.

"It's just that I've never done an actual relationship," Elizabeth said. "She's the only one I ever really wanted to have that with, and now I get a chance to see what that would be like without it being, you know, weird."

"Oh, I think you've managed to make it weird," Wendy said.

"Aren't you dating your employee while pretending to be her employee?"

"Weird can be good," Wendy amended. "But still—weird."

"And Wendy isn't pretending to be my employee. I can fire her if I want to," Janet stated calmly.

"Lace, I partway own the company," Wendy said.

"Try me," Janet replied.

Wendy focused on Elizabeth again. "It's not that weird. But doesn't this strike you as a little immoral? Scheming to void a prenup or whatever and helping a straight woman pass as a lesbian? That's like a black man helping a white guy put on blackface."

"But if the black man willingly put the blackface on him, wouldn't that make it okay?"

Wendy paused. "I…" She glanced at Janet. "Does it? We need to ask one of our black friends."

"We do not," Janet retorted. "And since when do you not like straight women pretending to be lesbians? That's every TV show you watch plus the porn."

"Name one!"

"*Velveteen—*"

"TV show!"

"*Xena: Warrior Princess.*"

Wendy laughed. "Lucy Lawless isn't straight!"

"She's married," Janet said.

"To a woman! Right?"

"No."

Wendy got her phone out.

43

Janet leaned forward to include Elizabeth in the conversation again. "It's fine to want a relationship. There was a long time after my wife left that I *didn't*, and then I wanted one. There's no rhyme or reason to it. But is this really how you want to start one? Even if it is with your 'lost love?'"

"I don't want a relationship," Elizabeth insisted. "I want Michelle. Just to pin down all this crazy neurosis bullshit I've had for the last ten years. And maybe, if it's something more…how else am I going to find out than by doing this?"

"You have found out," Janet said. "It didn't happen in college. Why is it going to happen now?"

"Because she just came into town sending every signal imaginable? What if she wants this too? What if this is her way of testing the water?"

"Oh my God!" Wendy exclaimed, and Elizabeth looked over at her, pissed, before seeing that she was staring slack-jawed at her phone.

"Okay?" Janet asked.

"I just need a sec…it's not even Kevin Sorbo. *That* I could understand…"

"She could be bi," Elizabeth pointed out.

"It's not the *saaaame.*"

"Why do people always say that?" Elizabeth asked. "What about liking men makes you worse at liking women?"

"Nothing," Janet said, "there's no reasonable adult who has a problem with—"

"Cooties," Wendy said, at roughly the same time. "Wait, no, what Jan said."

When Elizabeth got back to her own apartment, Michelle had already made herself at home, taking over one side of the closet and a drawer of the dresser. She'd already told Michelle about the cot that rolled out of the closet, and Michelle appeared to have changed the sheets and found a fresh pillow for it. "A couple sleeping on two beds in the same bedroom," Michelle said. "We can finally be like a fifties sitcom."

Right down to it being an act, Elizabeth thought.

Michelle seemed to sense her inner sarcasm. "That is, assuming you want to go for it…"

Elizabeth bit her lip. Suddenly, it was only down to one question: Could she go another ten years wondering what she and Michelle could've been like?

Even a hint had to be worth whatever it would cost her. "You want to go steady with me?" She smiled.

Michelle squealed and ran over to hug her. "Oh, thank God. Thank God for you, Liz. I'm just…so glad it's someone I can trust. There's no one else I'd rather have as my girlfriend."

Elizabeth felt herself blush. Already. *Stupid, stupid—* "So, ah, how's this work? I don't exactly read the society pages…"

"And I'm not a lesbian. But I think letting Facebook know is a good start."

She'd set her laptop up on an old writing desk Elizabeth used chiefly as an extra laundry basket, though the pile down in the footspace was gone. Now that she listened, Elizabeth heard the washer running. Having a significant other was paying off already.

Michelle sat down and logged in. "Oh, and here," she said, picking up a bag with the name of a fashionable, unpronounceable jeweler's name on it. "You got me a tennis bracelet."

She took it out of the box and showed Elizabeth, who had never quite figured out the 'tennis-y' quality of a diamond-studded bracelet. She didn't think she'd ever seen Serena Williams wear one. Still: "Wow, I have great taste."

Michelle put it on. "You got your phone? Take a picture of it, something about how you love spending money on me. That'll really piss William off. He *hates* spending money."

Elizabeth reached for her phone, remembered she'd plugged it into the charger on the end table as she came in, and went to fetch it. As she went, she heard Michelle typing, speaking aloud as she did. *Who does that? My fake girlfriend, that's who.*

"Dear Facebook, I've had my suspicions for a while, but it's finally official. Me and Lizzie have been dating. I know, right? Seems so weird that we haven't realized it all this time."

Elizabeth got her phone, automatically checking the messages as she carried it back to Michelle. In the interval, Michelle had posted and logged out. "Okay, gal pal, your turn."

Elizabeth sat down at the computer as Michelle backed up. She logged in, stared at the blank text field begging for her thoughts, went to her relationship status, and changed it to, "In A Relationship."

Really depressing how the 'widowed' option was just there, when you thought about it. You could go through a whole relationship just on that dropdown. Single, dating, engaged, married…then that. All in a tab on a profile page.

Jesus, I've been in a relationship for five seconds and I'm already Holden Caulfield.

"Short and simple," Michelle judged. "I like it. You might want to come up with something more elaborate over the weekend. Not pornographic or anything, just a bit more of an origin story. At least share my thing. Oh, and don't forget." She held out her braceleted wrist. Elizabeth photographed it and sent it on its way to Instagram: *I love treating my bae.*

Michelle smiled as her own phone jingled to let her know about Elizabeth's post. "Thanks for doing this, Elizabeth. You're the best friend a girl could ask for."

Then she began to take her clothes off.

"What're you doing?" Elizabeth asked.

"We have to make it look real, right? You 'catch me sleeping,' tangled in your sheets after a night of passion, take a few pictures…wait a few hours, then post them. Do lesbians not do that?"

"No, no—bikini waxing, that's what we don't do, as a rule."

"You're funny. I'll have to post about that." Michelle walked over to the bed. "Try to get my good side. Tomorrow night, I'll get you back."

Elizabeth made a solemn vow to herself. No matter what happened, she would not use the phrase 'friend zone' in *any* internal monologue.

Chapter 4

IT WAS FUNNY. A MONTH later, Elizabeth could look over her timeline and see the perfect life. There she and Michelle were, going shopping, dining out, taking in Broadway shows, always together, always happy, as cute a couple as Elizabeth had always thought they would be. It was the relationship she had never believed could really exist—and she wasn't in it.

Sure, Michelle was there when she came home from work with dinner on the stove. She was there when Elizabeth woke up in the morning, ready to eat breakfast with her. She was there to watch a movie or loan a book or just listen when Elizabeth had anything to say (almost anything). But they went to sleep in separate beds.

It was totally fake and Elizabeth still loved it, loved having a friend who was always there, loved being part of a family, loved being one half of a whole. Except what if she would love it more if *they* were more?

Still, it made a fucking pretty timeline.

Elizabeth took the subway home from work one evening, walking the three blocks to her apartment huddled in on herself against the piles of grimy snow that bordered the streets and sidewalks like scoops of ice cream from a dirty spoon. When she came up, Michelle greeted her as always. "Welcome back." If there was company over, she'd have kissed Elizabeth on the cheek. There wasn't.

There *was* a cookie cake the size of a Chinese checkers board on her table, the words 'Welcome to the family' written on it in frosting. A few pieces had been cut from it, giving it the maddening asymmetry of a jigsaw puzzle that was almost finished.

Michelle sat next to the cookie cake, the murder weapon in hand. The last time Elizabeth had seen her, Michelle had been doing a throwback look to her college years, mid-length hair covering the nape of her neck in a sensible, irresistible curtain. Now there was just a dark stubble crowning her cranium, fuzzing the pale skin of her scalp.

"Have you done something with your hair?"

Michelle compulsively ran her hand over her shorn scalp. "We are doing a lesbian thing, remember?"

"Yeah, lesbian, not Captain Picard."

"Well, I'm sorry to tell you this, but girl-girl kissing hasn't been acceptable proof that someone's a lesbian in a long time. I decided to do a little method acting."

"You got a cat?"

Michelle scoffed and picked up another piece of cake. "So my sister says hi."

"Patsy?"

"Anne." Michelle squinted. "The Instagram model. She's Internet famous. Or maybe she's regular famous. Or maybe we're all famous, I don't know anymore."

Elizabeth sat down beside her and, more pressingly, the cookie cake. "Unless some long-overdue adoption papers have finally come through, this was directed at me, right?"

"I suppose," Michelle said, which Elizabeth took to mean 'help yourself.' "Liz, I think we have to take this relationship to the next level."

That distracted Elizabeth from a slice with a whole letter of frosting. "Do you want a fake corsage?"

"I'm serious, Elizabeth. I know we haven't talked about it, but I need you to come home with me for the holidays."

"Wait, I thought you and your family were—"

"Distant?"

"I was going to say normal, but same difference I suppose."

"It's like this," Michelle said. "You know how my dad is, right?"

"Caught 'hippie' in the seventies and never really shook it?"

"Exactly. So we don't really do Thanksgiving. The Indians and all that. But my little sister—"

"Anne?"

"Patsy," Michelle corrected. "Her birthday is on December 20th, and we do that whole year's worth of holidays stuffed into a week thing, remember?

Ever since the first of us moved out, we all go back home to Ohio for her birthday, stick it out a week until Christmas, then go home."

"Get it over with all at once," Elizabeth surmised. "How Irish."

"I was going to try and beg off attending this year, say I was going with *you* to visit *your family*, but my brother—"

"Grady?"

"Shane," Michelle corrected with a sigh. "Anne's worried about him, so *everyone's* worried about him, so we all get to be there to microscope him together. Probably drive him crazier than he already is. But it makes Anne feel important, and that is our Christmas tradition."

Elizabeth paused, both to absorb that and to see if Michelle's essay on the subject ran any longer. This was why she didn't do relationships. Relationships were with people; people had families. "Not to sound insensitive," she said, "but can't you just tell them I couldn't make it? If you're so worried about them sniffing us out, I mean."

"Oh no. That would give it away for sure. They *love* William. If I come off as anything less than Sappho the poet—"

"Good reference."

"Thanks; they tell him, he tells his lawyers, and that's my divorce settlement fucked."

"So you want me to get off from work last-minute to go to Ohio and spend a week with your magically delicious family pretending to be your girlfriend?"

"Yes."

"I want the rest of the cookie cake."

"Done."

"I mean, you can have some," Elizabeth amended. "I honestly expected you to haggle. This is worth a whole cookie cake to you?"

"It's from my sister." Michelle rolled her eyes. "Which means it's going to turn into shit."

"Well, when I'm done with it..." Elizabeth smiled apologetically. "Can you put your hands on your head and say, 'To me, my X-Men?'"

When they'd about ruined their bikini bodies—but who gave a shit, it was winter—Elizabeth boxed up the rest of the cake in Tupperware and took it to work to share with Wendy and Janet. A phrasing that really meant 'snitched at it throughout the day and gave it to them once she thought there might be an alien embryo stirring inside her.'

"Babe," Wendy said, "can you start fake-dating someone who makes us cookie cake? I won't be jealous. I understand that women have needs…"

"Michelle didn't make it," Elizabeth said before Janet could reply. "Her sister bought it for us."

"Even better," Wendy said. "Janet, start dating Michelle's sister. Let's cut out the middleman."

"Speaking of cutting," Elizabeth began.

"Oop, here comes my goth phase," Wendy said.

Elizabeth kicked at her. "Janet, would you mind terribly if I took off a couple weeks at the end of the month?"

"That does seem fairly traditional," Janet said. "Though not for you. You've always had quite the unfailing work ethic. Don't tell me you're spending Christmas with your new family."

"I feel abandoned," Wendy said.

"Christmas and her little sister's birthday," Elizabeth said, making Wendy clutch her heart.

"Of course you can have some time off," Janet said.

"Yeah, we wouldn't want to cock-block you," Wendy added. "Or…no-cock-block you. Or, wait, you're not actually having sex, so… I'm going cross-eyed."

"Wendy brings up an interesting point," Janet said with a nibble on her piece of cookie cake. "By accident."

Wendy picked a crumb off her piece and threw it at Janet.

Janet let it bounce off her head without complaint. "Not to pry, but I assume being a beard does make for something of a dry spell."

"Though it shouldn't," Wendy said. "I'm gay as fuck, but if a guy pretended to marry me, I would at least give him a handy."

"I can give myself a handy, thanks."

"It's the principle of the thing."

"In that case, you should know I'm not 'stepping out' on Michelle when we're still…complicated. We have gotten very close. She is taking me to meet her family. I don't want to ruin that with a one-night stand just as she gets comfortable with her feelings for me."

"So, pretty much no sex since November," Wendy surmised. "You're really nailing this relationship thing. Pound it!"

She held her fist out to Janet, who bumped it. And then said, "Why did I pound that?"

"Good impression of my prom date there," Wendy complimented.

December 19

There was a moment Elizabeth tried to catch every year. It was that first winter moment when the snow really started to come down. The flurry of it drew a veil over the city like the finishing touches of a painting, and quickly covered over everything with a forgiving layer of pure white that hid all the dirt and grime and left the city clean.

It didn't last. Nothing like that did. The snowplows came to clear and salt the streets, the pollution fought that stark white cleanliness until it was a soiled brown, and the awed hush that fell over everyone at the citywide act of alchemy became disgruntlement with the tons of snow disrupting traffic, jamming up city functions, and otherwise inconveniencing people with the natural order of things.

In Ohio, though, that moment stretched on into infinity. The snow turned the dowdy, unimpressive plains into one giant diamond to be crossed. The trees sparkled, bejeweled, and the rivers were veins of silver ore that had never been mined. It was the winter of everyone's childhood dreams: icicles and snowball fights and bobsleds and snowmen.

It was a ten-hour drive from New York City to Watson, Ohio, in scenic Madison County. They'd planned to save money on a hotel by making it all in one go, getting lunch halfway through. Otherwise, no breaks, no stops. They'd set out in the morning and planned to make it there without any night driving. They'd rented a car, a Prius for the sake of the elder Harlow's blood pressure. Michelle did the bulk of the driving, being more comfortable with it than Elizabeth, who spent most of the trip semiconscious, lulled to sleep by the highway. That and a running engine were better than a CD of ocean sounds.

When she woke up, she knew they had to be getting close, because they were passing a billboard that said, 'HELL IS REAL.'

She turned to check that Freddy Krueger wasn't driving or anything, and asked blearily, "Did that just say, 'Hell is real?'"

"Yeah," Michelle confirmed.

"How very unlike the opening to any horror movie ever."

"A horror movie would be interesting," Michelle said. "That precludes it taking place in Ohio."

"I wouldn't say they *have* to be interesting," Elizabeth yawned. "Remember all those PG-13 remakes of Japanese horror movies in the Aughts? Jesus. All those ghosts with long black hair and pale skin—who knew that what really terrified the Land of the Rising Sun was Goths?"

"They're actually a type of ghost in Japan. Onryō. Now one more time. *Mi familia,* go."

Elizabeth stretched as best she could in the confines of an environmentally responsible car, climaxing with a crack of her neck. "Okay, there's your dad, Barry, I remember him. Widower. Shane's the oldest, then you, then Anne, and, ahh…" She faltered, half-asleep brain not fully functional yet. "Your other brother?"

"G," Michelle hinted.

"Grant? Gino? Gilbert? Gulliver? Gilligan? Gilbert Grape? Galapagos?"

"Yeah, we named him after the island, because there were Millennials back then."

"Your dad was a hippie."

"Grady! I remember you being a better study in college."

That's what she remembered about college… "Patsy, she's the youngest. She wrote that essay that pissed you off about how slaves didn't build the Washington Monument."

"Bitch. She can't prove that. Anyway, you missed one."

"I did not! Anne, middle child, right between you and Grady."

"Actually, I was talking about the dog. Limey, bull terrier, and here's what you've got to remember—"

"The weird love-hate relationship you guys have with him because he's a British breed, even though you've gotten three bull terriers over the years?"

"No, he has this esophagus condition. He can't eat normally, he'll choke, has to be in the high chair so gravity does the heavy lifting."

Elizabeth snapped her fingers. "Oh, right! Anne posted about it. Most adorable medical condition ever."

"Uh-huh, so don't give him anything, no matter how much he begs, unless you put him in his chair first. He knows he's supposed to eat that way." Michelle's attention was momentarily diverted to her dash-mounted smartphone, advising her on a turn, then she snapped back to the conversation, seeing she still had Elizabeth's consciousness. "Anne posted about it?" she asked.

"Yeah, she's been posting about the old homestead. Did one of her make-up videos about how to pack light and still look good."

"So you're Facebook friends?"

"More of a follower," Elizabeth said. "It's not like we Skype or anything."

Michelle grunted, which Elizabeth didn't think she'd ever heard her do.

"She has liked a few of my tweets," Elizabeth added. "But I am very pithy. Last Wednesday, I tweeted 'Jesus is returning, but they couldn't get all of the original cast to come back.' Funny, right?"

Michelle's thoughts on the matter were concealed deep beneath a furrowed brow. "So you're cyber-stalking her?"

"No, she friended me when she figured out we were dating, I friended her back to be polite because she's *your* sister, so now we're… cyber acquaintances. We nod to each other from across the information superhighway."

"Okay," Michelle said, each syllable drawn out into being not okay. "Little weird."

"Not really?"

Michelle squinted at her. "A little."

Elizabeth held up her hands. "Okay. There's a modicum of weirdness. What's that have to do with the price of tea in China? I thought I was supposed to get her on our side."

"You're supposed to sell that we're in this relationship." Michelle looked away. "I don't care where she is."

Elizabeth laughed a little in disbelief. "Okay, *what*? Did she feed the dog without the high chair?"

"Nothing. It's nothing. You just should watch out for her. She's smart."

"I'm good with smart women."

"Not like this. Never mind. Forget I said anything. She's not even going to notice anything's wrong."

Elizabeth rested her head against the window and tried to be lulled back to sleep. Something was *wrong?*

"You want me to drive?"

"No," Michelle said, "we're almost there. Don't even need the GPS for this."

And she turned the tinny little voice off so they drove in silence.

The Harlow estate was sub-suburbia, where there was practically a forest between individual houses. Turning off a slowly sashaying road, they hit a cement driveway that led up a slow incline toward a two-car garage.

One garage port was occupied by Barry Harlow's Prius. Elizabeth was gratified to note that it was a different color from her own rental. The other appeared to be a mid-range man-cave, holding a stack of firewood, a tool chest, and probably a calendar that featured more blonde hair than clothing, if tradition were being followed.

In the driveway before the permanently shuttered port was a vintage Airstream trailer camper, the kind that looked like something between a pod from an alien movie, a part that fell off a B-52, and junk.

The house itself—linked to the garage by a covered glass porch—was a strong post-war American Craftsman design. Two stories high and turreted in one corner, with the doors to a cellar barely noticeable among the snow-clad lawn ornaments. The gently sloping roof was a backdrop for a seasonal life-size decoration of a sleigh drawn by eight reindeer and manned by an African-American Santa Claus set tastefully against the chimney. It was the kind of house that had a chimney.

A '93 Dodge Intrepid idled on the lawn. A woman was bent over, leaning in through the window, presumably at first base with the driver, unless public indecency charges were a lot looser here than in New York State. The woman wore a ski bunny outfit: tight white pants, tight white sweater with a pink vest to set off all the white. Elizabeth had to say—strictly as a connoisseur—that it took a hell of an ass not to suffer in pants that were skintight and had the approximate thickness of tap water. And this ass didn't suffer, even though the pants were tight enough that if the wearer had an iPhone in the back pocket, Elizabeth could see what apps she had on it.

Michelle slamming her car door brought Elizabeth back to reality. She might watch ESPN now and then, but not tonsil hockey.

"My sister," Michelle said sarcastically, leaning against the car with Elizabeth. "The only woman with a fetish for getting bikini waxes. You're lucky it's winter. She usually dresses like a total slut."

"Do you have any pictures?" Elizabeth asked.

Michelle struck her shoulder. "That's my sister!"

"She's not *my* sister."

"Michelle, is that you?" Barry Harlow was coming down the porch steps. He was a stout man, shrunken and dumpy, his Dublin accent the biggest thing about him. He wore a sweater vest over an argyle shirt, both stretched over a large gut. His thick glasses and a gray herringbone cap provided adornment to a bald head. Instantly, Elizabeth compared him to the last time she'd seen him. He'd changed about as much as a tree would. A little grayer, a little wider, but under the bark, everything was the same.

"Daddy!" Michelle clapped her hands and pulled Elizabeth along to meet him, going so fast that Elizabeth nearly collided with a densely lettered sign in the lawn before sidestepping it. Barry came down, shrugging his way into a pea coat, and grabbed Michelle in a bear hug that dwarfed her despite her height.

"Guess you got those muffins I sent," Michelle said, patting his belly. He huffed a laugh the size of Rhode Island, coughed a little as it settled, then followed Michelle's gesturing hand to Elizabeth. "And you remember Liz."

"Aye, I do. Been a time, hasn't it?"

Elizabeth nodded, feeling nervous despite herself. She bounced on her heels and heard the snow crunch under her shoes. "Very nice to see you again."

Barry nodded. "It is, it is. Not no way I would've ever expected, but I suppose I'm not a very perceptive man at the best of times. Well, you're as welcome here as ever, Lizzie."

"Thank you, sir."

"Barry. Barry, please. I wouldn't be comfortable with this 'sir' stuff if you were knee-high." He waggled a bulb of a finger at her. "An' before we go any further, I thought I should come right out and say it: I do love living here in Ohio, it's quite nice, but I cannot countenance this 'Cleveland

Indian' nonsense. Absolutely unacceptable in this day and age. I've signed a petition and all, but still. The wheels of change grind slow. Sorry if you hear a radio or a TV playing one of their blasted games. I can't do much to help it."

"That's okay," Elizabeth said. "I'm not an Indian."

"Native American," Barry corrected.

"First Nation," Michelle further corrected.

Before they could get down to which individual tribes Elizabeth was not a part of, a snowball hit her square in the side of her head, blanking out the sound from one ear and sending her staggering.

"Oh shit!" came a female voice, contralto, and as amused as it was repentant. As Elizabeth straightened, she heard the gavel-bangs of crunching snow that announced someone was running up to her. "Shit, sorry, I thought you were Michelle."

"Thanks a lot," Michelle said. "My girlfriend's here one minute and you're already committing, like, a really crappy hate crime."

Elizabeth thudded the side of her head, knocking some snow from her ear, and turned. "It's fine, Michelle. You must be Anne. I recognize the aim." Then she got a look at her. —

The Anne she remembered was a gawky, freckle-faced girl with braces and carrot-orange hair who'd prompted Elizabeth to read *Anne of Green Gables* just to torture her. The annoying little sister who was a rampage every time the clan had visited Michelle.

The Anne she saw now had the same upturned nose, the same freckles, the same flaming red hair as ever, a throwback to the Irish country lasses that were the target of all those lustful Celts on the covers of paperback romance novels. But Jesus God, had she grown into them. The nose was pierced, once, with a cute little ring on one nostril. The freckles were downplayed by a bronze tint to her skin, a healthy tan replacing that fishbelly pigment of her earlier years. The hair, Elizabeth could only attribute to alchemy. Some magic spell had taken it from Little Orphan Annie to shampoo commercial. She had to have traded her firstborn for it, and it was worth it, spooling out from under a white beanie that she wore like a crown.

Her body was—again, speaking as a connoisseur—*amazing*, perfectly filling the fashionable clothes Anne wore while still irresistibly teasing with what was hidden. A perfect balance between showing too much to be decent and too little to be interesting, erring on the side of too much. She reminded Elizabeth of one of those Playboy models from before they outlawed subtlety, where instead of blonde hair and silicone there was an almost wholesome picture of health, an innocent but knowing sexuality that teased and hinted even when naked. Though, of course, Elizabeth would have to see her naked to be sure...

"To be fair, I remember my sister having hair, so I thought it stood to reason that Mrs. Jason Statham would be someone else." Anne smiled, almost mockingly, as if she could sense Elizabeth's thoughts and immediately count herself unimpressed. "So, you're Michelle's college lesbian fling," she said. "Little late, aren't you?"

"Anne!" Barry started to chide, but Elizabeth was quicker on the draw.

"You're the ass sticking out of the beater that's still trying to shift into gear," she said, glancing over at the Dodge Charger that had not yet turned over. "You guys do evening shows?"

"It was more of a one-night-only thing. A few encores, but I didn't buy the T-shirt." Anne reached out to brush some snow from Elizabeth's hair. She registered Barry's discontented stare and grumbling throat-clearances, and said to him "It's cool, we teased each other way back, too."

"I thought I just took your lunch money," Elizabeth said.

"I loaned it to you. Still waiting for it back. *Wow*, is your hair nice?" Anne bit her glove, pulling her hand out of it to stroke Elizabeth's hair. "Yes, I love it. This feels like a fairy just combed it for you." She glanced at Michelle. "You feel this shit? I don't know if you're into hair-pulling, but you should be. This is like the mane of a unicorn or something."

"Should I start petting your hair, too?" Elizabeth asked. "Are we doing that?"

Anne bit her lip. "Ah, no, Dad's giving me the no-go sign. Listen, how about I make up to you for that heinous, but well-aimed, snowball shot with the nickel tour?"

"I remember," Elizabeth said. "Christmas 2006. You get to know a place pretty well when you're laid up with food poisoning."

"I thought I remembered you not having a lot of Christmas spirit. Well, it's been ten years. We've changed a lot in the field of nothing. C'mon, Lana del Ray." Not giving Elizabeth a choice, she linked arms with her. "Front door!" she announced, jazz handing at it like it was a prize on *The Price Is*

Right. "Knocker, in case there are any boob jokes you'd like to make later, tiny windows for the voyeurs, and that dent there where Shane rammed his head, God love 'im. Inside, pop quiz, three ways to go, which one's the basement?"

"Stairs on the left?"

"Congratulations on not having amnesia. That's the rec room, we've got a secondary bathroom, a couch that folds out in the finest Autobot tradition, and one of those TVs so old it actually has a third dimension. Doesn't get broadcast ever since they stopped broadcasting, but if you want to watch a VHS tape or look at your reflection, it's great. I suspect this is where you and Riddick have your reservations. Where is she, anyway?" Anne looked back out the door, until she saw that Michelle and Barry looking under the hood of the Prius. "Checking the engine, vintage Dad."

"He knows it's a rental, right?" Elizabeth asked.

"Oh, he knows. We also have the cellar down there, all the Y2K prep you could ever want, with none of the carpeting. We've also got the washer, the dryer, Grady's quarter-life crisis. You want it, we've got it. That's the only storage space we have. Now on your right, please don't cheat by moving your head, what've we got?"

Elizabeth closed her eyes as if searching her memory. "Vomitorium?"

"We had that taken out. Dad gave up on his dream. But there is a kitchen cleverly disguised as a hallway. Those cupboard-looking things on the sides? They're actually cupboards. That refrigerator? Not fake, real. That breakfast nook? Not a breakfast nook, but you can eat there. Just unofficially."

Elizabeth grinned despite herself. Anne had the same madcap energy she'd had as a beanstalk, just a bit more refined, the dial cranked down until it was actually kind of charming. She wouldn't want to do shots with her, though. She knew Anne's type. A little margarita and that dial would go all the way back up.

A series of high-pitched barks in physical form scrambled into the kitchen, nipping at Elizabeth's heels so ferociously that she took a few steps back and was very glad sandals were out of season.

"Limey, no! No!" Anne said firmly, chasing the dog off with a series of chiding finger-wags. "Don't eat houseguests, you know you have that stomach thing! Now, love interest, you've remembered the basement, you've seen the kitchen, but are you ready for...the dining room?" Anne led Elizabeth in, pointing dramatically at the scarred dining table that'd been gussied up with a tablecloth, the cabinet of fine china, and the picture window with a pastoral view of the woods behind the house. "The window's actually new; Dad had to replace it after someone threw a baseball through it. Yeah, me. That's still a secret. Under your hat with it." Exiting the dining room led them into a hallway, Anne pointed toward the front door. Where the basement stairs went down, another set of stairs went up. "Lightning round: go!"

"Attic?" Elizabeth guessed. She'd only been here once, after all.

Anne made a buzzer noise, which struck Elizabeth as an extraordinarily cute thing to do with her lips. "Sorry, Hans, wrong answer. That is actually the second-floor bedroom, but I can understand the confusion. Now would you like to try for double jeopardy, where the scores can really change?"

"Hit me."

Pointing her other hand the other way, Anne circled her forefinger in the air. "What is...at the other end of the hallway?"

"Barry's bedroom, the bathroom, and Michelle's bedroom."

"It's funny, because I had to share that room with Michelle, then Grady went to college and she got the upstairs bedroom, but I had to stay in that bedroom and share it with Patsy. I didn't even get to change bunks. So I had pretty much no privacy as a child. At all."

"I couldn't tell; you have a great sense of boundaries."

"Thanks," Anne said. "I never thought I'd meet another woman who'd heard my sister snore. If I find out you take baths with her, too, I'm gonna get jealous. Bonus round!" Anne turned on her heel. Behind her, on the other side of the hallway from the dining room, was the living room. "Who is this lovely lady, when she's not jetlagged?"

Patsy, the youngest Harlow, lay asleep on the couch in the living room, the TV playing something that was trying very hard to be a sitcom but was in fact a reality show. Patsy was a Berkeley student with a minor in Goth. She was petite, splitting the difference between her father's shortness and her mother's slenderness, with the black make-up and fine white skin only making her look more fragile.

"Hi, Patsy," Elizabeth said.

Patsy snored like a chainsaw running out of gas.

"And that's the tour," Anne said, stripping out of her vest and sweater. Underneath her first two layers, she had on a T-shirt with 'I wish these were brains' written across the cleavage. Elizabeth couldn't agree with the sentiment. "Suggested donation is five dollars; please, take a pamphlet."

Elizabeth looked over at the near wall, and the side-door that went outside. Almost all of the rest of the wall was taken up by a massive cupboard, with closed cabinets on the lower half and bookshelves above that. Elizabeth automatically looked them over. Mysteries, mostly. Old ones. She remembered Michelle's mother, Margaret, had collected first editions of the James Bond books, the printing of *Casino Royale* making it look like a pulp detective novel. There were also secondhand shop copies of Matt Helm, Philip Marlowe, Ellery Queen, Mike Hammer, Hercule Poirot, Lew Archer, Miss Marple…

They were almost all paperbacks, old ones, too, with slight damage and yellowing pages. She'd always found something comforting about old books, even if she wasn't hipster enough to deny the convenience of a Kindle. But an old book was like an old dog. You could trust it, in a way. All it wanted to do was curl up with you, lay its head on your lap.

There was also a shelf that was a bit more contemporary, devoted to those cheesy old bodice-rippers that Elizabeth hadn't been allowed to read as a kid, and so had voraciously devoured. She pried one from its dusty place, pulling *Come Love a Stranger* far enough back to see its Fabio-licious cover art and run her finger over the embossed purple title font.

"Wow," Elizabeth said. "And I was wondering what started that unfortunate habit of calling it a 'dewy femininity.'"

"Please tell me Michelle actually does. Wait, don't," Anne said. "Mom used to keep them in her bedroom, but Dad moved them out here. Needed to make room for a bunch of books about the Bush administration."

Seeing that Anne wasn't objecting, Elizabeth pulled the book loose and dusted it off. "Mind if I borrow this for a bit? I have this funny habit of always trying to read someone else's books when I'm staying over. Like I'll get to know them that way."

"Just so long as you don't think we're any of the V.C. Andrews books," Anne said.

Sliding the book into her pocket, Elizabeth looked around the room. "TV's new," she said, nodding to the modestly sized plasma that was now the living room's centerpiece.

"All the shows are old," Anne said. "He watches *Matlock* in HD."

Michelle came in and made her way to the window seat, where she flopped down to make a cushion angel. "Is Grady here?" she asked Barry, who was easing himself into an easy chair over in the far side of the room, the rental car apparently having passed its inspection. With its piano, chessboard, and window seat, it was almost a separate room from the TV zone.

"Since he moved back in," Barry answered. "He went somewhere."

"Specific. And Shane?"

Barry shook his head. "Not yet."

"He is coming, though, right?" Michelle persisted.

"Last I heard. But you know how he's been lately."

"I talked to him," Anne said. "He said he and T are coming."

"T?" Elizabeth asked.

"No thank you, I prefer coffee."

Elizabeth glared at her.

"Shane's friend," Anne explained. "They're driving over from Jersey together."

"Jersey? That's where Shane ended up?"

Anne shrugged. "We all gotta go somewhere."

"And you?"

"Boston." Anne smiled. "Go Sox. Sorry again about snow bukkake. No hard feelings?"

"Nah," Elizabeth said. "I'll just get you back sometime when you least expect it."

"Good! That'll never happen, so I'm cool with it."

Barry lit a fire in the large stone fireplace—another feature of the household that made Elizabeth pine a little and wish that she could chuck everything and just live out here with a bunch of dogs.

They all sat around the fire and ate popcorn with homemade caramel ladled over it. Barry cued up a show for them to watch, evincing negative skill with his own remote.

Patsy woke up, or came close to it, trading hugs with Michelle. She proved to be as quiet and naturally shy as Elizabeth remembered, despite becoming the Crow, but she was good company. Elizabeth was happy to single her out for small kindnesses like taking her empty bowl to the kitchen or asking if she wanted a refill.

The show Barry ended up choosing, *Bad Lawyer*, was one of those network shows that Elizabeth had never heard of, outside of all the Internet articles that were all some variation on "You won't believe what they did this time!" Elizabeth was never sure if that was good or bad.

As they watched, Michelle found her way to sitting down next to Elizabeth, then leaning her head on her shoulder.

Elizabeth knew it was nothing—the first thing most people would think of to show that two people were together. But she thought of Michelle calling her 'my girlfriend' after she took a snowball to the face and the long, comfortable silences of the car ride and it *felt* like so much more.

"We have all the episodes of this on the DVR," Anne explained. She was sprawled on the loveseat perpendicular to the couch, her feet aimed at the TV screen, a bowl of popcorn on her lap. "It's like owning the DVDs, but stupid."

"So," Elizabeth asked her, "is it Bad Lawyer as in incompetent or Bad Lawyer as in evil?"

"I think it's Bad Lawyer as in the nineties. Want some?" She held the bowl of popcorn up to Elizabeth's face.

"I'm good," Elizabeth said, pushing the bowl aside.

Michelle took her hand then, and it felt so much like something it wasn't. No matter how much Elizabeth kept telling herself *it wasn't*, it kept feeling that way. Watching some dumb lawyer show about dumb people having sex and being dumb, but while they were pretty. And she felt like she was on her honeymoon.

"Hey," Michelle said, rubbing her thumb along a vein on the back of Elizabeth's hand. "You wanna do the thing again tonight?"

"What thing?" Elizabeth asked.

Michelle's voice dipped to a hush, taking on a honeyed flavor as it lowered. "You *know*. The *thing*."

She gave Elizabeth a wink that would've been arousing except for how broad it was. Elizabeth felt like she was in the audience of a Broadway play. "Yeah," she said, not sure how far to drop her voice when Michelle was clearly trying to put on something of a show. "Sure."

Michelle persisted. "I know you *hate* repeating yourself, but just this once, an encore *would* be nice."

Elizabeth felt a bloom of heat through her chest. Despite herself, it was a little...entertaining to picture herself in that role, to try on those clothes even if they weren't hers. It was just a little too hard to forget that Michelle pronounced 'encore' the same sibilant way Anne had: soft on the first syllable, hard on the second. That struck her, for some reason—that she was not just pretending to date Michelle, but to fuck her. That they were not just implying that but outright suggesting it now. The vehemence of the act made it feel less like a fun prank and more like a lie.

Anne took a bite of popcorn. Elizabeth guessed she'd been trying to hold off crunching into it while eavesdropping on them.

The commercial break came up. Instead of hitting fast-forward, Barry muted it and leaned in Elizabeth's general direction. "You ever watch this show before?"

"No," Elizabeth replied. "I don't watch a lot of television."

"Well, how do you like it? All the unbelievable plot twists and unpredictable mysteries?"

"I certainly can't believe it," Elizabeth said politely.

"They have a lesbian couple, you know. They were the ones eating in the diner."

"Yeah," Patsy said. "Sat together and everything."

"He wants to know what you think," Anne said, throwing a kernel of popcorn up in the air and catching it in her teeth.

"Don't go thinking I'm quizzing here now," Barry said. "I just happen to think they do a pretty good job with them and was wondering if you concur."

"Ah." Elizabeth scratched her nose. "I don't really care that much. It doesn't seem like they have much chemistry. It's not bad, it's just—there."

"So you think it's offensive?"

"No, I'm not 'offended' or anything." Elizabeth inwardly sighed. The show had come back on, but he'd paused it rather than unmuting. "It's good that they're catering to me, or at least catering to people who complain about not catering to me, but honestly? Okay, the main guy, what's his name?"

"Terence Grinder," Anne said with relish at about the same time Michelle said, "Terry Grinder."

"Really?" Elizabeth asked. "Thought I hadn't heard that right. Okay, so his wife has been missing for seven years in Namibia, presumed dead, and he's now dating the daughter of the mob guy, who is engaged to the other mob guy to stop a mob war. It's this whole big thing. The lesbians, they're just eating in a diner. It seems a little prosaic."

"But Lucille Coldyron—"

"Oh my God," Elizabeth muttered.

"She just got kidnapped," Barry continued. "You want Lana or Eve to get kidnapped?"

"No, it's just..." Elizabeth brought her hands up to rub at her eyes. "Honestly, it's like they're just there to be there? Like someone figured they'd get more of an audience if they had lesbians, but they're not really having an impact on the plot or adding anything to the show besides lesbianism. It's like they're just this obligatory thing. But I don't know, most of the romances in these things strike me as obligatory, so you shouldn't listen to me."

"So you don't like romance," Anne said. "That's weird, coming from someone who keeps having candlelit dinners with my sister."

Sometimes, Elizabeth regretted that social media was ever invented. "Okay, not most romances, but a good fifty percent of movies, TV, whatever, it's like they're just there because someone said, 'you have to have a romance.' And not even in ways that make sense! Like, the hero's Will Smith, he's going to punch an earthquake or whatever. It can't just be that he's in a happy marriage and he kisses his wife good-bye in the morning and then at the end he comes home and she's happy that he's safe. No, it has to be either that he's just suddenly met a woman at the earthquake and they fall in love while all these people are dying. Or! Or he's estranged from his wife, but somehow the earthquake gets them back together. And that's supposed to appeal to me as a woman. It's so condescending."

Barry's hand was jogging in the air, as if patting down an overly friendly dog that had turned invisible. "Now, now, I'll give you that some of these romances are unbelievable, but that doesn't mean they shouldn't try."

"Yeah," Michelle said. "Someone isn't much of a lesbian character if she isn't in a lesbian relationship."

"She is if she's a lesbian," Elizabeth said. "I'll make you a bet. I bet in all of the movies where you really like the romance, it's there because the creator really wanted to put it in. And when you don't like the romance, it's probably because it wasn't even there in the first draft of the story, but some moneyman forced them to put it in because they think women are obsessed with romance."

"So you don't think the boys here really wanted to put a lesbian relationship in?" Barry said. "They were just forced to."

"I don't know—" Elizabeth started to say, but Anne interrupted.

"No, no, I see what she's getting at. It's like *Raiders of the Lost Ark*, I buy that Indy and Marion are in love. *Temple of Doom*, they have whatshertits—"

"Willie Scott," Barry said. "Not senile yet."

"Willie Scott." Anne nodded. "And she's just there so Indy has someone to kiss."

"Exactly," Elizabeth said. "It's not as good because they weren't really passionate about it. And that's the thing about *Bad Lawyer*. I'd love if people who were passionate about portraying a relationship were doing…lesbian *Casablanca*, or whatever they want to do, but I don't want *more* obligatory romances."

"Well, *I* think representation is important." Michelle squinted. "And anything that increases representation can't be all bad."

"You haven't watched many lesbian movies, have you?" Elizabeth asked.

"Wouldn't you know?" Anne asked. "What do you two watch on movie night?"

"Nature documentaries," Elizabeth said quickly. "Least amount of straight people."

"Not the kind of cougars I had you figured for," Anne replied.

"This TV's gonna get plasma burn-in if it stays paused much longer," Patsy interjected.

Anne shook her head ruefully. "I've told him a thousand times. He doesn't even turn it off half the time."

"So you would like to watch more of the show?" Barry asked, picking up the remote.

"I wouldn't go that far," Elizabeth muttered.

Headlights shone through the windows, playing over the darkened room as a car swung in close on the road. They held there, winding patterns on the walls out of the curtains the light passed through.

"That'll be Shane now," Barry said. "Must be having car trouble. Anne, go see if they need any help with the bags."

Elizabeth didn't count herself in that relief effort, not having started the unpacking process herself, but Michelle gave her a dirty look. "You're not going?"

"Should I be?"

"You're not watching the show."

So Elizabeth reluctantly committed to wrapping herself up in a coat and putting her galoshes on.

"I'd take your bet," Anne said, meticulously reconstructing her winter ensemble.

"I bet a lot. It's an addiction. Specifics?"

"That all the movies with good romances have them because they wanted a romance and all the ones with bad romances had them because it was in the fine print or whatever. I bet there were a lot of people who were really passionate about delivering an epic, soul-stirring romance and they just sucked at it."

"So you're the one who wants every movie to have a romance in it," Elizabeth said as they went from the living room to the hallway to the dining room to the kitchen to the porch. "How does it feel to control all of Hollywood?"

"Not all of it. The guys who did *Platoon* didn't listen to me. I think they really missed out."

Outside, the sun had fully set and the moon had come out, turning the snow a kind of blue that seemed to hum faintly. Elizabeth was surprised by how cold it was. She saw a car circling around, boxy as the old Ford it probably was, and as it rounded the curb and started up the drive, a set of asses slapped against the windows. Not good asses, either, by Elizabeth's reckoning. Asses that could only be improved by hemorrhoids.

"McQuarries!" Anne shouted, and was off like a bolt. She ran out into the yard, stooping to grab a rock from the gravel abutting the driveway. The Ford sped up, making a fast turn as it peeled off and side-swiped the sign posted on the curb. As it roared into the night, Anne let fly with the rock, hitting one of its glowing red taillights. The red flickered and went out, leaving the taillights one baleful eye staring back at them as the Ford drove off.

Elizabeth jumped down from the porch. Anne stood by the fallen sign, dialing on her smartphone. Three numbers. "Hello, police? Yes, I'm on 514 Mary Lane. A car just passed our house driving very erratically. One of the taillights was out, you can't miss it. Okay, thanks."

Elizabeth considerately waited for her to hang up before asking, "What the hell was that all about?"

"It's called civic duty, Elizabeth." Anne saw the sign that had been knocked over, sighed, and picked it up to try to peg it back into place. Elizabeth could only see faintly by the moonlight, but now she recognized it as one of those signs that seemed designed to advertise hashtags: Black Lives Matter, Science Is Real, Love Is Love, Black Girl Magic Is Real...

"You know, I never did figure out what Black Girl Magic is," Elizabeth said as she knelt down to help Anne dig out a new hole to post the sign in. The snow cleared away easily, but the ground was hard.

Anne handed Elizabeth the sign, then took out a pocket knife to tenderize the soil. *Yeesh*, Elizabeth thought.

"Actually, Penn & Teller did a special on it. Turns out it's all done with smoke and mirrors," Anne said.

Elizabeth smirked. "Not a big believer in love, science, and black people?"

Anne rolled her eyes. "The sign just seems a bit much. Common decency as bragging rights. Whatever happened to humility?"

"The woman in the three-hundred-dollar leather boots complains that not enough people are humble?"

Anne met her eyes, grinding the point of the knife into the ground like a pestle into a mortar. "Four hundred dollars."

"Nordstrom?"

"Stuart Weitzman. Don't hate the playa, et cetera et cetera..." She pulled back the knife, wiping it in the snow before retracting the blade, and Elizabeth was able to slide the signpost nicely into the hole she'd dug. Anne shored it up with loose dirt and snow.

"So really, what's with the 'McQuarries?'" Elizabeth asked, imitating Anne with wide eyes and an overly dramatic voice.

Anne shrugged. "They killed our mom. C'mon. Fire's getting lonely."

"That's very poetic," a man said.

"Jesus!" Elizabeth cried, and as she tried to stand up, her feet slid out from under her and she did a nine-point landing with her ass.

Anne, of course, laughed.

"Did I spook you?" the man asked.

Elizabeth realized who he must be now, that sullen, leaden voice, a big guy with the stoutness of his father and a pudgy belly under an untucked shirt and down jacket. He had one of those beards for just his chin that men seemed to think were fashionable. The hair was dark on his face and a bright Celtic red on his close-cropped head.

Grady Harlow offered her his hand. Elizabeth took it and let herself be yanked to her feet. "Don't sneak up on people like that."

"I parked the car on the curb, got out, and walked through two inches of snow while weighing two hundred and twenty pounds. What were you so into you couldn't hear me coming?"

For a panicked instant, Elizabeth didn't quite have an answer.

"Fixing McQuarrie battle damage," Anne answered for her.

Grady grunted and rolled his shoulders, seeming to say it figured while forming as few syllables as possible. "I did some Christmas shopping. Got you something," he said to Anne, then fixed Elizabeth with a stare. "Not you, though. And Shane called, said he and T are stopping at a hotel for the night, be in tomorrow."

He started for the car he'd parked by the curb, a Plymouth Acclaim with one door colored in primer like a silver tooth in a set of dentures. Anne grabbed his arm. "Whoa, hold on, you aren't that memorable. Elizabeth, this is Grady. He's having a nervous breakdown."

"It's a cleansing moment of clarity," Grady replied with an air of pedantic correction.

"He has Asperger's, so all he does are movie references and disdainful silences. Here comes a disdainful silence."

Grady unzipped his jacket in a slight huff. His T-shirt was black with a blue triangle in the center. "My silence isn't disdainful. It's intellectual and detached."

"Nice T-shirt," Anne said.

"You got it for me."

"You wore it."

"It fits!"

"I'm going inside," Elizabeth said.

In the house, Anne took over the duty of telling Barry that Shane and his friend wouldn't be making it that night.

Barry made a sympathetic noise and worked himself to his feet. "Suppose Michelle was right then. Not much point in waiting up." Before he disappeared down the hall, he added, "Elizabeth, we've got you and Michelle in the basement. Grady, you'll be sharing the bathroom, so try and let the girls shower first."

"Grady lives out in the trailer," Anne explained. "It's a nervous breakdown thing."

Grady grunted and turned to leave. Then he stopped and wheeled around, pointing a finger lazily at Elizabeth. "Just so you know, you can use the soap and toothpaste and mouthwash and everything, just not the washcloth."

"Got it," Elizabeth said.

"I use the bar of soap for most washing, so it should be fine for you. It's just I wouldn't want to touch something to my face as well as...other places."

"He means his undercarriage," Anne said.

"I get it!"

"I did mean that," Grady added as she walked away.

Elizabeth went down the stairs to the basement, every step creaking and moaning in a way they hadn't when she was twenty. She told herself she didn't weigh *that* much more; the house was just getting *really* old.

Elizabeth went through her little travel rituals, laboriously arranging her luggage and swapping out the provided pillow for her own. She heard water running in the bathroom; Michelle washing off her make-up. It almost amazed her, how they could have this bodily intimacy of being comfortable with each other's nudity, each other's morning and bedtime rituals, each other's *lives*, but there was still something that hadn't quite clicked, something that stopped it from being real. A key that couldn't get into a lock.

Elizabeth tried not to think about it. She was doing this for Michelle, after all. And the money. And the helluva story she'd get out of it if she survived this week. Did she even look like the sort of person who used a stranger's washcloth?

"So Mickey," she called, "what's with the McQuarries?"

"Huh?" Michelle asked, shutting off the water. She started brushing her teeth.

"The Hatfields to your McCoys? Don't tell me Ohio has gang wars now."

"No, no," Michelle garbled before spitting. "Nothing like that. We just don't get along, that's all. Grady and Anne care more about that stuff than I do."

"But Anne said they, uh, killed your mother?"

Michelle made a choking noise before Elizabeth realized she was gurgling mouthwash. She spat. "God, *really*? She should be an actress." Michelle came out of the bathroom and climbed into the fold-out, lying on her side to face Elizabeth, who was on her stomach. "Mitch McQuarrie, before he retired, was an insurance adjustor. When Mom got sick, there was this experimental treatment that she wanted to try. Mitch ruled that it wasn't covered by our policy. The boys were pretty pissed off. So was Anne—Patsy's lucky, she was really too young for all that. I guess they pulled some pranks on Mitch and his kids, they started coming back at us—it's all really ridiculous."

"So everyone but you and Patsy have this family feud going?"

"Mom had lung cancer, Liz. She wasn't going to get better. If it helps the others to blame someone, fine, but God, it's been years. You'd think we'd have enough shit to deal with just being under the same roof."

"Well, they did moon us. Lot of cellulite they forced us to see."

Michelle slapped Elizabeth's ass through the covers. "Yeah, somehow I don't think you retaliating would have the same effect. Get some sleep. The day starts pretty early around here." She turned over, pressing her face into her pillow, then reached her arm out across Elizabeth's back. "Thanks for doing this, Liz. Really."

"Anytime," Elizabeth said, wondering how she could have everything she wanted and yet have it feel completely wrong.

Chapter 5

December 20

ELIZABETH WOKE UP TO THE sound of a vacuum cleaner breaking down next to her ear. She looked around frantically. Michelle was gone, and the noise was coming from the cellar, reverberating through the closed door. Elizabeth got up, wearing boxer shorts and a white tee with black blocks replicating the LED display of an old Tamagotchi. She grabbed the kimono Janet had gifted her in 2012 and threw it on as she went to open the cellar door.

Grady was there, working on a sheet of plywood with something that looked like the juicer from hell, giving it the same treatment that a bad actor got in a *Saw* movie. The space had been converted into a one-man shop class. Elizabeth stared at it blearily.

Grady noticed her there and came to a stopping point, possibly not in that specific order, and turned off the juicer. He was wearing goggles and earmuffs. He took the earmuffs off. "You really should have eye and ear protection if you're going to be in here. It's a little hazardous." Then she saw him scowl as he looked at her shirt. "Have you had that shirt since the nineties?"

"I put it on at ten, which was three hours before you woke me up with your buzzsaw!"

Grady checked his watch. "No, it's twelve-oh-seven. In the afternoon. And it's not a buzzsaw, it's a plunge router. I'm using it to make a dado for a nightstand."

Elizabeth blinked. "And you're doing that at twelve in the morning?"

"I always do it at twelve. Stop at two, get food, then keep going till four, five, whatever."

"You woke me up," Elizabeth said pointedly.

"You were asleep at twelve."

"It's my vacation. I sleep in on my vacation."

"Until twelve? You missed breakfast. Anne made pancakes."

Elizabeth seethed, figured this was not a matter that was worth arguing over for the next six days of her life, and closed the door. Then she opened it again. "You come into my room while I was sleeping?"

"It's not your room, it's a basement. And no, I went through the cellar door."

"I sleep with a gun under my pillow," Elizabeth said, and closed the door again.

"You sleep a lot with a gun under your pillow!" Grady called through the door.

Upstairs, Michelle was waiting for her in the kitchen nook, wearing a tasteful sweater and black pants as she read *Of Human Bondage*. Elizabeth had always loved her for her mind. The black pants didn't hurt.

"I knew Janet was working you too hard," Michelle said. "I saved you some breakfast in the fridge."

"Trust me, she works some a lot harder." Elizabeth opened it up, finding a Tupperware container with scrambled eggs, bacon, and grits. "No pancakes?"

"Sorry, couldn't save you any. Three siblings and counting."

Elizabeth took the container to the microwave, popping it in and setting the timer for two minutes. She was just settling on her heels to watch the little plate rotate when Michelle grabbed her about the hips and pulled her down into her lap.

"I saved you a seat," Michelle said, and kissed Elizabeth's shoulder as she whispered, "Play along; she's been up to something all morning."

"Who?" Elizabeth started to ask, when Anne came into the kitchen.

She looked a little like a porn parody of Michelle, wearing ripped jeans and a white T-shirt with 'I have no tits' printed on the front. There was a slash in the middle of her cleavage, opening it to her bra, just to be contrary.

"Getting an early start, Liz?" she asked, helping herself to a mug and some coffee. "It's weird you two don't wake up together. I had this old boyfriend, once we started sleeping together, we always woke up about the same time. He'd be off in an entirely different city, but first thing in the morning, I'd see him post something on Facebook."

"Sounds inconsiderate," Michelle said. The microwave dinged. "Anne, you mind? Elizabeth here was just getting comfortable."

Anne took the Tupperware out of the microwave and set it down on the table. She eyed Elizabeth as she did so. Green eyes scorching her. Elizabeth gave it right back, centering herself and projecting BITCH into her chakra's subwoofer, or however that third-eye stuff worked.

Anne stole a piece of bacon and left with it poking out the side of her mouth.

"Such a cunt," Michelle said under her breath when she was gone.

"I wouldn't go that far," Elizabeth said. "Hey, what's with Grady and his Bob Vila act downstairs?"

Michelle squinted. "Huh? Oh, it's some...thing. I don't even know. He used to do some data entry thing over in Des Moines, but about a year ago he quit his job, moved back in here, started building furniture to sell online. The whole handcrafted hipster thing. I guess he makes some money, and Dad can use the company, but other than that, I don't know *what's* up with him."

"Reassuring," Elizabeth said.

"Oh, he's a pussycat. I don't know if he even thinks about girls that way. I mean, I *guess*, but who's gonna date someone that does woodworking in a basement all day?" Michelle rolled her eyes. Then took a sniff. "You shower?"

"Maybe I've watched too many horror movies, but I don't want to shower while there's a guy in the other room holding a buzzsaw."

"You can use the upstairs one. The worst you have to worry about is Anne and the electric carving knife she keeps in the nightstand."

"Oh my God."

"Yeah, she figures if someone busts into her and Patsy's room, she needs enough knife for both of them."

"Know what to get her for Christmas: a Taser."

"Play your cards right, she might ask you to film her using it on herself—"

Limey caught Elizabeth's attention, trotting through the kitchen to his water bowl. She pitched her voice to a babyish level. "Hi, Limey!"

The dog let out a growl like he was auditioning for Wolverine.

"Limey!" Michelle scolded him, as if scandalized.

"Am I wearing the same perfume as the mailman or something?"

"Maybe he's just jealous that you don't have to sleep on the carpet," Michelle teased.

For all the good it did her. Elizabeth rolled her eyes.

Outside, there was a squeal of tires, several honks almost muting the crunch of gravel coming up the driveway.

"McQuarries?" Elizabeth asked, once again mimicking Anne. She got off Michelle's lap to check the window over the sink.

There was a Buick Century parked in the driveway, the driver's side door hanging open, and she heard a flurry of snowy footsteps outside, jovial screams back and forth, and something wet and pulpy bursting. Michelle went to the front door just in time to be nearly stampeded as it burst open, two men flying in one after the other.

Shane, Elizabeth recognized. Tall as his mother's side of the family could go, but with a smattering of exercised muscle giving him a broader chest and wider arms than necessary. He wasn't a bodybuilder or anything, just a bit of a triangle, with shaggy hair and one of those oxen beards that men thought made them look like Navy SEALs.

He was being chased by a black man of about the same age, tall and wiry, with natural hair and a neat mustache. He was holding what looked like a humungous jelly bean, and in the time it took for Elizabeth to realize it was a water balloon, he threw it at Shane, Shane ducked, and it hit *her* square in the chest.

Elizabeth was reminded that water and white T-shirts were not her favorite duo.

Making them a trio with not wearing a bra didn't help.

"Oh shit, sorry," Shane said as she wrapped her arms around her chest. He grabbed the black man in a rough sorta-hug. "Just trying to get this asshole back for executing me with a water pistol at point blank range!"

"You put it in park, man. You left yourself wide open. Hey, I'm not made of steel here—" He looked over at Michelle, staring at her shaved head as if looking for his reflection in it. "I didn't know they gender-swapped the Transporter."

"Shane!" Anne cried, flying into the kitchen to get straitjacketed by one of his hugs. "You finally made it. *God*, it's been boring!"

While they reunited, Elizabeth tried to make do with just one arm covering herself while she grabbed a dishtowel to see about drying off. Water balloons. Honestly.

"You must be T," Anne was saying, giving the black man a smile. "Shane has told us so much about things other than you."

"This is my G, Typhos Jones," Shane told her, thumping the black man on the chest. "He didn't have anywhere else to be during the holidays, so I figured I'd let him gawk at you losers."

"Typhos Jones?" Anne repeated. "Sounds like you own a jetpack."

Typhos extended his hand for a shake. "Nah, call me T-Dog."

"Really?"

He grew serious. "No, it's Typhos."

"Please don't expect to shake hands with me," Elizabeth said, feeling mildly put out. If she was going to be a one-woman wet T-shirt contest, the least people could do was let her be the center of attention.

Shane looked at her again. "You're Michelle's girl? Fuck, no wonder she went gay."

"Shane!" Michelle slapped his arm.

"What, that ain't the technical term? Where's Grady?"

"Doing his woodworking thing," Anne answered.

"*Still?* Fuck, what happened to ADD? Doesn't that shit work anymore?"

Anne seemed to sense the bad vibes coming off Elizabeth like radiation at Chernobyl, and came to collect her while Shane trampled down the stairs to reunite with Grady.

"C'mon," Anne said. "We'll get you a nice shower in the upstairs bathroom. I'll go get some clothes for you. Deal?"

Elizabeth nodded to Typhos in passing, waggling her fingers in a weak hello. "Nice to meet you."

"If it's any consolation, you're lookin' *good*."

Anne waited until they were through the dining room to say: "He's right, y'know. Those are primo tits."

"I'm glad they're getting such widespread approval," Elizabeth said, tightening her grip on herself. "Want to stop at Barry's room and see what he thinks?"

"Nah, I'm pretty sure he'd like them." Anne steered Elizabeth to the bathroom, which was clean and respectable, if a little bit Kubrickian. White plaster was a bad pairing with white linoleum.

Elizabeth showered quickly, wondering who would be giving her more trouble over Christmas, the Harlow boys or the Harlow women? At least the shower was nice. Like the one downstairs, it was a bath/shower combo, and the water pressure was like a brisk massage compared to the shower in her apartment that the super still hadn't fixed. She didn't even have to tie a washcloth around the showerhead to keep a spraying leak from dousing the rest of the bathroom.

Thinking of washcloths got her thinking about Grady and undercarriages. A relationship in a nutshell, that's what that was. Taking a shower with someone else's cock washer in there with you. Someone like Michelle might make it worth the trouble, but what was she even up to? Feeling out the relationship, trying it out…? She certainly didn't have to be so demonstrably affectionate to sell that they were girlfriends. The Harlows were Irish; sitting next to each other was probably overly emotional by their metric. And they'd cuddled—who cuddled if they didn't want to do more than cuddle?

"Knock knock," Anne said as she came in, hauling Elizabeth's tote bag and suitcase with her. She tossed both on the bathroom counter and opened them up as Elizabeth poked her head around the shower curtain. Anne had opened her luggage and was going through it.

"You don't dress much like a lesbian, you know."

Elizabeth kept her sarcasm down to a dull roar. "And how do lesbians dress?"

"Functional, not much style, a lot of pockets—you know, like men."

"I know that's insulting to someone, but I'm still working out who."

Anne pulled out a tee that flashed color as she swished it around, looking it over. "This is cute," she said. "I'm borrowing it."

Elizabeth was about to start in on the outrage when Anne went ahead and stripped off her shirt. And while Elizabeth might not've dressed like a lesbian, well…

There was a cheetah-print bra. And a tattoo along her lower belly that Elizabeth didn't have time to read, and wondered why she had tried to.

Elizabeth was weak. Weak and gay.

"Is this weird because you're gay?" Anne asked, pulling the shirt over her head.

"Pan," Elizabeth said.

"At least wait until I've got the thing on before panning it," Anne said through the shirt.

"No, I'm pansexual. And it isn't weird."

Anne straightened the shirt down to her belt. It was one of Elizabeth's lounging tops, like the Tamagotchi shirt, and Elizabeth was a little surprised that someone as fashion-conscious as Anne would try to pull it off as a look.

It was a white T-shirt with the Spider-Man face logo shaped into a heart. Either the tightness of the T-shirt was enough to distort the logo, or Spider-Man's eyes had gotten really big since the last reboot.

The shower curtain slipped and started to slide away from her. Elizabeth grabbed it in both hands and pressed it against her body.

Anne was checking herself out in the mirror, but Elizabeth had the impression of being in the corner of her eye at all times. "Yeah, not weird. You're Michelle's girlfriend, after all, so it's not like you'd be interested in somebody else. People are so puritanical, but it's just our bodies. Man, woman, pan, straight—just because you see something, doesn't mean you'll do something. What's a pansexual anyway?"

"It means I'm attracted to all genders."

"Oh, all right. So what's the difference between a pansexual and a bisexual?"

"About ten hours of arguing on the Internet." A flush of heat struck Elizabeth as she watched Anne look good and *know* how good she looked in *her* shirt. "You want me to scribble something on it about your tits?"

"Maybe on the back, you could write 'If you're reading this, you're missing out on the other side.'"

Shit, that wasn't bad. "Could you—Agh!" Elizabeth shrieked.

The water had turned icy cold. Somewhere, someone had flushed a toilet. She went through a complicated series of maneuvers intended to hold the shower curtain in place, shunt the showerhead away from her, and move her body away from the stream of Arctic water. She mostly succeeded in not slipping and breaking her neck.

Anne casually ignored her as she unfolded Elizabeth's prize boucle jacket from Chanel, black with white accents. "This is cute. Let's see what we can do with this." She hung it up on a hook on the door, then rooted through Elizabeth's suitcase like a pig nearing a truffle.

"You wanna stop going through my stuff?" Elizabeth demanded.

"No, that's okay, I can keep going," Anne said, all her attention on a Breton-striped top in the same chiaroscuro color scheme as the jacket.

"The operative words there were 'stop going through my stuff.'"

Anne picked up a pair of black leggings, gave them a considerate hum, and hung them with the top and jacket. "Make me."

Elizabeth ripped down a towel, wrapped it around herself, and was in Anne's face by the time she turned her freckled mug around. They stared each other down, neither giving an inch, and Elizabeth found herself acutely aware of Anne's body. Not her attractiveness, as she'd been when Anne switched shirts, but Anne's physicality. The teeth grinding behind her set lips, the unblinking eyes holding their blunt stare, the nostrils steadily moving with tranquil breaths as she kept her cool.

It made thoughts of her own weakness run through Elizabeth's head. That she was dripping wet with shampoo in her hair and only a scant towel between her and Anne. And even if Anne was as straight as a Disney character that got more than five lines, not to mention the sister of her fake-girlfriend, the fact was that *Elizabeth* found her attractive, and there was just something about someone she liked in that way—that stupid, body-centric, damn-the-brains sort of way—having some…advantage over her.

It didn't help that Anne had the face of an angel, freshly fallen. And… was she blushing?

If Anne couldn't take it, Elizabeth certainly couldn't. She decided to call a truce while there was still warm water. "What is this, first day in prison? Beat up the toughest inmate so no one messes with you?"

"I probably don't think about women's prison as much as you." Anne plucked a trailing end of Elizabeth's towel and tucked it into place. "Because the only thing I know about lock-up is to try to use the bathroom before they put you in, 'cause all they have in there is single-ply toilet paper."

Elizabeth held her fierce gaze, trying not to show how much she was wondering *what the fuck did that mean?*

Because it sounded a lot like her crush's little sister was hitting on her, and *that* only happened in pornos. And the only person she knew who was living in a porno was Janet.

"Thanks for the shirt," Anne said at last. "You can have mine, too. Bit more truthful with you."

After she'd left, Elizabeth picked up the shirt she'd abandoned. 'I have no tits.'

She knew little sisters were supposed to be annoying, but surely *that* stopped outside the nuclear family.

She stepped back into the shower and found that the universe had rewarded her patient and compassionate nature by allowing the hot water to run out.

Years of secretarial work had taught Elizabeth that sometimes it was best to play peacemaker; you could always stab someone in your imagination. She put on the ensemble Anne had picked out for her, which looked remarkable on her, though Elizabeth refused to give Anne credit for that. They were her clothes—they all looked great on her.

She went into the living room, finding Barry in his customary spot on the easy chair, and Shane lying on the floor with his back against the couch in one of those stances that seemed comfortable to boys. She sat down on the other end.

"Just so you know," Barry was saying, "I think I speak for all of us when I say we're really, truly, absolutely sorry for slavery."

"That's okay," Typhos said distractedly. "Just don't let it happen again, I guess."

Elizabeth picked up the *TV Guide* and flipped to see what was on, wondering if the kind of people who listened to vinyl and thought cassette tapes were vintage also totally knocked themselves out looking up when the next rerun of *Law & Order* was playing.

"Would you like to watch something, dearie?"

"I mean, if there's anything on..."

Barry tossed her the remote. "Go right ahead. I think I'll go and see what Patsy wants for her birthday dinner."

Michelle, bearing filtered water in a commemorative McDonald's glass, passed Barry as he left. She sat down beside Elizabeth and watched her channel-surf while Shane yawned, flexing his toes as if fascinated by their dexterity.

"Hey, babe," she said, pressed against Elizabeth from shoulder to hip, just this *warmth* that Elizabeth felt like she should've noticed was missing.

Michelle took a long sip, ice cubes rattling against her teeth, reached across Elizabeth to set the glass down on an end table, and kissed Elizabeth's cheek. Her lips were wet and cool, goosing Elizabeth like the touch of metal in winter, so cold her tongue could get stuck. Elizabeth let out a little yelp, not sure how she should react, and Michelle teasingly brushed an ice cube along Elizabeth's earlobe.

"Just play along," Michelle whispered.

Elizabeth didn't have to be told twice. She turned her head, feeling Michelle's corpse-cold lips against hers, her tongue delving for the warmth of Michelle's mouth. And she wondered if a relationship could be like this. Sitting down beside someone. Kissing them. It wasn't much to add to her friendship with Michelle, was it? Not so big a leap at all.

"I think *Frasier* is on," Shane said, checking his watch. "You guys want to watch *Frasier* or keep making out? Or you could just go and have sex like adults."

"I'm on my period," Michelle replied, twisting around and resting her back against Elizabeth.

"Don't those sync up?"

"If you really want to know about our menses," Elizabeth said, "you should check the FAQ."

"Relax, babe," Michelle said. "Shane's a post-feminist feminist. He doesn't mind buying pads or anything."

"Really?" Anne asked, passing through the hallway. "Incoming!"

She threw a pen at Shane, who twisted around like a wet cat to get away. Elizabeth laughed and was a bit embarrassed to see Anne smiling, too. She would've preferred to think the only thing Anne found funny was Adam Sandler movies. Maybe puppies with cancer, too.

"Who throws things, honestly?" Shane picked up the pen and tossed it back at Anne. "We throw things in this family now? Is that what we do?"

"It had the cap on, pussy," Anne said.

"Elizabeth," Barry said, ignoring the antics of his offspring, "Patsy's vegan again, so would you mind going to the store and picking up a few extra veggies for dinner? I'd ask one of the others, but you and Michelle have the only hybrid, so it's best for the environment."

"And I'm still the only person who can get the oven to work for an hour?" Michelle asked.

"God's given you a gift, Michelle. So how about it, Liz?"

Elizabeth was already up, stretching, thinking maybe a long winter drive would provide some of the clarity that her time with Michelle kept pushing away. "Sure. I do have this nice jacket to pair with my outfit."

"I'll come with," Anne said, popping up like a kernel of popcorn that had decided to explode long seconds after the microwave timer had reached zero. "I have some stuff I need to pick up."

Elizabeth couched a pleasant offer with 'fuck-you' civility. "That's okay, I'll get it for you. Just add it to the list."

Anne smiled back at her with such an impressive 'and-the-horse-you-rode-in-on' politeness that Elizabeth felt like she was getting roasted by the entire state of Minnesota. "Nah, I wanna touch base with Ginger, too. She's a cashier over there. Her sister down in Delaware just had twins, so I want to give her a hug in person, get her to pass that on to the new munchkins for me."

Holy shit. Elizabeth hadn't been sure anyone she wasn't related to was capable of that level of bullshit on the fly.

"That's nice of you," Barry said, with the cheerful obliviousness any father developed when his daughter hit her teens. "You don't mind, do you, Elizabeth? A long car ride like that goes down easier with a little company."

"Or a radio," Elizabeth muttered.

"You know any of the radio stations in Ohio?" Anne asked, buckling her seatbelt.

Elizabeth pushed the start button with her middle finger. It was a little satisfying. "No. I have this system where I turn on my phone and then it plays music I bought instead of British women singing."

"Yeah, I don't like One Direction either. Here." Anne thudded on the radio and spun the dial until it landed on 93.7. It was playing some decent music, so Elizabeth let it slide, but Christ, did some people have a way of finding new nerves to be the last nerve they could get on.

Elizabeth checked the road, pulled out, and drove.

"Turn left at the stop sign," Anne said, reclining her seat.

"I have a GPS. I know which way."

"Does it tell you the speed limit? Hint: add ten."

"It's winter, we're in Ohio, everyone else drives pick-ups, and we're in a hybrid. Knowing how hard people work to shovel their driveways, I sure would hate to ruin one with our flaming wreckage."

Anne looked around the Prius. "I don't think this thing can explode. Queef, maybe…"

"I know what you're doing," Elizabeth said, wringing the steering wheel as if it were a neck. "You're vetting me. Like, usually Michelle's big brother would come and give a boy a whole speech about how if he broke her heart…"

"He'd break your neck?"

"That's catchy. I'll have to remember that."

"Don't," Anne told her. "It's from *The Fast & The Furious.*"

"Oh, never seen 'em."

"You haven't? There've been like ten movies. You haven't even seen one by accident?"

"The first one seemed dumb. I've avoided everything after as a matter of principle."

"Finally, some moral fiber in the universe."

"The point is, you don't have to treat me like I'm the wicked stepmother marrying your father or something. I just want Michelle to be happy. That's all."

"Oh, I believe that," Anne said. "Michelle has a way of finding people who *just* want her to be happy…"

There was a minefield *there* that Elizabeth wasn't interested in playing Princess Diana to. She held her tongue as the radio station did its identification. "Keep listening to 93.7, The Split, Ohio's LGBT headquarters."

Elizabeth rolled her eyes. "Thanks for tuning into this. I hate listening to straight music."

Anne straightened her seat up. "They play *good* music. That's more than I can say for anything else on the FM dial around here."

Elizabeth scoffed, though the radio bore out Anne's point by playing "Suffragette City." She would've focused on the road, but they were at a red light. "You know why that is, right?"

Anne put her feet up on the dashboard. "Why what?"

"Why gay music is better than straight music."

"Okay, I know Prince was a little girly—"

Elizabeth overrode her. "Gay music is better than straight music because gay people dance. Once you know you're writing music that people dance to, it's like you actually bother to have a rhythm."

"Hence EDM, I suppose."

"Screw your EDM. Freddie Mercury, David Bowie, Mick Jagger—these are not people who have only touched their own junk. All of rock is at least bicurious."

"Hip-hop?" Anne retorted. "Rap."

"Rappers can be gay!"

"Personally, I think that's what got Tupac killed."

"Oh my God..."

"It would be a twist, you have to admit. No one would see it coming."

"Are we almost there?"

"What am I, a navigator? Check your GPS."

The grocery store was doing a holiday thing that was almost cute, like it thought it was the Mall of America. There were paper snowflakes on the glass and one of those midget Christmas trees by the cash registers. All Elizabeth could think was that some minimum-wage worker had to put all that crap up. It was enough to make you a Marxist.

Elizabeth got a shopping cart and Anne hopped into it, reclining against the far end of the cart with her feet up against the child seat. Her heels were black with red on the bottom. Elizabeth narrowed her eyes at them. *If I kill her, I can take those. So, two reasons.*

"You can walk," Elizabeth said.

"You can push," Anne replied. "And of the two of us, who is wearing five-inch heels?"

"I'm not taking you to get your thing," Elizabeth said.

"S'okay. I found it." Anne reached over and plucked a box of Q-tips from the endcap of the aisle they were entering. She hugged it to her chest. "I'm good. Let's buy some kale!"

Elizabeth reached into her pocket, took out the shopping list Barry had given her, and shoved it in Anne's face. "Here. Navigate."

"I like that you trust me."

"I like your shoes."

"I like your outfit."

"You picked it out."

"Yeah, I'm great that way." Anne unfurled the list and read. "Frozen spinach. Probably with the frozen foods, but I like to look for clues anyway, see if there's a twist ending coming."

Elizabeth pushed the shopping cart along, pointedly ignoring the looks she was getting. If Anne could take it, so could she. "So, what're you into?"

They rolled into the refrigerated aisles, Anne holding the list between her thumb and forefinger, tapping it with her middle finger. "Don't ask me that. I don't try to find common interests with people."

Elizabeth opened a frost-stained door and pulled out a package of chopped spinach. "Really."

She tossed it onto Anne's gut, completely casual. Anne brushed it between her legs, also completely casual. "Nah, waste of time. What you've gotta do is find stuff you both hate."

"Cynical," Elizabeth said. "What's next?"

"Feta. Probably in the—"

"I've shopped before," Elizabeth said.

"I'm sorry for taking my responsibilities as navigator so seriously on this loosey-goosey boat." Anne looked over the elbow she'd parked on the side of the cart to check out her reflection in the passing glass doors. She hummed with approval. "You like kittens?"

"Yeah," Elizabeth said, thinking of feta cheese.

"I like kittens," Anne said. "Common interest. Now I hate Scientologists. Isn't that a bigger deal than liking kittens?"

"I think a lot of Scientologists would say so."

Anne poked her tongue into her cheek a moment. "Relax, I don't hate Scientologists. They do a great job running Hollywood."

"Could do with less reboots, though." Elizabeth grabbed a package of feta and tossed it at Anne, who batted it away from her breasts.

"Watch the merchandise! Onions and, while we're in the produce, anything you can imagine going in a smoothie."

Elizabeth steered them towards produce.

Anne wiggled her toes, tapping the tip of one shoe against Elizabeth's forearm, and Elizabeth felt uncannily like she owned a cat.

"God, reboots," Anne said nastily. "They're not even remaking the good stuff anymore. Now they're remaking shit I didn't like the first time around. And they're changing the races and the genders and shit, like I should run to go see a Little Tramp movie in 2017 because he's black now. I wouldn't give a shit about the Little Tramp if they 'reimagined' him as a robot that pooped dinosaurs—"

"Yeah," Elizabeth agreed. "And I don't hate *Hamilton*. I haven't seen it, but the fans…"

"Jesus Christ, the fans!" Anne rolled her eyes. "At least *Phantom of the Opera* fans were funny."

"At least *Phantom of the Opera* fans had seen it. Ninety percent of the won't-shut-up fans haven't even seen *Hamilton*, they've just read thinkpieces about it. They're not fans of the show, they're fans of the thinkpieces!" Elizabeth grabbed a bag of onions and threw it to Anne, who caught it and stuffed it to the side.

Anne kept up the juggling act as Elizabeth threw some more greenery at her. "I hate thinkpieces. 'This show about murders showed a murder, here's why that's a bad thing.' And they're all written like someone ran a dorm room through a thesaurus." Anne glanced at the list. "Olive oil."

"I can top that!" Elizabeth said, jolting into motion. "People who have pets and say they're 'parents?'"

"Oh God!"

"You want a kid, adopt someone, don't take your dog to a spa."

Anne's foot tapped against Elizabeth's arm again, her tongue poking out between her lips, pink and wet, as she thought furiously. "Pugs and bulldogs."

"Okay, if you're one of those people who think bulldogs eat babies…"

Anne grabbed hold of either side of the cart and hauled herself up to face Elizabeth. "No, but they're bred to be unhealthy just for this dumb aesthetic. Old English Bulldogs can't clean themselves, they can't mate, they can't give birth, not on their own…people need to stop breeding them that way. There are these guys in Germany breeding a different kind of pugs called Retro Mops. They have longer legs, smaller eyes, they can actually open their nostrils to breathe… I'm not saying we need to destroy pugs, but we need to phase them out and get healthy pugs instead so there aren't a bunch of dogs suffering for no reason!"

"You're very passionate about eugenics all of a sudden," Elizabeth teased, dropping the olive oil into Anne's lap.

"Minced garlic," Anne said. "Yeah, everyone loves everything from Victorian England, but the moment I bring up my love of selective breeding, *I'm* the bad guy. And I love selective breeding."

"You wouldn't know it from the way you dress."

"Garlic's to your left, smartass," Anne called, and Elizabeth snatched it up.

"What else?" she asked, placing it on top of Anne's head.

Anne eased from one side to another, trying to keep it balanced. "Nothing. That's the whole list."

"So, do I have your blessing to hold hands with your sister?"

"Oh, God no. You're way too cool for her. You need to get something else going immediately."

"What do you mean by that?" Elizabeth asked, feeling compelled to jump to Michelle's defense. "I think Michelle's plenty cool."

"Don't let her hear you say that." Anne took the garlic container and rolled it around in her hands. "Furiosa's smart, I get it, but she's one of those smart people that thinks they're the *only* smart people. Like watching *Doctor Who* and sipping tea makes her better than anyone who likes football or wears a push-up bra. It's tiring."

"She's not like that," Elizabeth said. "She doesn't even like *Doctor Who*."

"Probably too mainstream for her now. Now she'll only like the stuff where the Doctor is some lumpy guy who wears a scarf." Anne blew an unimpressed gust of air through her lips. "Don't listen to me. She's *your* girlfriend, right?"

"Right." Elizabeth picked a chew toy off the shelf. They were in the pet aisle.

Anne caught it. "Trying to tell me something?"

"It's for the dog. Honest."

Preparations for supper were well underway when they got back. Their grocery bags just added to the confusion. Barry had marshalled everyone but the birthday girl into some task or another, occupying the entire kitchen with only mild slapstick. As guests, Elizabeth and Typhos were exiled from the cooking. She saw him talking with Patsy, so she went out onto the patio to read in climate-controlled nature.

She'd made it about halfway through her borrowed book when Barry came to collect her, his Oxford shirt and wetly combed hair marking it as a special occasion. "The food is ready, dear."

"Great," Elizabeth replied. She went for the front door, but Barry blocked her.

"Just one moment," he said, looking behind him to see that they weren't overheard, then facing her. "You know the friend Shane brought, Typhos—he's African-American."

"I noticed," Elizabeth said.

"Aye. Not that I think you'd have anything against him, just that he might be sensitive to certain subjects, you know? Jokes."

"I didn't know I was in the habit of telling black jokes."

"No, no, but all it takes is one, from one of us, and then he'll probably think all of us are against him, and then where will we be? I'm sure you wouldn't like it if one of the others made a little funny and set him against you, so I've told everyone to mind their tongues."

"Okay," Elizabeth said bemusedly. She would've thought the thing having everyone on eggshells would be the lesbian lover of the eldest daughter, but apparently that didn't rate compared to a black friend. Ellen had taken all the edge out of being a dyke.

"So just don't say anything too nice about the police or poverty or just anything you think wouldn't make for a polite conversation, that's all."

"Got it," Elizabeth nodded. Overbearing father figure: check.

They went through the warzone of the kitchen to the dining room, where Shane was in the middle of a story: "So I did mean it when I said, 'I love you,' I was just talking to the *dog*."

Typhos laughed, leading the chorus, and pounded Shane in the shoulder. "Classic, bro!"

The food looked slightly unlike food. There was some oddly prepared fish, something that looked like dough, various bowls of rice, curry, and porridge, and an incongruously placed birthday cake under a dome cover.

With Patsy at the far end of the table, eating off a Happy Birthday plate, and Barry at the head, Elizabeth ended up wedged between Michelle and Anne. They faced the three boys, Elizabeth across from Shane.

After Barry had said grace, he cast his reel at Typhos. "So, Mr. Jones, how do you like the food? We decided to try something new and fix a traditional African dinner."

"I've never been to Africa," Typhos demurred.

"Oh, it's very inspiring," Barry said guilelessly. "You should go. The motherland, you know."

"Actually, my family immigrated from Haiti."

"Yes, but, you know, they came from Africa originally."

"Didn't everyone's family come from Africa?" Typhos asked. "Originally? Cradle of civilization and all that."

"That's Mesopotamia," Michelle said.

"Can you spell it?" Anne asked her.

Elizabeth redirected. "Can you pass the, uh, bread dough?"

"You wanna cook it?" Shane asked, making Typhos laugh. He picked up the dough.

"It's asida," Barry said, mainly to himself.

Shane handed it to Elizabeth. "Thirty, right?"

Elizabeth guessed there'd never been a 'you're eating with a lady' speech from Barry. "That's right."

Shane accepted the conveyor belt of passing food, serving himself, then passing it on. "Don't worry, you're gonna love your thirties. The great thing about it is that you *finally* don't have to worry about being cool."

"Oh yeah?"

"Yeah. Teens, you gotta be cool. Twenties, you gotta be cool. Thirty—who's left to impress? The guys at the office? Who gives a shit about them? *I've never listened to Fifth Harmony.*"

Elizabeth shrugged. "They're not bad."

"But c'mon, would you ever choose to listen to them?" Shane gesticulated so wildly, he almost knocked over his water. He was mildly calmed down by being forced to take a bowl of something Barry called kapenta with sadza. "But I have listened to Katy Perry. It's great. Lame, but great. I remember only being able to listen to cool stuff in my twenties—I spent five years just listening to Kanye and Radiohead. It was awesome, but really repetitive."

"I couldn't ever get sick of listening to Radiohead," Anne said. "*OK Computer* was the last great rock album, and they should've gotten the title song on *Spectre*, not some weepy *American Idol* contestant."

"Harry Styles actually put out a pretty good rock album," Patsy said.

Shane shook his head. "It's your birthday, so I'm gonna let that slide."

"Muse does pretty good rock," Grady said, barely looking up from cutting his food. "They're rock, right?"

"Not compared to *OK Computer*," Anne said.

"Anne used to be a huge rock chick," Michelle told Elizabeth, leaning over slightly, but not so far the rest of the table couldn't hear. "The moment she got to high school, it went like growth spurt, rock and roll, boobs, *this*." She gestured off-handedly at Anne.

Anne smiled back at her. "I'm still a rocker, I just took the aesthetic as far as it could go. Once you've pulled off a Mohawk, you've pretty much rebelled as much as you can."

"Oh, if only that were true," Barry said. The phone rang from the kitchen. He sighed, unhitched his napkin from his collar, and went to answer it.

Shane was the first to pick up the conversation when he was gone. "You know there's some guy who calls himself The Weeknd?" he asked Elizabeth. "Not a band! One guy! He doesn't even spell it right!"

"I think we should go back to the pulp fiction with that stuff," Elizabeth said. "*Weekend Jones and the Temple of Time!*"

"Did you know," Anne said, "that if you interweave tracks from *OK Computer* and *In Rainbows* you get seamless transitions? I mean songs that complement each other perfectly?"

"I think you might be the one person who's impressed with Thom Yorke's dancing," Elizabeth said.

"It's as good as Drake's," Anne said.

"I don't think you can throw out the last twenty years of rock just because something was your favorite album when you were a kid. I mean, the White Stripes, Kings of Leon, Queens of the Stone Age, Gomez, Wolfmother, The Strokes..." Elizabeth bit her lip as she groped for another name. "Eddy Current Suppression Ring..."

"Muse," Grady said. "Are they not rock? I thought Chris Brown was a rapper, but apparently he's not, so..."

"Muse is rock," Michelle assured him. "They're just not that good."

"They're pretty good," Patsy said.

"They were in *Twilight*," Shane said.

"So was Anna Kendrick," Typhos pointed out.

Shane clutched at his heart.

"And Peter Facinelli," Grady said.

"Who?" the others chorused.

"He was in *Fastlane*."

Shane pounded the table. "*Fastlane* was the shit! Like a *Fast & Furious* movie every week!"

"Elizabeth wouldn't know about that," Anne said. "Never seen any of 'em."

"Maybe it's a lesbian thing," Shane said.

"If Michelle Rodriguez is in them, it's not a lesbian thing," Anne said.

"Well, I'm not gonna watch a movie just because Michelle Rodriguez is in it," Elizabeth said. "As proven by most Michelle Rodriguez movies."

Barry came out of the kitchen, going to the coat tree in the hall by the stairs. "That was Bill Garrick. His car broke down and he's supposed to be leaving for Christmas with his family two hours ago. They're in Maryland, of all places…"

"Can't he call someone else?" Patsy asked.

"He did, two hours ago. They dicked him around, then said they couldn't send anyone until tomorrow." Putting on a scarf, Barry came back to kiss Patsy's forehead. "I'll be right back. You kids finish eating—just don't cut the cake without me."

They all said quick good-byes as he left. Elizabeth tried the bread dough, aware that hers was about the loudest noise being made besides the door opening, closing, being locked, and then the rattle of an engine turning over in the garage. She guessed it was something about having a family she wouldn't get.

"So, Typhos," Anne said a moment later. "What do you hate?"

"'Scuse me?" Typhos asked, dabbing his mouth with a napkin.

"It's this theory she has," Elizabeth said. "Hating something gives you more in common with people than liking something."

"I don't know." Typhos tapped his spoon against his plate. "I'm a pretty laid-back guy. Shane here, he could go on forever about some movie he doesn't like; if I don't think I'll like a movie, I don't go see it."

"Yeah, but if it's a Terminator movie, you've gotta see it," Shane said. "Just for Arnold."

Typhos stuck out his chin, thinking hard. "I guess it's always bugged me when there's a movie or a book or something where two people go at it doggy style and it's supposed to be demeaning or some shit?"

"Because he's not looking her in the eyes as they *make love*," Anne said, affecting a French accent.

"Yeah, that shit. *That's* the line we're drawing as too kinky? Not butt stuff—"

"Not sloppy blowjobs," Shane added.

"No, doggy style. Who doesn't like doggy style?"

Patsy raised her hand hesitantly.

Anne booed. "Okay, I'm letting you get away with that because it's your birthday, but *sis*—"

"It's like, what am I supposed to do?" Patsy asked. "Just…hold the pose?"

"Yeah," Michelle said. "If a guy likes the pose so much, maybe he can just take a picture."

"I don't enjoy having my picture taken *that* much," Elizabeth said.

"Well, hey," Shane said. "If even the lesbian likes it…"

Elizabeth held up a finger, signaling for quiet as she swallowed her last bite. "Not a lesbian, I—"

"Shit, Michelle," Anne interrupted. "How bad a girlfriend are you?"

"Ha ha," Elizabeth said. "I'm pansexual."

Grady counted off on his fingers. "LGBTA…"

"It's pronounced la-gah-bee-te-ah," Anne said. "It's French."

"You know what the A stands for?" Elizabeth asked her.

"Anonymous."

Elizabeth reached out and spun her glass of water so the Winnie the Pooh printed on it was more properly facing her. "Pansexual is just someone who loves people regardless of gender."

"So you're bisexual?" Typhos asked.

"No, that's two genders. I'm also attracted to people who don't fit the conventional gender binary."

"What, like horses?" Shane asked.

"Shane, c'mon," Patsy chided.

"Yeah," Typhos said. "There are still boy horses and girl horses. This is more like robots."

Elizabeth huffed a sigh. "It's more like no one really feels entirely male or entirely female, and there are people who are biologically male, but really don't feel that way, or female for that matter, and I don't consider that a factor in finding them attractive or being romantically interested in them."

"But if there were a robot," Grady said, "it's possible you'd be sexually attracted to them?"

"I don't know. I don't think someone would program a robot with a sexuality of any sort."

"They're going to," Grady said confidently.

"What, did you invest in a Kickstarter?" Michelle teased.

Grady leaned a little ways across the table. "Think about the people who are likely to build a robot. Do you really think they're going to have girlfriends?"

"Or boyfriends," Anne said.

"You're right," Shane agreed. "Or boyfriends, they might be gay."

Elizabeth rolled her neck. "It seems like if someone's going to make a robot for sex, they're going to make it look like a person. So that seems just like a question of being attracted to a person, not a robot. I mean, people aren't 'robosexual' because they use a vibrator or a sex doll or whatever..."

"So you'd consider it?" Shane asked.

"Consider what?"

"If there was a robot that looked exactly like Jennifer Aniston, I mean it was completely lifelike—"

Grady rubbed his chin. "If it's absolutely lifelike, how do I know it's not alive?"

"Okay, Turing, calm down, we're just talking about fucking robots."

The doorbell rang. There was a moment of echoing silence as they looked among themselves, before Anne and Michelle stood up.

"Dad back so soon?" Michelle asked, squinting.

"Without his key?" Anne replied.

"Could've lost it."

"Then how'd he drive home?"

Her curiosity piqued, Elizabeth went with them to the front door. There was a faint crackle as Michelle unlocked it, then she opened the door and orange light poured in, the sound of fire sawing at their ears, the flame right on the steps of the porch. The wide-open door let the acrid smoke pour in.

Elizabeth moved automatically, going to stomp it out, but Anne stopped her. She took a firm hold of Elizabeth's shoulder and vaulted past her, making Elizabeth feel like a hobby horse before Anne kicked the fireball, lobbing it out into the yard. It hit a snowbank and sputtered to a trickle of smoke.

"McQuarries," Anne said, chewing the word.

"You can't know that," Michelle said, squinting.

"If it smells like dog shit," Anne said, stepping off the patio to wiggle her kicking foot in the snow. "Glad I wore my mowing sneakers."

"Yeah, don't think the smell can get much worse," Michelle said.

Anne rolled her eyes as they tromped back inside, rubbing their hands together, shaking off the cold.

"Okay," Anne said with a sudden air of command. "We squad up, we think up something to drop down their chimney or whatever…"

"I'm not sure that's a good idea," Michelle said. "It's just a prank. No need to escalate things."

"They've hit us twice," Anne said. "They're not gonna stop unless we show 'em we're not going to be fucked with."

"Or they've had their fun and now they're going to knock it off. It's Christmas, Annabelle. You really want to bother with this nonsense on Christmas?" Michelle looked to Elizabeth for support. "Liz, tell her. Don't we have better things to do than get into some infantile prank war with them?"

Elizabeth hesitated. Her own thoughts were more along the line that anyone who brought dog shit to her place outside of an untrained puppy needed to get his ass whipped. But it wasn't like it was her place to judge. "Mickey's right. It's just a dumb prank."

Anne stared at her. "Wow. Guess even someone with a pussy can be pussy-whipped."

"Anne," Michelle said firmly. "Think. Is this really what you want Shane to be stewing about right now?"

Anne ground her teeth and fumed. "Fine. *Fine.* But this had better be the end of it."

"It is," Michelle said. "I've got a good feeling about it."

The doorbell rang again.

"Oh hell no!" Anne flung the door open. Except this time the only piece of shit on the doorstep was Michelle's husband—Elizabeth recognized him from Michelle's Facebook.

William Bridger was the kind of man Michelle usually went for. Tall, active, strong cheekbones, dimple in his chin, blue eyes. He was holding a package and, seeing Anne with her fists raised, held it in front of himself defensively. "Easy! Easy! I come in peace, promise!"

"Oh, Will, it's you," Anne lowered her fists. "We thought you were someone else."

"A faithful husband, maybe," Michelle said.

"Michelle, I know it was wrong, but I only cheated once."

"No," Michelle insisted with exacting precision. "There were two women!"

"But at the same time." Will grinned haplessly, like he'd been caught pulling a practical joke and was trying not to give it away.

"They were twins!"

"Well, I think it's nice that they can do things together."

Elizabeth stepped in. "Maybe if it weren't *you* they were doing—"

Will looked her over, the slightly amused smile not leaving his face. "You must be Elizabeth. I'm actually here for Patsy. I know it's her birthday, and I brought her a gift." He glanced from Elizabeth to Michelle. "Looks like the judge saw things your way. The papers will be ready to sign on Boxing Day. I couldn't bear to make my lawyers work Christmas."

"Mine are Jewish," Michelle said.

"So are mine, but they've married shiksas." Will shrugged. "Maybe I should give 'em your number."

"Will, c'mon," Anne said, voice exasperated but fond. "Elizabeth and Michelle are very happy together."

"Then I'll leave you to it." He gave his box a shake. "Soon as I'm done with the birthday girl."

He swept into the dining room like a one-man parade. The girls could only follow. Will gave off a quick karaoke of the birthday song as he set the box in front of Patsy.

"Here you are, Pat. Sorry, Grady, Shane, Typhos—didn't get you anything."

"Always next year," Shane said cheerily. "If the divorce doesn't go through, I mean."

"Did you get the chair I sent you?" Grady asked.

"I did!" Will answered, his eyes flitting back to Patsy as she opened her present. "Very comfortable. Did you make that posture-pedic?"

"No, just gave it…gave it a bit of a hum. It's actually kinda interesting…"

"What is it?" Patsy asked. She had disemboweled the gift wrapping to find what looked like a robotic organ transplant, done up in the sleek transparent silicon of an Apple Store.

"That," Will said excitedly, crouching down beside her, "is the toaster of the future. Tell me, what's the worst part of making toast?"

"Burning it," Michelle answered, hanging in the doorway with her arms crossed.

"The wait," Will corrected her seamlessly. "Now what's the first thing you do in the morning?"

"Pee," Grady said.

"Pee," Shane echoed.

"Check my phone," Typhos said.

"Exactly!" Will enthused. "The Toasty is the world's first Internet-capable toaster. Connects to an app on your smartphone. You put the bread in at night, go to sleep, wake up, check your phone, the app automatically starts the toaster, so when you go to the kitchen, the toast is ready *already*. Genius, right? You're holding one of the first production models. My start-up's building two thousand of those bad boys. Only costs a hundred-fifty. Wave of the future. Well, I have got to go, but it was great seeing you all. Anne, loving the podcast—"

"Vlog," Michelle corrected mercilessly.

"Grady, can't wait to see the next mofo to come off your lathe. Shane"— he bent over and gave Shane's shoulders a shake—"take those pills now, right? Give Barry all my love. I'm going. Happy birthday, Patsy. Elizabeth, good luck, you're gonna need it. Merry Christmas. God bless us everyone!"

And that carried him out the door.

Michelle faced the dinner table. "You know he cheated on me, right?"

"Oh, yeah," Shane said. "We're definitely going to kill him. But other than that, he's great."

"I may not like him," Grady said, "but I respect him. And I also like him."

Barry got back not long after, and the conversation settled into a jokey recounting of the repair work, then they went through cake and presents. Elizabeth had gotten Patsy an Amazon gift card—the gift that keeps on saying "I didn't know what to get you." With that all done, they settled in to watch the latest episode of *Bad Lawyer*. With every available surface in the living room covered by a Harlow, Elizabeth begged off, saying she would be lost on season six when she hadn't even finished season one.

She knew it didn't make any sense, but she was still a little surprised when a show she didn't watch went six seasons. It felt weird to be that out of step with the mainstream. Like hearing that polka music had conquered the Billboard Top 100.

Elizabeth went downstairs, securely closing every door she could, and drew a bath in the basement bathroom. There was a lot she liked about living in New York. Everything the tourists liked, really, just less obnoxiously. But for an apartment that she paid an obscene amount of zeroes for, she had to take showers. And, were she to live in a basement in Ohio, she'd get to take baths.

Life wasn't fair.

Just the muted shout of the water pouring from the faucet and filling the tub with scalding, steaming heat was magnificently relaxing. The warm steam flickered under her clothes, prying at them as she undressed, and she could feel the light touch of that heat on her body as she bared herself to it, pulling and tugging magnetically at the iron in her blood. It'd been far too long since she'd poured herself into a bath and had a long soak.

As she toed the surface of the water, biting her lip at its brisk heat, Elizabeth promised herself she would take a bath every day she was here. Maybe invest in some bath bombs while she was at it. She committed her foot to the hot water, gritting her teeth as the heat flushed up her leg, just on the edge of bearable. She stepped in with her other foot, then lowered herself down, only stopping to press play on her iPhone's 1960's classics playlist, then seeping down after the lower half of her body until she'd sunk completely under.

She stayed there a heartbeat, feeling the glossy tickle of her hair brushing against her cheeks, and then she rose. The bathtub even had a pillow opposite the faucet for her to lay her head against. She did, knowing vaguely that she should get her hair done at least before relaxing, and promising herself she would get to it in a minute…or five…or ten…

Steam kept wafting off the rippling surface of the water—Elizabeth took a moment to admire her own nudity, because if you didn't, really, how was anyone else supposed to? She closed the shower curtain, trapping the steam in with her, and basked in its press against her face, her skin, her pores. Fuck spas; *this* was all she needed.

She tried to remember if Janet's apartment had a bath, and wondered if there was any possible way to ask to use it that wouldn't be taken very inappropriately.

Elizabeth didn't hear the door to the bathroom opening and closing, or the rustle of clothing being lowered. But she did—with the preternatural knowledge that people have of their cell phones—know that hers had been picked up.

She drew back the curtain and saw Anne sitting on the toilet, her pants around her ankles and Elizabeth's phone in her hands, being manhandled.

"Relax," Anne said. "It's only number one."

"Do I just put out a pheromone for you?" Elizabeth demanded.

"No, it's all your charming personality. Two bathrooms, Irish family, and I can't write my name in the snow. You're an only child, right?"

"Hopefully. Would you put my phone back?"

"Why, so it can keep playing…" Anne scrutinized the screen. "*My Little Runaway* by Del Shannon?"

"Hey, this is music," Elizabeth told her.

"You sound like one of those archaeologists who finds a little bone thing and says it's a comb."

"That would be an anthropologist," Elizabeth snarled.

"Like anyone can even know that," Anne said. She was swiping left and right. "Caravan Palace, not bad… Oh, Taylor Swift. You are human after all. And Britney! You're a girl."

"So, I'm a human girl. Does that about cover it or would you like to know more?"

Anne's nose wrinkled. "Lonely Island, really?"

"You don't like Lonely Island?"

"They made Michael Bolton cool again. Fuck 'em. Here, I brought you something…" She leaned over, giving Elizabeth a view of—

"Oh my God!" She pulled the shower curtain shut. "I just… I'm informing you now of a policy I have where every conversation I'm in should have at least one pair of pants being worn."

"Not much for pillow talk, eh? Can't blame you. Here." Through the vinyl of the curtain she saw Anne setting a CD case on the sink. "*OK Computer*. Find me a better album than that in the last twenty years and, I don't know, I'll owe you a Coke."

"Are you still peeing? What did you do, drink a water cooler?"

Anne flushed and did all the attendant business while Elizabeth stared at the bath's soap dish. It was a really cute soap dish. Carved like a little cherub's wing or something. Her soap dish was pretty much just a missing tile.

"And by the way," Anne added, washing her hands. "Your little runaway song doesn't count, since it came out before Radiohead. During the Great Depression, if I don't miss my guess."

"Have you ever been punched in the mouth?" Elizabeth asked. "It really seems like you haven't ever been punched in the mouth."

Anne opened the door, letting a cool draft of air in to prickle Elizabeth's exposed skin. Elizabeth sunk into the water up to her nose. She fumed, snarling into the bathwater. Then Anne ripped away the shower curtain, kneeling beside the bathtub, so shockingly close to Elizabeth that she could smell Anne's perfume. It reminded her of cinnamon.

"I *know* you're not really dating Michelle," Anne said, her voice dropping an octave. She played her hand through the water lazily but pointedly, and having Anne in the water with her even to that minute degree made Elizabeth's ears heat up like fireworks about to explode.

"You can hug and snuggle and cuddle all you want, but I've *seen* the way Michelle looks at you and she doesn't want to *fuck you, Elizabeth*, not one bit. So, your whole story is bullshit and I don't know what the real story is, but I'm going to find out, and if you're fucking with me or anyone else in my family, I am shutting you down, you got that?"

"You don't know me," Elizabeth said. "You don't know shit." She slammed her fist into the water as hard as she could and was very satisfied when most of the splash landed on Anne.

Anne stared at her, damp T-shirt clinging to her skin, water running down her face and turning her hair into dripping strands of fire across her cheeks. She brushed a wet strand behind her ear.

"And you don't know my sister," she said, getting up and closing the shower curtain. Her silhouette disappeared out the door.

She at least had the decency to close it.

Chapter 6

December 21

ELIZABETH WOKE UP TO THE find Michelle standing in the open door to the bathroom, getting dressed before the mirror. Not the worst thing to see first thing in the morning. She stretched out, unkinking her body, and wondered how much she was allowed to enjoy the show. One eye's worth, she decided, burying most of her face in the pillow. The bed was still as comfortable as a warm blanket on a cold day could be.

"So much for us waking up together," Elizabeth said.

"Huh?" Michelle asked, stripping off her blouse to try on another one. "Yeah, I guess. Another late morning?"

"Nah. I do have some circadian rhythm. That was just a lot of late nights catching up to me." Elizabeth decided that staring at Michelle was getting creepy so she dragged the sheet over her head and stared at that instead. Long-distance relationships had nothing on relationships that weren't really relationships. "Hey, what's up with Shane?"

"Hmm? What about him?"

"Exactly. You're all kinda tiptoeing around him. I'm just wondering what's going on there?"

Michelle stripped off another blouse. "Nothing *interesting*. He's bipolar and sometimes goes off his meds. Why, what'd Anne say?"

"What makes you think Anne said anything?"

"You're a horrible liar. She's a drama queen, middle-child syndrome, so she's appointed herself his guardian, her and Grady, who really ought to know better. Middle-*children* syndrome, plural." Michelle's words became muffled as she applied lipgloss. "Anne seems to think he's going to run off and have a lost weekend if he stubs his toe. It's sick. Like Munchausen by proxy. She knows if she's the Shane expert, she'll get all sorts of attention, so there you are."

"But he's cool?" Elizabeth asked.

"I think so. Don't play Anne's game. Shane's a big boy, he can handle himself." There was a creak of floorboards as Michelle stepped out of the bathroom. "Hey, Casper, what do you think?"

Elizabeth pulled the sheet away. Michelle switched two blouses in front of herself on hangers, flashing her bra in-between them.

Elizabeth resolved to make very sure which blouse looked better.

Michelle looked at her, suddenly serious. "Hey, can I ask you something?"

Elizabeth was torn between gay-girl *here we go* and the fact that it was Mickey asking. "Sure."

"Right, this is a little awkward, so I'm just going to ask—what does pussy taste like?"

Elizabeth wasn't sure if she'd ever seen someone's jaw literally drop before, but she was pretty sure hers just had. She just wasn't prepared for the words 'pussy' and 'taste' to come out of Michelle's mouth in that order.

"I know!" Michelle ducked her head into one of the blouses, giving Elizabeth a weirdly shocking look at her bra. "I know. But what if it comes up? You've met my family. They're not always the most...circumspect."

"Yeah, but I don't think they're going to ask you what my pussy tastes like. Unless there are other pussies now?"

"No, no, you're the only fake relationship I'm in." Michelle sat down on the bed, a long, lean gulf of her side showing up to the insubstantial strap of her bra, just a hint of ribs there like they were outlining a path. "It's not like I would tell them, but they'd know if I didn't know, so..."

"So?" Elizabeth asked, unconsciously flexing her thighs. Oh, that was bad. That was really bad. She clamped her legs shut and hoped Michelle hadn't noticed.

"I should have something of a secret." Michelle smiled at Elizabeth. "You are my best friend. We should have secrets, shouldn't we?"

Elizabeth bit her lip. With Michelle sitting on the bed, the waistband of her jeans was standing away from her body, and Elizabeth could see down the small of her back as it started to curve into her panties. "It tastes like... like pussy!"

"Liz," Michelle said dismally, batting her eyelashes like she was trying to spare Elizabeth the hardship of her burning gaze.

"Well, what do you think it tastes like? It's not like it comes in Gatorade flavors."

"I assume it tastes good." Michelle rolled her tongue in her cheek. "I mean, if it didn't, you wouldn't...you know. So it has to taste at least—nice."

"Yeah," Elizabeth said slowly. "I guess. It's sort of an acquired taste. And everyone's is different, obviously."

"Obviously," Michelle agreed, nodding in such an eager-to-please way that Elizabeth felt a crazed twitch around her thighs. This whole confusing moment was bookmarking itself for future daydreams, along with the words 'let me show you.'

"I guess it's like when you kiss someone. That...intimate taste. Only stronger. You're smelling them and feeling them...her...seeing her... It's less of a taste and more of an experience. Like she's sharing something with you. The way she closes her eyes, or meets yours, or looks away. The little shapes her lips make. The flush that goes through her as she gets more and more excited. Sometimes I can even feel her get warmer. Like I've set her on fire. That's what I remember about a girl. Not just her pussy."

"And," Michelle asked, lying down on one elbow, "do you remember that about me?"

Yes. "I mean, it was such a long time ago," Elizabeth said, looking away to spare herself from Michelle's gaze. It was like the woman was pouring boiling oil on her, which would suck if she didn't feel so fucking cold...

"You're blushing," Michelle said, which made Elizabeth feel like her temperature was jumping another twenty degrees. "But that was a good answer. I'll have to remember that."

When she got off the bed, Elizabeth was finally able to breathe.

"Uh-huh," she said belatedly.

She needed a shower. She needed a *long* shower.

Elizabeth was feeling showy, so she dressed up a bit—pulling a purple Melanie Wiggle Dress from Glamour Bunny over her hourglass figure, black bra, black panties, and pantyhose, coming out looking like Jayne Mansfield at her most va-va-voom. She paired the look with a coral belt, wishing she'd been able to pack more shoes or a purse to match and really outdo Anne. She settled for a choker. A simple look, but elegantly so.

She went to get the newspaper and found Shane and Grady outside, standing on one foot, Shane expounding as if training a championship boxer. "This is great leg-training, Grad. Your leg's only used to taking half your weight, so you give it twice that, pretty soon you've got one swole leg. Trust me, man, this is how Chris Hemsworth does it."

"Boys," Elizabeth said, waving to them.

They waved back. To Elizabeth's slight disappointment, neither of them fell over.

"Care to get some training in?" Shane asked her. "Hardcore workout I'm putting my baby bro through. Not everyone can keep up."

"Nah, I get my exercise from running away from my problems," Elizabeth said, and brought the newspaper inside.

There was a hearty breakfast, with a selection of leftovers on the lunch menu. Elizabeth gave Limey his chew toy. He nearly snipped her fingers off. She thought she was getting through to him.

Patsy had found a *Law & Order* Christmas Special on the tube. Elizabeth couldn't say no to that. An hour later, the brothers came in, Shane thumping his way up the stairs to the second story while Grady beached himself on an easy chair and massaged a knee. Elizabeth checked the time and decided that 'training' had pre-empted woodworking. She left McCoy wishing everyone a happy new year—she loved it when both the detectives and the attorneys shared the screen—and went downstairs, hoping to kill at least one book in private before the evening and Barry's mandatory family fun.

"Hey, guys, this is Anne Harlow, welcome back to my channel: Who What Wear. Today I'm going to be reviewing the Tiger line of pressed powders by Sophie Takai. No spoilers, but I bought an extra case of this stuff for my little sis's birthday, so after the review, I'm going to bring her in for a second opinion, see how she's liking this gunk. I hope she liked it, because it's crazy expensive, so if she didn't, I'm gonna have to scrape it off her face and see if I can get a refund. Just sweep it back into the container."

Elizabeth opened the door to the cellar, where Anne had set up some kind of…amateur porno set. There was a massive roll of green paper hung up on the wall behind her, a card table in front of her with a number of make-up products and props and sheaves of paper, and a camera facing her. And was that a boom mike set up over her head?

"What are you doing?" Elizabeth asked from the doorway.

Anne wore a shirt that read "lol they blocked me" with a swishy skirt and the kind of make-up job that didn't obey the Geneva Convention. It was almost overwhelming, but she'd stopped just short of 'plastering it on' at a 'shade overdone, glam rock' sort of look. And she'd put her hair in pigtails, which Elizabeth didn't think was a good look at all.

Anne gestured around. "Camera, make-up, the long speech I'm assuming you just heard about me reviewing make-up—you got me, it's my one-woman performance of *MacBeth*."

Elizabeth held up the book in her hand. "Well, I was going to enjoy some peace and quiet and literature, so maybe you could do this somewhere else?"

"Maybe in a universe where noise doesn't carry and I don't have the biggest family since the Hapsburgs all under one roof. But on this Earth, I need to use the cellar. You were already resigned to Grady using it, right? I got him to let me use it instead, so the way I see it, you're losing the sound of a circular saw going at a block of wood and gaining my sparkling repartee."

"Well, I'm not in the habit of clearing out when Grady 'woodworks' since it's only happened once, and I had my heart set on using the basement, because I have ears too and it's hard to read when I have to listen to your big brother and his friend having another impromptu wrestling match."

"Why don't you go hang out with your girlfriend, Eleven? Since you're so in love and out and proud and stuff?"

"Why don't you go hang out with your boyfriend? Do you have one of those, or are you waiting for Sophie Takai to send you one for review?"

"It's hard to find a boyfriend when he has to be real and not a beard for a real-estate scam, or whatever it is you're doing."

"That's—" Elizabeth faltered. "That's true, it is hard to find a good man, but you still suck."

"Why don't you just close the door and let me use the cellar while you use the basement?"

"Because I'll still hear you talking about 'the Tiger line of pressed powders.'"

"Then maybe you can learn something about wearing make-up that isn't stolen from the set of *Mad Men*."

Elizabeth slammed the door shut. She heard Anne say, "Note to self: edit out all that." Then, very charitably and with lots of goodwill and much love in her heart, she got out her cell phone, turned up the volume, and started Del Shannon again. It wasn't quite the best soundtrack to read a paperback copy of *Meet the Tiger* by Leslie Charteris, but it went great with Anne's discontent.

A minute later, Anne opened the cellar door and pointed her camera out at Elizabeth. The red light was on and everything.

"You got me," Elizabeth said, not looking up from her book. "I'm the Blair Witch."

"I know this doesn't matter much to you," Anne replied, "but this is my livelihood, so maybe you could look into your heart and find some feminist, working girl, professional courtesy—"

"You're going to play the solidarity card after you pried into my relationship like it's any of your business?"

"My family, my business."

"Well, I'm queer and my life is hard enough already, so maybe you could find some human decency, good person, 'What Would Jesus Do' courtesy..."

Anne lowered the camera and crossed her arms. "Are you screwing with my family, yes or no?"

Elizabeth sighed and told herself it wasn't a lie. "I'm just here as your sister's date. I don't have an ulterior motive." *Michelle does, but I don't.* "And I really don't want my week here to be a series of sparring matches."

"Fine. You turn off the soundtrack, I get my show over with, we call it the Aristocrats."

Elizabeth couldn't believe she knew that reference. "God, you're niche. Fine. Record away."

Anne withdrew into the cellar, closing the door behind her. Elizabeth could hear her talking through the wall, but it was as indistinct as hearing the radio in a car as it drove by. She could tune it out easily enough. Even put earphones in, if the thought of doing so didn't make her feel like an uber-bitch for not thinking of it earlier.

The doorbell rang. Grateful for the distraction, Elizabeth headed up the stairs to investigate. When no one else came to answer the door, she opened it and found an elderly black man arranged precisely on the welcome mat. His face was boyish despite a thick mustache and thicker set of glasses, and he wore multiple layers of comfortable but fashionless clothing, like he was three English professors merged into one. He bore a wicker basket under one arm.

"Oh, hello!" he said, evincing surprise in an unexpectedly high-pitched voice. "I was expecting one of the Harlows. You must be their houseguest, Elizabeth?"

"That's right," Elizabeth said. "Are you here to see someone?"

"No, not as such. I'm Jonah Slade, pastor over at the Good Shepherd Northview Church, and I live next door. Say, do you know what church you're attending for the Christmas service? We are a predominantly black congregation, but I promise you, it's just like a white church, only we think Tyler Perry is funny."

Elizabeth smiled. "I'm not really religious—I guess I'm just going with the Harlows wherever they're headed."

"Well, they're good people. Our carolers have been coming here every Christmas for as long as I can remember, which isn't much these days, and Barry Harlow always has enough hot chocolate to go around. Now isn't that sweet?"

"It is!" Elizabeth said.

"Anyway…" He held out the basket. "This is just a little thank you in advance from us next door. Some cookies, candy—God knows my wife loves making it, but I can't have it under my roof or I won't be able to fit out the door much longer."

"Oh! Thank you very much. Would you like to come in?"

"No, no, I've got a trunk full of those things to give out. But, just between you, me, and the walls, y'all are my favorite."

Limey came running up, barking excitedly, and Jonah stooped to scratch him behind the ears.

"And I put in a bone for the mutt here. See that he gets it next time he's in that high chair of his."

"I will," Elizabeth promised. "Say, I have a weird question…"

"Shoot."

"What's something that you hate?"

Jonah scowled. "You mean, like a group of people or—"

"No, no, nothing like that, just…*something*. A song or a type of car…"

"Vanilla ice cream," Jonah said confidently.

"Oh?"

"Yes, sir. No flavor. Why buy an ice cream with no flavor? If you're gonna get ice cream, why not get ice cream you like to eat?"

"I suppose people like to put toppings on it," Elizabeth said.

"That makes no sense to me. Say you want Oreo cookies on your ice cream. You buy cookies 'n cream, right? Or you buy vanilla ice cream, for just about the same price, *and* Oreos for half again as much, crumble the Oreos up yourself, you get the exact same thing as cookies 'n cream at twice the price. If you want to be boring, *chocolate* is boring, but at least it tastes good!"

"I guess you're right," Elizabeth said. "I've never really thought about it, but I don't think I've ever bought vanilla ice cream."

"So we have that in common."

"Yeah, I guess we do."

"Does that answer your question?"

"Yeah, I think it does."

They wished each other a good day, and Elizabeth went to put the basket on the kitchen table, taking a Zip-loc of raisin cookies for herself. She resolved not to feel guilty about it. It couldn't be that anyone else liked raisin cookies, could it?

Grady came into the kitchen then to refill his water. Seeing the basket, he called out to Shane that there were cookies, which brought both Shane and Typhos *tout suite*. Elizabeth left them talking about "*Blart*, a gritty R-rated distant finale focusing on a broken-down old Paul Blart trying to defend his mall during a zombie apocalypse," and went to enjoy her cookies in peace.

But there was an odd itch left from her encounter with Anne, something unsaid that bothered her like a hard-fought game coming to a tie. What was the damn point of a sport that ended in a tie? You needed sudden death overtime, best two out of three. It was either the agony of defeat, the thrill of victory, or nothing.

Elizabeth dug up her laptop and went to the bathroom for some tub privacy, where she got comfortable and did a search for Who What Wear. It was mildly complicated by not knowing if it was spelled Who What *Where* or Who What *Wear*, and the other one was porn. But she finally found Anne's YouTube channel.

The videos went back almost ten years. The first few were from high school, reviews of rock albums mostly, Anne wearing flannel vests and a biker bandanna and other adorable things like that. As the descriptions had warned, they were very early, and Anne wasn't much of a performer, but she definitely had an It quality, a bit of Marilyn Monroe's laugh, a bit of Diana Dors's shimmy. She wasn't Beyoncé or anything, but another woman could have the same measurements as Anne, say the same things, and just not be as magnetic.

The videos kept going, becoming a vlog in college with sporadic updates, then offering an eclectic mix of content after graduation. Movie reviews, music, books, theories on this and that, reactions to this and that, and pleasantly free of the clickbait nonsense that made everything on the Internet read like a tabloid headline. She was a bit more low-key than that, with titles like "You wanna talk about Kylo Ren?", "I think the Jurassic Parks should've stopped at *The Lost World*, you guys," and "Fuck you, I still cry at *Titanic*."

On camera, in the vignettes Elizabeth skipped through, she was chummy and easygoing but fiercely individualistic. Girly, but tomboyish. Good-humored, but not a comedian. Thoughtful, but not serious.

As time went on, the beauty stuff took center stage, with one show a week on this or that. Apparently, when there was nothing else to talk about, she entirely covered viewer mail. There was still the occasional discussion or review posted; at various times, she'd corralled Shane, Grady, and Patsy into appearing for a second opinion on this or that, with even Barry showing up.

That brought Elizabeth to present day, where Anne was apparently also a model on Instagram. Some of the videos showed the shoots she did. It was risqué, but mild by Internet standards. She'd show her bra, but in an unbuttoned shirt or a plunging neckline. It reminded Elizabeth of something on the side of a WW2 bomber—Janet would love that—and she considered how carefully Anne must control her image while still being spontaneous and open. It seemed a tough tightrope to walk, and that nearly invisible effort impressed Elizabeth.

And *shit*, did she look good on January 4, 2015. Orange—who knew?

The stairs groaned as someone's weight ambled down them. Elizabeth shrunk the window, then closed her laptop. So she was sitting with a closed laptop on her knees when Barry arrived at the bottom step.

Not suspicious at all.

"Mr. Harlow," she said, launching a charm offensive. "Hi!"

"Hey, Elizabeth." He leaned against the wall, adjusting his stance after he brushed the light switch. "So, how are you finding Christmas with the Harlows?"

Elizabeth smiled at him. "Oh, you know…as long as the coffee's fresh, I'm happy."

Barry laughed, scratching behind his ear. "Well, I don't want you thinking we're ignoring you or not being sensitive to yours and Michelle's leanings. If you need anything, I'm sure any of us would be happy to help."

"Yeah, I'm fine." Elizabeth shrugged. "No complaints."

"In fact, though, I was thinking maybe we could do something—as a family—that's considerate of you and Michelle, the same way you've put up…not put up…the same way you've participated in our little shenanigans."

"I don't need any special treatment," Elizabeth demurred. "Warm bed, hot meals, I'm good."

"No, no, it's our pleasure. I want to treat you to something that appeals to you, not just what we like."

Elizabeth held in a long-suffering sigh. "Sure. Why not?"

After the vague anxiety attack of riding with Michelle on icy roads while she followed Barry's speeding Prius, Elizabeth reached Club Gumb. Whatever else you could say about the entertainment scene in Ohio, it wasn't short on parking. They were able to park close enough to the door for the bass to rattle their windows. She and the girls walked to the door, got a pass from the bouncer, and went inside to meet up with the boys. Elizabeth figured acclimating to deafeningly loud noise worked on the same principle as swimming in cold water. The best way through was to just dive in and hope no bodily malfunctions occurred.

Inside, the club had a jump-start even on the wintry dusk—pitch-black except for glow necklaces that were bestowed upon them like leis. The music that had struck Elizabeth outside as being vaguely Mordor in origin turned out to be Russian rap, a combination that didn't do favors to either side, or to sound in general. The current karaoker—karaokee? karokette? —at least looked to be having fun, which to Elizabeth's mind covered a multitude of sins.

Maybe it was NYC provincialism, maybe it was just snobbishness, but the place struck her as plasticky, a theme park version of a gay bar. Or maybe it was just that she was thirty and cool wasn't her go-to anymore, like Grady had said. It had been a while since she'd frequented a place like this, preferring either partying nights on the town where she could find someone in her social circle who was guaranteed non-crazy, or the trendy, high-maintenance nightspots that she considered Bring Your Own Orientation. Not so selective about sexual identity as long as everyone inside was fashionable and had nice skin.

The Ohio scene, on the other hand, was eager to please and desperate to prove itself; a combination that tried her patience. The clientele was mostly queer, and seemed comfortable and happy enough, so maybe it was just her, her internal wavelength not jibing with what this place was sending out. It'd been known to happen.

They played seeing-eye dog for Barry, who stumbled through the club's Late Dank Basement aesthetic, and finally were seated in an ungodly amalgamation of booth and table. Elizabeth pictured a Chuck E. Cheese birthday party for gay kids. But then, who would the mascot be, Richard Gere's gerbil?

She laughed to herself and thought how ashamed she should be for thinking that.

There was a community theater stage on the far side of the room, as if they'd deposed a high school play to put on a prom for scene kids, and most of the light in the room came from the ghost lights on it, which were set to a disco ball display. There was also a light above their table, and all of the other tables as well, but it was a blacklight that only illuminated the writing on the menus and the bodypaint on the waitstaff. It made Elizabeth feel like she was ordering off an episode of *CSI*.

"Quite the production they've made of this place, wouldn't you say?" Barry asked sunnily. "Very much its own."

"Very much so," Anne agreed, possibly because she'd read the menu and found the disturbing similarities between the names of the meals and the contents of Urban Dictionary.

The waiter came by, reminding Elizabeth once again that while she was attracted to men, she still didn't get the appeal of twinks. She'd always held that the less a prospective lover reminded you of Justin Bieber, the better. But he took their orders professionally, with none of the sadism Elizabeth

110

would take in seeing the middle-class Irish order things that made a Sex on the Beach look subtle and skimpy on innuendo. The waiter took off, and they were all left reconsidering their open-mindedness.

Barry clapped his hands together. "So, Mr. Jones, did you notice the Christmas decorations back home?"

"Mmm?" Typhos asked, still studying the menu. "Oh, yeah, the nativity scene. Looks nice."

"That's the Slades', actually," Barry said. "Our next-door neighbors."

"Well, it's on our property, too," Michelle said. "So it's a little ours."

Barry took an overly patient breath. "I consider it theirs; they made it. The Santa Claus on the roof, that's ours."

"Yeah, that is crazy!" Typhos said. "Getting all that stuff up there. Is that safe?"

Barry waved a hand about. "It's fine. We get very mild weather here in Madison County."

"Yo, why is Santa Claus black though?" Typhos asked.

Barry blinked more than was strictly necessary. "I'm glad you asked, Mr. Jones. The historical Santa Claus, Saint Nicholas—"

"Santa Claus was a real guy?" Shane asked.

"It's one of those 'every legend has a bit of truth' things," Michelle said. "Like King Arthur."

"And that Clive Owen movie!" Typhos said, nodding. "That was tight."

"I thought it was okay," Elizabeth said.

"You didn't like Kiera Knightley?" Anne asked.

"They had Mads Mikkelsen and Hugh Dancy years before *Hannibal*," Grady said. "And Mads keeps talking to Hugh about how great killing is."

"Now *Hannibal* I liked," Elizabeth said. She conjured a European accent that was somewhere in the East, but nowhere specific. "'A recliner is a type of chair that can bend backwards to give additional support. Tell me, Will, how much would you bend to support a friend?'"

Barry raised his voice. "But anyway, Saint Nicholas was black..."

"Oh, okay," Typhos said. "I just thought that before you'd make Santa black, you'd make the Jesuses Middle Eastern. They were all born in Bethlehem, right?"

"Grady, you doing okay?" Barry asked a moment later, his tone mildly accusatory. "You look a little uncomfortable."

"I always look uncomfortable."

"I thought there'd be more leather," Shane said.

"You're thinking of an S&M club," Elizabeth said. She kept her voice only slightly chiding. "Gay equals liberal equals vegan. Not a lot of leather."

"Hey, real quick," Michelle cut in. "Saint Nicholas is usually depicted as dark-skinned, but he was actually Greek."

At that moment, the background music was replaced with the piped in sound of a drumroll and all the lights on the stage snapped on. A drag queen whose make-up game allowed her to do a reasonable impression of an early Pixar character was dressed as a candy striper, while another, who had the understated class of one of Trump's ex-wives, lay on a hospital bed, dressed as a 1950s housewife.

Elizabeth groaned. "I get that they're supposed to be women, but why is that one a nurse? Why can't she be in drag as a female doctor? They have those now."

"I don't think you're getting the whole vibe they're going for," Anne said.

"Mrs. Mounds," the nurse said, hoisting a comically oversized syringe.

Prop comedy, Elizabeth thought. *The last refuge of the scoundrel.*

"I am here to give you your injection!"

"Oh, are you me husband?" the housewife asked in a bad Cockney accent—not that Elizabeth had ever heard a good one.

"You may feel a small prick!"

"Oh, but you're definitely my husband. OOOOOOH! I think I got the point."

Elizabeth held her head in her hands. "This is where all those dick jokes they couldn't tell on *Leave It to Beaver* go to die…"

"It's a drag show, lady," Shane said. "What are you expecting?"

Elizabeth shook her head, still in her hands. "I never got the big deal about drag queens putting on make-up and dresses to look like women. You men do know that we do that to look like women, too, right? First thing in the morning, I look like Christian Bale trying to win an Oscar."

"I believe you," Anne said.

Elizabeth let *that* slide. But she did say pointedly: "And I don't like the implication that all women are these catty, slutty, obnoxious caricatures…"

"That's not every drag act," Patsy said.

"No, that's just people in general," Grady said, scratching behind his ear. "I've seen it on reality TV. People seem to find it amusing."

"When have you watched reality TV?" Anne asked.

"Michelle has it on sometimes when I'm getting a glass of water. Real housewives of whatever." He shrugged. "Can't see how you wouldn't prefer the fake housewives."

"They're not making fun of women," Typhos said.

"Thank you!" Anne replied.

"They're making fun of black people."

Anne shook her head. "They're white!"

Typhos made a show of pointing things out to Anne. "Look at 'em! They're all doing these stereotypical ghetto queen bits, but they don't put on blackface, so nobody cares. It's a minstrel show."

"Minstrel show?" Michelle asked. "That seems a little strong."

"I'm standing by it," Typhos said. "It's a bunch of white people pretending they're Queen Latifah."

"It still seems strong."

Elizabeth heard something go *fuck it* deep in her subconscious. She didn't disagree with Typhos, but damn if he was going to be the only one speaking up while she shut her mouth and checked her phone.

"Honestly," she said, "I'm not sure why you brought me here. If you wanted to take me out to do something just for me, that's great, that's very thoughtful of you, but why a gay bar? I enjoy other stuff! To say nothing of the fact that people mostly go to gay bars to hook up and I'm dating someone, clearly, so why not take me rock climbing or to get a massage or to play laser tag? Or just ask me what I'd be into!"

"I asked Michelle," Barry said.

Elizabeth took a deep breath. "It's just not for me. And while I'm on the subject, *Bad Lawyer* looks like a horrible show. I'm glad it has gay people, but I'm not going to watch a show I don't enjoy just because two women might kiss in it. Trust me, there are other ways I can see that."

"Well, the first season isn't great," Anne said, "but it gets a lot better if you give it a chance."

"I don't want to sit through twenty episodes before it works out the kinks. I go to work, I don't get twenty days to stop sucking before they fire me. And are you going to agree with me once tonight?"

"Should I?" Anne asked.

Elizabeth spread her hands.

"Clearly," Barry said, clearing his throat, "this was a tad ill-advised. I'm going to stay and get my order, sort out everyone else's refunds, but if anyone wants to leave, we did bring two cars."

"I'm hungry," Shane said. "I'm staying."

"I'm out," Grady said, standing.

Michelle and Typhos got up, too.

"I'm with them," Anne said.

"Thought you liked drag shows," Elizabeth said.

"In general. These guys suck."

It had started snowing again outside, the wind kicking up, flecks of white shining against the early night in the glow of the streetlights. It would've been pretty if it weren't so cold.

"So, Typhos," Grady was asking. "That's a Greek name, right?"

"Hey, man, just because the Greeks are all broke…"

Elizabeth held her London Fog trench closed tight against the snow. The hemline had been a bad idea. "Can we circle back to this where there's central heating? There are five of us, we drove Priuses, and we've still got three people enjoying the Buffalo Billiards Bar. What are we doing?"

"We could always go back for them later," Grady said.

Michelle imitated her father. "That wouldn't be too good for the environment, boyo."

Anne was on her phone. "Okay, they're going to text us when they're ready to leave."

"So four of us can go and one of us could stay here," Michelle figured.

"I brought a book," Grady said. "If there's a coffee shop or something around here, I could just hang out."

"No, no," Anne said. "It's Christmas. We came out here to spend time as family. Leave no man behind!"

Michelle asked, "What do you want to do? Get some overpriced lattes and watch Grady read?"

"Applebee's next door has a bar," Elizabeth suggested. "We get a quick drink, hope the others don't order dessert."

"I could go for a beer that doesn't cost ten bucks," Typhos said.

"Guess I'm still designated driver," Grady said.

"Well," Shane reasoned, "you still don't like beer."

"It's a restaurant," Anne said. "They'll have mixed drinks."

"I'll get a Dr. Pepper."

"Freak," Anne replied off-handedly.

"You just have to drink it warm." Grady shrugged.

"I'll ask them to microwave it."

The restaurant was playing music that worked the 'classic' in 'classic rock' to within an inch of its life, but at least Elizabeth could see her hand in front of her face. The bar was open, the stools free—in Ohio, there weren't nearly as many people drinking away the holidays as there were in New York. Talk about Norman Rockwell...

Elizabeth took off her coat to sit down and crossed her legs. The looks were worth the frostbite. Even Anne had to glance at her and admit, like a witness on the stand, "Nice dress."

"It is, isn't it?"

Typhos signaled for the bartender, who was pulling double-duty, delivering drinks to a table in the back. The wait had him tapping his fingers on the bar.

"I just don't think it's funny," Grady was saying. "It's basically amateur stand-up, right? Well, they're not funny. I don't get how that stops being important when they put on dresses. Eddie Izzard, he wears dresses, he's really funny."

The bartender came over. Typhos nodded and dropped a fiver in the tip jar that read 'Stacy's Boob Job Fund.' "Sorry they got you working so hard, brother. Bourbon."

The bartender gave a straight-guy 'de nada' gesture as he poured. He assiduously kept his own counsel as the others ordered and received their drinks, the conversation continuing around the exchange like traffic around roadwork.

"So the standard has been set," Anne agreed, drumming her hands. "You can be funny even when you're a man wearing women's clothing."

"Oh, I think men can be funny, as long as they're not too handsome," Elizabeth said. "Fat men, automatically funny."

"Especially when they fall down," Anne said sarcastically.

"Well, they have to say 'whooooooa' or something," Elizabeth replied.

The last drink poured, the bartender moved off, Michelle's eyes following after him and his tight jeans. Elizabeth wondered if anyone noticed or if she was the only one paying attention.

Typhos savored a whiff of the bourbon before he took a sip. "Speaking of all things gay, when does a lesbian lose her virginity?"

"When she has sex," Michelle said. "Duh."

"I'm not a lesbian," Elizabeth said. Not that anyone was looking at her.

"Oh, do I have a chance then?" Shane asked.

"She's pan," Anne said. "Remember? It's like being bi, only she does robots, too."

"That's right, that's right—but c'mon, who wouldn't fuck a robot if it looked like Scarlet Johansson or whatever? A liar, that's who."

Grady shook his head. He was nursing a Pepsi; they hadn't had Dr. Pepper or even Mr. Pibb. "No, no, for it to count, you would have to want to fuck...a Transformer with the *consciousness* of Scarlet Johansson."

"Bullshit," Typhos said. "There's no lesbian who would fuck a gorilla just because it had the mind of a lesbian, am I right?"

"I don't know," Elizabeth said. "Dating prospects can get pretty bad."

"Wait, wait, wait," Typhos said. "I know you're pan and all, all into those expansion-pack genders that the kids seem to like, but we still haven't heard your opinion. When does a lesbian lose her virginity?"

"Michelle said it. When she has sex."

Grady coughed. "I think what he means is...is your fourth base our third base?"

"Which is that?" Michelle asked. "Fingering or tongue? I can never remember."

Anne giggled. "If you can't tell the difference, no wonder you broke up with Will."

"I'm not talking about fingers or tongues," Elizabeth said. "I'm talking about any emotionally meaningful sex."

"So if Ben Affleck stops into town, fucks an eighteen-year-old, he doesn't give a shit, she doesn't give a shit, then she's still a virgin? She ain't got no hymen!"

"I would've thought dildo," Michelle said.

"But a woman can fuck herself with a dildo. That's the dictionary definition," Elizabeth argued.

Typhos moved the tip jar to let Michelle know where to stick it. "Well, a man can fuck himself with a fleshlight. It's still not sex unless there's someone else there."

On Typhos's other side, Anne passed him a fiver. "This is exactly why this whole virginity thing is so ridiculous. I don't even believe in that shit."

"You can't just not believe in it," Grady said. "It's a thing."

"So was the Earth being flat!"

"So was alchemy," Elizabeth agreed. "And phrenology."

There was a burst of laughter from a table in the back, and Elizabeth reflexively turned. She caught a fleeting glimpse of flashing eyes pointed her way, and then they turned back—as if she were the noise and they'd been looking for her.

"They laughing at us?" Grady asked.

"Nah." Elizabeth turned back. "I'm changing my answer. I'm going with Anne here."

"You can't change your answer," Typhos said. "That's the coward's way out."

"She makes a good point," Elizabeth said. "What does virginity have to do with anything? How is someone who's never had sex *that different* from someone who's only had sex once? And then *they're* not at all different from someone who's only had sex twice?"

"Oh, there's a difference," Michelle said. "Eventually."

"Unless they're married, which I also don't get," Anne added.

"Marriage?" Elizabeth asked.

"No, just why it makes such a difference, premarital sex and marital sex. That one's on the way out, and we should send the whole virginity mess with it. Like the four humors, or Pluto. Let the world move on."

"Fair point," Typhos said. "I'm going with Anne, too."

"What happened to not changing your answer?" Grady asked.

"I didn't have an answer. I asked the question, remember? And when in doubt, always go with the hottest chicks in the room."

Michelle squinted. "Is this because I'm a lesbian?"

Grady scratched his head. "Is what because you're a lesbian?"

"Anne's straight, Elizabeth's pan, I'm off the table, so…"

"It was just a stupid joke," Typhos said.

"Yeah," Elizabeth said. "Take it as a win for feminism."

"Nah, I'm not a feminist," Typhos replied.

There were more gales of laughter behind them. Elizabeth didn't turn at first, but when it kept going—when it seemed to be right behind her—she turned and saw a glint of metal. The ring on a finger, pointed her way, before the hand was withdrawn. They were being laughed at.

"Don't mind them," Grady said, narrowing his eyes to scrutinize the group. "They're assholes."

"McQuarries," Anne muttered darkly.

"*Those* are the McQuarries?" Typhos asked. "The dogshit McQuarries?"

"Good description."

"What do you mean you're not a feminist?" Michelle questioned.

Elizabeth tried to head that off. "I'm almost done with my beer. Let's go see what's taking the others so long—"

"I mean I'm an egalitarian," Typhos said.

"Great, a men's rights activist."

"No, nope, one of my problems with feminists is that they've got attack dogs going around saying shit, doing shit, and no one's on the inside policing them."

"Attack dogs?" Anne repeated dubiously.

"Yeah, fucking insulting people, going on the offensive, with a wink and a nod from everyone else. And I'm not saying the MRAs are better. They do the same shit, so I'm not with either side. I just believe men and women are and should be equal. Egalitarianism."

Michelle held up a finger. "Give me just one second while I figure out how to phrase this… Okay, how can you not want to call yourself a feminist just because some of them step out of line? As a black man, do you not know what the feminist movement has done for you?"

"Yeah, they've made us march at the back of suffragette protests. That kind of shit is still going on, by the way. Not that I want this whole self-pitying, 'white people are the worst' shit from white people, the martyrdom routine, but there's stuff to work on."

"And there isn't with 'egalitarianism?'" Anne asked. "None of *them* have ever stepped out of line?"

"I don't see it as a movement, I see it as a philosophy."

"Okay," Michelle said, "how many people in your philosophy have actually done something for abuse victims, for rape survivors…"

"Don't all gang up on him," Elizabeth said, though her words were nearly lost in an irksome squeal as a chair was pushed back from a table. One of the McQuarries was on his feet.

"I'm not going to get on my phone and look up statistics," Typhos said. "I'm talking about a personal stance here. There's all this stuff about being a proud black man. Black heritage, black excellence, and I love that shit, we need that shit. But then you turn around and while you can be proud of being black, you can't be proud of being a man."

Michelle squinted. "I wouldn't say that's feminism's fault, precisely."

Typhos blew a puff of air out of his lips. "Well, there ain't no men going around saying you should run down the whole gender. Look at music. It used to be about how women shouldn't be with scrubs, they should find good men, and men shouldn't *be* scrubs, they should be a good man to a good woman. That's feminist, or at least it used to be. Now, it's all men ain't shit, women are goddesses, and us fellas just have to put up with it. I'm not saying women aren't goddesses, I'd never say that, but how you not gonna let a man be a king, be a badass, be a warrior? If you don't want a man, fine, but why wouldn't you want a man who's just as good as you?"

Grady coughed.

"Oh, you're on his side," Michelle said.

"He is saying men and women are equal."

Michelle narrowed her eyes. "That's facetious."

"I say men and women are equal and you automatically think I'm facetious?" Typhos asked.

"Do you need to look the word up?"

"Michelle!" Elizabeth put in curtly.

"Well, what do you think?" Michelle asked. "You've been oddly quiet here."

"I think that if someone has issues with something, you can't just dismiss it out of hand," Elizabeth said.

Michelle scoffed. "Someone has issues with everything."

"And nothing's perfect," Elizabeth said.

A small tray—the type used to hold a receipt and pen—dropped down to the counter beside them. It wasn't set down. It was dropped. All of them looked at it, wondering if it was theirs, before noticing the stocky man standing over it. He was a little below average in height, with his curly hair giving into baldness, and an abrasive smile coarsening a nondescript face into sandpaper.

"Yo, we're leaving," he called over to the barman. "There's your credit card, get it while it's hot."

"Vinnie McQuarrie," Anne said, leaning an elbow on the bar. "Usually I'd figure you for the drinking alone type, but I guess somebody turned over a really big rock."

"Annabelle Harlow," he replied, leaning on the bar himself. "Heard one of the 'Clan Harlow' went lezbo. Glad it's not you, sweet cheeks."

"Well, the night is young and *you're here*."

"Vinnie, Anne, come on," Michelle said. "If nothing else, can't we just pretend we don't see each other?"

"I wish," Grady said, and Anne pounded his shoulder in a silent 'good one.'

Vinnie snorted. "Yeah, 'bout what I'd expect from a Harlow. The self-righteous act, then bam, my windshield's caved in."

"That was an accident," Anne said. "You know it was. Slashing the tires on my mom's car, though. Classy. She loved taking a taxi to her chemo."

Vinnie shrugged, unapologetic. "Didn't know it was your mom's car. But hey, better things to do than hear you bitch and moan about everything your family's been through." The bartender had slipped in and, with the speedy stealth of someone who wanted no part in an argument, replaced the receipt and credit card on the tray. Vinnie took his card and signed the slip without adding a tip. "Tell your sister I said hi."

"Hey." Typhos flicked his finger against the tip jar, making it chime. "Aren't you forgetting something?"

"No. I remember waiting forty-five minutes to get a steak." Vinnie wagged his finger. "Nuh-uh."

"It's part of their wages, man. It's Christmas, they're understaffed, and it's busy. Cut 'em some slack."

"You cut 'em some slack, bro."

"Bro?" Typhos asked.

"Bro," Vinnie confirmed. He reached into his jacket pocket and brought out a pair of sunglasses. "Listen, you ever have a Hydrox cookie?"

"A what?"

"Hydrox cookie," Vinnie repeated, slipping the sunglasses on. "It's basically an Oreo. Like, the store brand Oreo. Only it actually came out four years before the Oreo, in 1908, when Sunshine Biscuits thought to use an industrial press to make their chocolate wafers have the imprint of a flower—"

"Holy shit," Elizabeth interrupted. "Are you doing a monologue?"

Vinnie lowered his sunglasses. "I'm...I'm telling you about Hydrox cookies. They're basically Oreos—"

"What do you think this is, prestige TV?" Elizabeth looked around for support from the Harlows, but none of them seemed to get the reference. "You know, those shows about people who seem cool but turn out to be assholes?"

No response.

"No one ever turns a light on?"

No response.

"Occasionally you see someone's ass?"

"Oh, like Ryan Murphy shows?" Michelle asked.

Elizabeth groaned inwardly. "Yeah. And there's always some guy who wants to make a point and instead of just coming out and saying something, he has to tell a whole big story about some weird shit he saw or like a Bible verse. And since the show is an hour and a half long, he'll go on for five minutes or so, just on this little fairy tale that's supposed to prove his point. And you don't really mind, because it's some cool guy like James Spader who could probably make reading a phonebook sound cool, but c'mon, who does that in real life?"

Vinnie blinked. You could see it behind his lowered sunglasses. "No, but the Hydrox cookie came out before the Oreo, but the Oreo cookie caught on instead!"

"He makes a good point," Anne said. "It does lose something if he just skips to the end. I think if we heard the whole Hydrox saga then it would come off better."

Grady raised his hand. "I actually already know what a Hydrox is. But did you know that Jacob Loose, the guy who owned the company that made Hydrox, ended up getting rich off the Cheez-It?"

Vinnie looked at him. "Why don't you just kill yourself? That is the Harlow way, right?"

There was a roar of motion as the Harlows cleared their stools, Grady's actually clattering to the floor. Then there was an equal and opposite roar from across the restaurant, as the McQuarries jumped up from lounging around their table, rattling it and the empty plates left on top.

Typhos stood as well, hands balled into fists.

Anne grabbed Elizabeth by the shoulder, pulling her back. The whole gang retreated a few steps.

"Good, good," Michelle said. "They're leaving anyway, so we just—"

Anne interrupted her like she wasn't speaking at all. "They threw the first punch."

"What?" Elizabeth asked as Anne walked up to Vinnie. "What?"

Anne stood in front of Vinnie, reminding Elizabeth of a cat that stood up to a dog without time for piddling concerns like the dog being a Rottweiler and the cat being a cat. "I've had a lot of time to think about this," she said, "because it's genuinely a mystery of the universe to me. Now a bully, such as yourself, will not be the smartest guy—otherwise he'd think of something better to do socially than the equivalent of flinging his own feces around. But it's like they have this sixth fucking sense of knowing just how far they can push people so that person will snap and get into trouble while *they* walk away scot-free. They were only joking, after all. It was just one big joke. To a man, any given bully in any city on Earth will have this precise calibration to play the victim while still being able to torture someone as much as they want. Someone like me, someone like my sister, someone like my brother. But what really gets me is this. Every now and then, that bully who is so used to getting his jollies on someone weaker than him, will just happen to run into someone who they just absolutely should not have fucked with."

"And I just ran into someone like that?" Vinnie asked dubiously.

"No," Anne said. "You ran into three of us."

A ballerina couldn't have been more graceful, lifting her Converse sneaker from a dead rest to the modicum of space separating his testicles. Anne was like a cheerleader doing a high kick, popping her hips and leaning back slightly as her foot flew up, then sweeping her leg back down to catch her weight underneath her. Elizabeth was genuinely impressed.

Then feet were stomping on linoleum and cheap vinyl furniture was being shoved out of the way as Vinnie's siblings—all four of them—came running. Elizabeth had about a second before the stampede hit. Michelle had thrown herself over the bar, Typhos had raised his fists—they'd been balled for a while—and the Harlows were running at the McQuarries like the snap had just come in a football game.

Elizabeth didn't have time to ask herself if she wanted any part in this family feud. She just had time to grab an empty beer bottle and swing it as hard as she could.

Chapter 7

THE FIGHT HADN'T LASTED LONG. There was a donut shop next to the restaurant. Personally, Elizabeth would've thought a gay bar, sit-down dining, and a donut shop on the same block were eclectic even for New York, but there was no accounting for taste. They spent about an hour locked up in holding, with the McQuarries chained together on a bench outside the cell to keep them separate. It seemed to Elizabeth that not being locked up was a privilege, not a right, but then she saw that one of the deputies had 'McQuarrie' printed proudly on his name bar and guessed that had something to do with the family breathing free air.

She also noticed that the toilet paper in the cell was only single-ply. That annoyed her far more than the incarceration. Not that she needed to go—it was just that it meant Anne was right about something.

The McQuarries were taken to the sheriff's office to be interrogated, one by one, and then they started in on the Harlows and the Harlow-adjacent. Grady was the only one spared. He'd suffered a broken jaw and was at the hospital getting treated. Deputy McQuarrie brought Typhos back to the holding cell.

"Elizabeth Smile?" he asked, and she picked herself up.

"Present."

He held up a small evidence baggie. Inside was one of Elizabeth's press-on nails. She'd last seen it in Phil McQuarrie's scalp, after she'd jumped on his back to keep him from breaking Anne's pert little nose. He, in return, had thrown his head back and caught Elizabeth's face with his thick skull, which was probably where she'd picked up the bruise on her eye that everyone else was so excited about.

"You wear press-on nails?" Anne asked.

"I have sex with women. I need to be able to take them off."

"So instead of acrylics, you're shoving acetone up people's cooches. Considerate."

"I have a system. You start by using organic glue…"

Deputy McQuarrie opened the cell door.

"Oh thank God," Anne said.

The sheriff's office struck Elizabeth as almost exactly like her old principal's office, although she remembered her principal as a tall, lean man, impressive stentorian. Sheriff Byers might've had the voice of Powers Boothe, but he had the build of Truman Capote. Yet, seated behind his desk in a leather chair, his chubby fingers folded together, and his bulldog face set into a grimace behind oversized glasses, he might as well have been the guy who showed up at the end of a superhero movie to show how screwed the superhero would be if they greenlit a sequel.

"I've got a pretty good idea of what went down," Byers said, now striking Elizabeth as somewhat reptilian. It was all in how his folded fingers didn't budge, and his lips barely moved beneath his bulbous spectacles. "And I realize you're not a Harlow and you just got dragged into all this because you were at the wrong place at the wrong time. So, tell me the truth. Who started it?"

Elizabeth had had a full hour to think it over now. She'd heard from Anne that they wanted to know who'd thrown the first punch. She could still see Anne kicking that fat fuck in the happy place. A thing of beauty and a joy to behold.

"They did, Sheriff," Elizabeth said. "I couldn't tell you which of them because I'm new to the area, but it definitely wasn't any of the Harlows."

Byers sighed. A deep rattle in his lungs. "That's what I figured. Come on. Up."

They went back to the holding cell and the benches. Byers signaled to Deputy McQuarrie, who started unhooking his kin, and he himself opened the holding cell. "Well, seems there's no way to say for certain who did what. I've got people saying it was McQuarries and people saying it was Harlows. So just for the sake of the holiday season, I'm suggesting something here. If everyone here drops the charges against everyone else, I'll kick you all loose to spend Christmas with your families. Assuming, of course, that *both* of you pay for the damage to the restaurant. And not just half and half. The full expense, from either family."

Vinnie had apparently been elected the McQuarrie family spokesman. "That's fine by us," he said. Elizabeth was surprised his voice wasn't higher-pitched.

"We're good, too," Anne said.

"All right then," Byers said. "Go on home. And I expect both of you to stay out of each other's way from here on out. It's a small town, but it's not that small. You wanna kill each other, do it somewhere the paperwork won't find me."

They began to file out, both groups eying the other like Little League teams forced to clap hands after an unsporting game.

"And one other thing," Byers called after them. "Both of your last names are banned from the Applebee's."

It was near midnight by the time they exited the police station, and truly dark. In the reshuffling of everyone and their vehicles, most went home with Barry in his car, while Elizabeth found herself volunteered to go with Anne and rescue Grady from the hospital. She didn't mind too much, especially with Barry lecturing people on conflict resolution in the other car, while Shane asked Typhos for a play-by-play. He was pissed, as if he'd been in the bathroom while the winning touchdown was scored. Even Anne's company was better than Shane talking about how *he* would've gone *muay thai* on someone's ass, and Barry clucking over what a failure in communication that was.

It was a slow drive, the headlights revealing an endless bead curtain of snow. Elizabeth sat in the passenger seat, checking out her black eye in the mirror. She chided herself for several of the Johnny Depp jokes that came to mind. Michelle was in the back. She'd fallen asleep while everyone was going over seating arrangements.

Anne turned on the wipers. The only damage she had taken in the fight was having her lip split open, which had already healed into a scab that only made her look cuter.

"So that guy, Vinnie," Elizabeth said. "What was he—"

126

"He was talking about Shane," Anne said. She spat the words out like they were too hot to hold in, but her next sentence was cooler, a little apologetic. "And it's really not any of your business."

"Sorry." Elizabeth leaned her head against the window, thinking that maybe she should've just ridden in the back with Michelle. Cuddled with her. Breathed her in like Michelle allowed her to. It was just that she didn't question herself so much with Anne. She knew where she stood—in some vague, hard to define way. Anne may hate her, but at least she was *resolved* to hate her.

"Listen," Anne said. "You were pretty good back there. Maybe I'm just saying this because you kept all my teeth in one place, but you didn't have to do that and you did. I appreciate that."

"Anytime," Elizabeth said. "Well, not before a date or anything. I look like the end of a Rocky movie."

"Yeah, you look like your mom had a close friendship with Rocket Raccoon, if you know what I'm saying."

"I don't think people not knowing what you're saying has ever been a problem for you."

Anne grinned slightly, wincing as she did so. That cut on her lip couldn't have been too much fun. "True enough. But I still don't think you and Michelle are going to be prom queens. Since she's not a lesbian and you seem like you barely know her anymore."

"I...know her..."

"Whatever," Anne said, taking one hand off the wheel to gesture. "The point is, whatever you're up to, you're good peoples. I don't think you would've backed us up like that if you were screwing me over. So, whatever the game is, have fun, I guess. Probably not my business anyway."

"Thanks," Elizabeth said. "I think."

Anne shook her head, smiling. "And I can't believe you smashed a bottle of Pepsi over someone's head."

Elizabeth shrugged. "They didn't have Coke."

Grady was zonked out on painkillers when they picked him up from the hospital, so he didn't offer much conversation on the ride home. Or hand gestures, since that was the limit of his vocabulary at the moment.

Anne didn't say anything either, seeming sheepish after all she'd said before. Elizabeth didn't mind. Things with Anne seemed to have found an even keel, and she didn't feel the need to jeopardize it by saying anything. She was perfectly content to ride in silence.

Typhos was sitting on the porch when they pulled up. He came out and helped Grady get out of the car and stay on his feet. Grady wrapped an arm around Typhos's shoulders and gave him a tight squeeze.

"Guess that means he likes me," Typhos said.

"You punch a family unit together and you're friends for life," Anne observed. "That's male bonding for you."

"That's OxyContin for you," Elizabeth corrected. Grady smiled, displaying the wiring that held his jaw shut. "Or maybe he's just always hated solid food..."

"He's autistic," Anne said. "Having this good an excuse not to talk to people is right up there with DC Comics actually making a good movie as far as he's concerned."

Grady gave her a thumbs-up.

"He can walk," Anne said, "I got him. Elizabeth, can you make sure the car's all locked up?"

"You're worried about Ohio car thieves?" Typhos asked.

"I'm worried about McQuarrie car thieves."

"I'm on it," Elizabeth said.

While Anne kept a hand on Grady's shoulder, guiding him inside, Elizabeth went back to the Prius and tried the doors. None opened. For good measure, she went to check the other Prius, but Typhos was already getting it.

"Guess we're getting the full 'A Very Harlow Christmas' treatment, huh?" Elizabeth asked him.

"Yeah, about had my fill of this McQuarrie shit. Any more of that, I'm seeing if someone else has room at the inn this Christmas."

Elizabeth laughed. "It's funny. Barry was pretty worried about you going, 'fucking white people.' Guess I should've taken him a little bit more seriously."

"Nah," Typhos said. "I wouldn't talk that way about my friends."

In the living room, Grady sacked out on the couch while the rest sprawled over cushions and pillows on the floor, forming a triage center.

Barry had gone to bed, his worry no match for his advancing age, while the rest of them were too wired to sleep or, in Typhos's case, supposed to stay awake in case he had a mild concussion. With nothing better to do, they formed a game of Uno on the floor.

"We play by house rules," Shane said. With his father asleep, he'd busted out a small bag of weed and rolled a joint, which Anne had seemed surprisingly shocked by, but she'd acquiesced to taking a puff like a girl about to see talking bees in a PSA. Shane now held the joint clenched between his teeth, with the baggie thrown on the floor beside the cards he was shuffling. "Fuck Off Uno," he declared. "The way it works is, someone makes you draw cards, you tell them to fuck off, or you have to draw an extra two cards. It's very cathartic."

"Y'all need a rule for that?" Typhos asked. He was holding an icepack to the back of his skull.

Shane dealt out the cards. "I'll start. And the conversational topic, in deference to our LGBT brethren, is...if you had to sleep with a member of the same sex, I mean had to, who would it be?"

Michelle was sitting on the easy chair, sorting through the day's mail. "Am I supposed to participate in this conversation, because..."

"Grady can't even talk, you don't see him complaining," Shane said, gesturing at his brother.

Grady tapped his forehead. One arm hanging off the couch, he checked his cards. On painkillers, they must've been enthralling.

"I know what he'd say," Patsy said. "'Why would I *have* to have sex with a man?' And then we'd say something like, 'a genie showed up and offered you a billion dollars to.'" She tapped the weed bag and Shane passed her the joint.

"Hey," Anne said, getting up from the floor. "Liz, leak? You're leaking?"

Elizabeth touched her forehead. A cut had decided to start bleeding again in a sluggish trickle down her temple. Abruptly Anne was there, pressing a blot of tissues to the cut. Elizabeth thanked her and took over with the tissues.

"If we're all done oozing?" Shane said, returning to the subject at hand. "And then Grady'd say, 'It's a question of would you have sex with a man for a billion dollars?'" He laid down a Blue 4.

"Of course," Elizabeth said. "No one's that straight." She laid down a Red 4.

"Burt Reynolds is," Anne said, playing a Red 2.

"Sean Connery," Shane said, as Patsy played a Red 9.

"Michael Jackson," Typhos said, playing a Yellow 9. "Takes a real man to be confident enough to own a monkey."

"Chimp," Michelle corrected.

From the couch, Grady laid down a Yellow 3, then formed a circle out of the thumb and forefinger of one hand, poking the forefinger of the other hand through it.

"Okay," Anne said. "He'd have sex with a man."

Grady shook his head and gestured in a circle with two fingers.

Anne's brow furrowed as she tried to puzzle out his sign language. "But...but..."

Grady rubbed his fingers together.

"The money! Is the genie good for the money?" Elizabeth translated. Grady snapped his fingers and pointed at her in agreement.

"Shit," Shane said as he played a Blue 3. "The rest of us idiots are getting snookered into having gay sex on spec. This mother's going to clean up on *his* gay sex."

"Elizabeth, you gonna play?" Anne asked

"Yeah, yeah. Sorry about this." She dropped a Wild Draw 4 on the deck.

"Fuck off," Anne said, biting her lip as she took her cards. "You're what's wrong with America. We've all been wondering, trying to figure it out, but it was you, all along."

"Creative. Green, by the way," Elizabeth said.

"So how can you be sure the check will clear with a genie who has a zen for gay-for-pay?" Anne asked.

Patsy leaned forward so Shane could relight the joint. Belatedly, she played a Green 5. "Trial period. He gives you a billion dollars for a week, and if you want to keep it..."

Typhos rearranged his hand. "So, you've got a billion dollars for a week, why not just buy whatever you want, then tell the genie to screw off, you've got bearer bonds?"

"Doesn't work like that," Elizabeth said. "He takes it all back."

Typhos dropped a Green Draw 2 on Grady. "Sorry about it, bro."

Shane jerked a thumb at Grady. "I know it's Fuck Off Uno, but maybe we should waive the rule for people with speech impediments."

Grady gave Typhos the finger.

"That works," Shane said, and played a Green 4. "It's a genie, all right. They're the original lawyers. They've got it all sewn up. And you really need a billion dollars, no matter how straight you are."

"I'm not sure this counts," Elizabeth said, playing a Blue 4, "but I'd have to say Michelle."

"You're already pan," Anne said. "I don't think making her pick which woman she wants to sleep with is keeping with the spirit of the game." She played a Blue Draw 2.

"You're a trollop," Patsy said. "And we can't make her pick which robot she wants to have sex with either. Oh, and fuck off."

Typhos played a Red Draw 2. "Sorry, Grady, I just got a bunch of these."

Grady bit his thumb at Typhos.

"Literary." Typhos drew two cards for him and slid them into Grady's deck. "Back to Elizabeth—what about animals?"

"Let's just skip me," Elizabeth said. "I don't want to open that can of worms with this family."

"If you are ever in that situation, don't pick horses," Anne told her. "Trust me, I saw a documentary about it once."

"There's a documentary about horse-fucking?" Shane asked.

"There is."

"And you watched it?" Michelle asked.

"Why does no one believe I watch documentaries?" Anne retorted. "Shane, it's your turn, right?"

"Oh, is it?" Shane studyied his cards as if trying to read a fortune from them. "I know which guy my little bro would fuck. Vladimir Putin."

"I didn't know he was a Republican," Elizabeth quipped.

"No, we've discussed it. Putin has that big homophobia thing, right? If it got out that he fucked a dude, he'd be ruined. Right, Grady?"

Grady nodded, then painstakingly laid a Red 3 on the pile. He stared at it as if he expected it to reveal a treasure, like in an Indiana Jones movie.

"But what if Putin wants to top?" Patsy asked, horrified.

Anne shrugged. "Can't be that bad. The man is clearly compensating for something."

"Can we go back to how Shane and Grady have discussed which man they would have sex with if they had to have sex with a man?" Elizabeth asked.

"We're Irish, what else are we gonna talk about?" Shane scoffed. "Our feelings?" He laid down a Red 7.

"Okay," Patsy said, "so is the person we pick, do they become gay, or are they getting a billion dollars, too, or—"

"Shit, good point," Elizabeth said. "You do not want a straight girl going down on you."

Anne's eyes flickered with interest. "Oh? How can you tell?"

"Trust me, you can tell. They go at it like they're on *Fear Factor*. If you ever want to feel like your lady parts are minced buffalo testicles or something…"

"Who wouldn't?" Anne replied, watching as Elizabeth played a Red 2. She played a Green 2.

"Do you guys have to lawyer everything?" Typhos asked. "I feel like I'm watching C-SPAN, only I actually watch C-SPAN when I'm high and it's entertaining. Listening to you argue about gay fucking while I'm high is like watching C-SPAN when I'm not high. I'll tell you who I'd have sex with. Shawn Mendes, done."

Patsy blew air between her lips and dropped a Reverse card on the pile. "I suppose…Gal Gadot. She seems nice and cute and… Buffalo testicles, really?"

"John Boyega," Shane said. "Because, and I'm just saying here, a lot of white in the choices so far. Not many people in this game down with the swirl."

Typhos high-fived him.

"Elizabeth," Anne said, and Elizabeth looked at her, shocked. Anne held up a Wild Draw 4. "Payback's a bitch."

She dropped it on the pile and said, "Yellow."

Elizabeth took her four cards quietly.

"Take two more. You didn't tell me to fuck off, and I deserved it."

"Your whole life," Elizabeth said with forced lightness.

Anne's head tilted. "What, you didn't think I was saying that I would go gay for—"

"No, of course not," Elizabeth said quickly.

"Because that would get us on Springer."

"Springer's still going?" Typhos asked.

"Everything's either still going or coming back," Shane said. "You know they just did a *CHiPS* movie? What's the audience for that, people who fuck to TV Land?"

"Are we done with this subject?" Elizabeth asked. "Did everyone get their bicuriosity out?"

"More or less," Anne said. "Michelle didn't go."

"I'm not playing," Michelle said distantly, absorbed in a letter she'd just opened.

Patsy rearranged her hand. "So, Typhos, how did you and Shane meet?"

"Fencing club," Typhos said. "We both liked broadswords, struck up a friendship, and when Shane heard I didn't have a place to go for the holidays, well…"

Michelle stood over them and flung a letter on the cards. "See? You see? Look at that! You all love Will so much, then look!" She was an unbecoming red with anger. "He's actually *taking me to court*, that's how in denial he is that I'd leave him for a woman. But you're all just going to forget about that the next time he comes over and acts like one of the boys!"

Shane picked up the letter but Elizabeth snatched it away. She'd read enough legalese in her time to get the gist of it: Will's lawyers were saying that Michelle was trying to pull a fast one and they could prove it.

"You want me to punch him?" Shane asked. "I'm the only one who hasn't gotten to punch anyone today, so I'm due."

Elizabeth almost pointed out that Michelle hadn't been involved in the brawl either, but stopped herself—it wouldn't seem supportive. "They don't have any proof," she assured Michelle, though privately, she wondered if they did…and where it could've come from.

Elizabeth found an old Discman among the detritus of the cellar. Once a new pair of batteries had been put in, and she'd taken the earbuds off her iPhone, she had a perfectly reasonable way to listen to *OK Computer* as she lay awake in bed, willing herself to get tired.

Michelle came down eventually, undressing and crawling in beside her, throwing an arm over Elizabeth.

"Is there any real need for that?" Elizabeth asked, pulling out the earbuds. When Michelle had pressed in on her from behind, the heat of her body felt remarkably like a chill.

"For what?"

"The cuddling. You don't want to do it, right? And it's not like anyone's going to walk in on us and wonder why we're not spooning."

"So, what, you mind?" Michelle pressed.

"A little," Elizabeth said. "I'm just trying to get some sleep here."

"Okay," Michelle said, squinting. "Fine. I just could use a little support and I thought I could get it from you."

Like I've ever gotten it from you. Elizabeth bit her tongue, unsure how to respond to that. It surprised her, the venom of that first thought. "Why do you need support, Michelle?" she asked diplomatically.

"*Think*, Liz. Will thinks he has proof. Where could he have gotten that? And just *now*? It has to be someone here."

"They're your family, Michelle."

"Exactly. *Anne*. She's always been jealous of me. It's like they always say, pretty girls want to be told they're smart and smart girls want to be told they're pretty. I'm sure *Will* tells her she's smart."

Elizabeth flushed with indignation at Michelle's implication. She hated the thought of lecturing Michelle on her own family, but she also hated thinking of Anne as some traitor, especially motivated by the paltry jealousy and sexual intrigue that Michelle suggested. As annoying as Anne could be, it just felt wrong.

Then again, hadn't everyone who had ever been manipulated thought the same way? If Anne was as persuasive and underhanded as Michelle thought she was, then couldn't Elizabeth be feeling exactly the way Anne wanted her to feel?

"Help me, Elizabeth," Michelle said plainly, putting a hand on her arm. Elizabeth could feel Michelle's knees on the backs of her thighs, Michelle's closeness all down the rest of her body. And it felt—no wonder it'd been so easy to pretend.

"With what?"

"Anne. She's trying to get close to you. I can see it. So let her get as close as she wants and show her we have nothing to hide. Prove to her our relationship isn't a lie."

Again, Elizabeth was surprised. This time by thinking immediately *it is*.

Chapter 8

December 22

THE DAY OF THE GREAT Aspirin Shortage of '17.

Elizabeth woke up to find Limey sleeping next to her on the bed.

"You have got to be kidding me." She yawned and turned over to watch him sleeping, wondering if he would flap his paws as he chased a dream squirrel. She'd never actually seen a dog do that. It sounded crazy cute.

Instead, Limey woke up, whined, and padded right over her stomach to jump off the bed and head upstairs.

"Diss." He'd activated her bladder with his weight, so she had to get up, too.

Wanting to keep up good relations with the Harlows—now that they might be all that was standing between her and a horde of vengeful McQuarries—Elizabeth went to take Limey walkies and found Grady rooting through the garbage can, the painkillers having evidently worn off.

He noticed her and waved a slight acknowledgment. Then he kept going through the trash. Elizabeth picked up the newspaper from the end of the driveway, tucked it under her arm, and went to see if Grady was foaming at the mouth or anything.

He seemed pretty rational overall, though to complete the picture, he'd need to be sorting through back issues of a magazine or something, not imitating a raccoon.

"So, maybe this is a stupid question, but what'd the trash can do to you?" Elizabeth asked. "Like, what, do people do drug drops there or something?"

Grady shrugged and made a noncommittal noise, then pulled out a pill bottle. It rattled, half full. He wiped it off with some snow, then stuck it in his pocket.

"Holy shit, they *do?*" Elizabeth exclaimed. "I am definitely retiring here."

With Grady out proving that the world was far more like an RPG than Elizabeth had realized, she went in search of breakfast. After she'd finished washing her dishes, she asked herself if whatever was up with Grady meant that Anne was having another recording session in the basement. She went down and found that Anne's passionate voice was indeed ringing through the door to the cellar.

She grabbed her book, went to the door, opened it up, and sat down with her back against the doorframe, facing Anne. Anne looked right back at her. She was wearing a choker-wrap crop top with short sleeves, all in a beige-y nude, which blended seamlessly enough with her creamy skin to make you think, if you saw her in a bit of shade, that it was a lot lower cut than it really was. High-waisted jeans did what they could, but didn't hide much of the lean belly that her top left bare.

It made Elizabeth fidget a little. All she wore was a ribbed mock-neck black top from Maje and a matching circle skirt with white polka dots. For once, she felt underdressed. "And we were getting along so well," Anne said, putting her hands on her hips. She was cute when she was angry. Even cuter when it was this *fond* anger, like she was savoring it. Not that she was *cute*-cute...

"Détente," Elizabeth said. "If I have to put up with you in the background, you have to put up with me in the background."

"Why can't you just go into the bathroom and read on the toilet like a normal person?"

"Hey, I ignore you, you have to ignore me, too. Fair's fair."

"Fine," Anne said, picking up a sheaf of papers and shuffling them on the table. "But no comments from the peanut gallery."

Elizabeth wondered if Anne could be this proof that Will had told Michelle about. Woman's intuition said no—on some strange level, she trusted Anne. Maybe she should just go with her gut. But maybe everyone who'd fallen for a con artist had thought something along those lines.

Not that she'd *fallen*-fallen for Anne...

Anne faced the camera with a light grin that favored her cut lip and paused for a moment—Elizabeth guessed to make for an easier edit. Then she launched into her spiel. "Now let's get into some viewer mail. ParkerPalmerParker writes..."

"Did you actually print those out?" Elizabeth asked, brow furrowed, her voice carefully composed into genuine curiosity, with only an undercurrent of wickedness. Maybe if she pulled Anne's pigtails enough, she'd get a confession. It worked on *Law & Order*. "Sorta defeats the point of e-mail, doesn't it?"

"I thought I said no comments from the peanut gallery," Anne said, her voice making it clear that she was quite certain on the point.

Elizabeth gave her most innocent smile. "In my defense, I don't know what a peanut gallery is."

"Do you know what a cue card is?" Anne waved the paper in the air. "I'll give you a hint: the weatherman doesn't *really* memorize the weather every single day before the news comes on."

"Now I know what to get you for Christmas: a tablet."

"Oh, don't splurge. You get me an expensive gift like that and I'll have to get you a real girlfriend."

Elizabeth laughed despite herself. She hated when people were funny while she was arguing with them. Only she was allowed to do that. "All right, fine, I'm done. Keep going."

She licked her finger and turned the page of her book.

"I wouldn't put that in my mouth if I were you," Anne said. "Do you really know where it's been?"

"Your sister."

"If you say so."

"Yeah, as it turns out, it feels much better when someone else does it for you. Don't believe me? Try it."

"That's not my brand. Try the other ninety-nine percent of the Internet."

"I will."

Elizabeth would've made a poor spy, even though she'd look great in a leather catsuit. Could the fact that Anne was so charming—but not *charming*-charming—be evidence that she was working with Will? Was that how a spy would act, or just someone who was legitimately a cool person? And what the hell was *charming*-charming anyway?

Anne huffed and reoriented herself on the camera. "'Dear Anne of Queen Labels, you're so good at showing off these different kinds of make-up, but how do they really work? Why does putting one chemical or another on your face make you look more attractive?' Well, Triple P, in my case it's because I want to keep people guessing as to how much sleep I've been getting. Because like all gingers, I don't sleep. I wait."

"Are you going to give an answer or just do stand-up?" Elizabeth asked. *Nothing to hide*, she thought. *I'll just be nice and funny and sweet because I've got nothing to hide.* "I'm not expecting *Bill Nye the Science Guy* here, but *Beakman's World* at least..."

Anne swiveled the tripod so the camera faced Elizabeth. "Guys, you all remember my plucky sidekick Liz from the last video. Well, you all wanted to see her again, so looks like you get your wish. Please note that she's been using someone's fist in her eye instead of shadow. Let's see how that look plays on the catwalk."

"It's not like it's a hard question," Elizabeth said, dropping the book into her lap. "Humans have mating rituals just like any other animal. They signal availability, healthiness, ovulation..."

"We put on lipstick to show we're ovulating," Anne said. "Makes sense."

"It does, actually," Elizabeth insisted. "Humans want to show they're eligible as breeding partners, so they try to look younger. That's half of all make-up right there."

"The other half," Anne announced dramatically. "Ovulation!"

"The skin around women's eyes is naturally darker than it is on men, so eyeshadow makes us look more feminine. Mouths, also darker, so lipstick makes us look more feminine."

"I wear red lipstick," Anne said. "It's kind of my color."

"That's ovulation," Elizabeth said, twisting the knife with her words. "Ovulating women have more estrogen in their blood, making them more easily aroused and giving them redder lips. So when we put on lipstick to make our lips look redder, it's saying that we're more easily aroused. Because of ovulation."

"Also explaining why men find tampons so exciting."

Elizabeth scowled. "That increased blood flow also pinkens women's cheeks. Hence...*blush*."

Anne smiled like she was an actress desperately trying to stay in character while sharing a scene with Robin Williams on cocaine. "So that's—*hence* blush." Anne snickered.

Elizabeth found herself tittering as well. She didn't know why. It wasn't that funny. It was science.

"Okay, shut up now," Anne said. "I'm ignoring you."

"Is that an angry flush I see in your cheeks?" Elizabeth asked. "Easy to mistake for a blush. *Hence* why some women look cute when they're angry."

"You haven't seen me angry," Anne said.

"Well, God, I have a soul. What more does it take to piss a ginger off?"

Anne dropped her head to the card table and cackled. "Just so you know!" she said, pointing a hand out through her hair. "This is just making my shoot take longer!"

"I don't mind," Elizabeth said quietly, holding up her book but really looking over the page numbers at Anne as she laughed and laughed…

"Okay, here. Come over here."

"What?" Elizabeth asked.

Anne was beckoning her in. "I just thought of a great new segment for the cage-fighting portion of my audience. 'How to Hide a Bruise.' In case you haven't noticed, my friend here has quite a shiner because of a barfight she got into the other night…"

"You started it," Elizabeth declaimed, getting up and walking over to the set.

"And despite how that sounds, we were on the same side," Anne told the camera. "Really."

"Well, obviously. You do still have a face, after all."

"Sit," Anne said, pushing Elizabeth into a folding chair. "Don't worry, you can still read all you want. I'm just going to help you look less like Frankenstein's Monster while you keep literature alive."

"Someone has to," Elizabeth grumbled. "Did your fans really say they wanted to see me again?"

"Yeah, they seemed to think you were funny, which is why you can't trust what you read on the Internet."

"No, I got that part, I just can't believe you have fans."

Anne blew her the most sarcastic kiss Elizabeth had ever been blown. She picked up a vial from the table. "First, we use concealer on the bruise."

"You're really blowing the lid off the make-up industry's secrets here."

"Keep talking, Dita von Teese. You'll be drinking this concealer."

"Beats your dad's cooking."

"Okay, don't box me into defending that. It's dirty pool."

Time flew as they shot the video. Elizabeth figured out why Anne was so popular. She really was good at this stuff, like the one-in-a-billion perfume salesman you wouldn't mind cornering you at a mall, or a big sister showing you the ropes. They talked like the camera wasn't even on. Elizabeth admitted that her guilty pleasure was the film noir look she went for, all femme fatales and Girl Fridays. Anne came up with an impromptu history lesson on how women had worn make-up during World War II, painting Elizabeth's legs and drawing on stocking seams to show how a woman might pretend to have pantyhose on when the war effort was taking up all the nylon.

Afterward, Anne said she had enough material for her next four shows. "People are going to be disappointed on the fifth," she said. "When you stop showing up."

Elizabeth smiled at her. "By the way, I don't know how to tell you this, but your shirt doesn't have anything funny written on it. It doesn't even mention your boobs once."

"My bra does. See?" Anne peeled her top up. Her bra was black—naturally—with glistening silver studs on the cups that looked like braille writing.

"Clever," Elizabeth said. "What's it say?"

Anne lowered her shirt. "That I'm not into blind guys."

They went upstairs together. Shane was in the kitchen, stirring a pot of hot cocoa on the stovetop. There was an open bag of mini-marshmallows and a pyramid of coffee mugs stacked nearby.

Typhos was out on the porch, sitting on one of the patio chairs, cradling a steaming cup of cocoa. A group of carolers sang "God Rest Ye Merry Gentlemen" down the block. It was late afternoon, and the sun was already starting to nestle itself into the horizon.

"Help yourselves, but leave a little for the Baptists, eh?" Shane said, standing out of the way as Anne slipped in to fill her cup from the pot. She filled one for Elizabeth, too. "We're all watching it in the living room, if you wanna."

Anne stiffened, but nodded almost imperceptibly. She took her mug and moved into the dining room, but there was something lost about her that paradoxically made Elizabeth want to follow. She went through the dining room to the hallway, the sound of the carolers fading. She heard the crackling whooshes of an old home video.

"Using that thing already?" Anne said on the TV. "You should've given me time to put my face on!"

"There's always next year," Barry said, his voice oddly disembodied behind the camera. "You look quite well without your face."

It wasn't Anne on the video, of course. Anne was the little girl ransacking the area underneath the Christmas tree, getting all her presents into a pile distinct from Michelle's and Shane's and Grady's. No Patsy yet.

The woman was Margaret, their mother, and as well as she'd aged, Elizabeth could tell the difference with a prolonged look. There were laugh lines flanking her red lips and crinkles at her bright eyes, white snowing into her red hair. But there was also something Elizabeth could only see from knowing Anne. There was this glow, this absolute glow, and it wasn't that Anne didn't have it, but that she kept it hidden, guarded, and Margaret... didn't.

Elizabeth heard footsteps going up the stairs. Then, a moment later, Shane pushed past her to sit cross-legged on the floor. They were all there. Barry. Michelle. Grady. Patsy was even misty-eyed.

Elizabeth didn't get the feeling she was unwelcome, just that this was private. Too private for someone like her—a fraud, a con artist who may have been invited there but still didn't belong. She went upstairs, thinking about how in love Margaret had looked, how Barry's camera had followed her with such fondness and glee, how happy they'd been watching their children on Christmas morning.

A happy marriage. A perfect relationship. And how had it ended? With Barry alone, watching the memories, seeing which would decay first—the video tape or his pain.

Anne wasn't in the upstairs bedroom, spartanly decorated, with a pair of duffel bags open at the foot of Typhos and Shane's beds, like military men at a new posting. Elizabeth looked around, wondering how the hell

Anne could've left a room with only one exit. And then wondering why someone would open a window in the dead of winter.

Snow lightly powdered the slanted roof, just enough to show Anne's footprints. Huddled into one of the boys' coats, she sat in the empty sleigh. Her tiny figure seemed incongruously out of place, an element of a child's drawing, a tableau of the chimney, the black Santa approaching it, the flicker of Christmas lights that shone up from below. Further graffitiing the scene was a cloud of cigarette smoke hanging over her head like her own personal raincloud.

"You want to know the punchline?" she asked. "Mom died of lung cancer." She shook some ash off the end of her cigarette. "The real kicker—she wasn't even a smoker."

Elizabeth sat down against the sleigh, bumping Santa, then steadying him quickly. It was a hell of a view. The carolers in the street, the nativity scene in the lawn, an empty road and an open forest and a frozen pond in the distance.

"Anne," Elizabeth said, "tell me about something you *do* like."

"You won't believe me."

"And you're letting that stop you?"

Anne took a long drag from her cigarette. It tinted her exhalation a languid gray. "Weddings."

"Weddings."

"Can't help it. I wanted a wedding under trees, beautiful trees, New Zealand trees, with birds singing in them…singing to all the people in their Sunday finest… I was six."

"I don't have anything like that," Elizabeth said, pulling her knees up to her chest and wishing she'd grabbed a coat, too. She thought she'd be a much better friend if she were somewhere much warmer. "Although I did once think it would be funny if there were a wedding where the groom had a female best man and the bride had a male maid of honor. Then I watched *Made of Honor* with Patrick Dempsey and realized it wouldn't be."

"I like Patrick Dempsey, too," Anne said. "I think people see him only as McDreamy and he is so much more than—OH FUCK!"

The cigarette had burned down enough to singe her, and she'd dropped it to the floor of the sleigh.

The sleigh made of wood.

Smoke began rising, encouraged by whatever ecofriendly, highly flammable material Barry had varnished it in.

"Put it out!" Elizabeth cried.

Anne stomped on the floor of the sleigh. "I'm trying!" The sleigh skewed out of position, its runners grating against the roof.

"Look out!" Elizabeth grabbed for Anne and hauled her out as the contraption started slipping down the rooftop, sawing through the shingles with an awful racket. Down below, the caroling broke off. Pastor Jonah looked up with a horrified expression at the sleigh tipping forward.

"Oh Jesus, no! Jesus God, no! No! Lord! Don't!"

The curling tip of the sleigh's front runners hooked on Barry's beautiful Christmas lights and ripped them clean from the guttering. They tore off in one long string from the eaves, front and back, lashing wildly in the night air.

"God, no, not the lights!" Jonah cried.

Anne and Elizabeth both ducked as the string of lights whiplashed past their heads, missing them by inches. Santa was not so lucky. The Christmas lights snagged on his neck and he was ripped from his perch. The flaming sleigh sparked off the gutter and launched out into the starry night.

Anne and Elizabeth dived to either side, rolling away from the speeding Father Christmas as he was dragged between them.

There was a moment of stillness, a pause in the bustle of the holiday season, a small suspension in time filled with fear, panic, and a little bit of the magic of Christmas as the fiery sleigh, festive lights, and a garroted Santa arched up, up, up into the night sky. Then—

"Lord Jesus!" Pastor Jonah screamed. "Get down! Jesus! Everyone, down!"

Elizabeth raised her head from her hands, just in time to see the choristers dive for cover. Above their screams, the jangle of the sleigh's silver bells rang out like the laughter of the damned, as the sleigh careered toward the neighbor's nativity scene.

The impact of the sleigh against the nativity was brutal. The wise men were plowed under. Mary and Joseph were pinned against the back of the stable. Baby Jesus and his manger? Mangled. The flames hit the straw and the nativity went up like Harry Potter books in Alabama.

In less than half a chorus of "Good King Wenceslas," the neighborhood was shrouded in billowing smoke and traumatized choristers.

The front door clicked open and Barry ran out with a baseball bat in hand. "What happened? Is everyone okay?"

"I burned my finger!" Anne called from the roof, holding it up to all to demonstrate. She had, of course, burned her middle one.

Elizabeth's hands embraced her face.

Sheriff Byers's office still looked like a high school principal's. He still looked like the head of SPECTRE when he was behind his desk. He still seemed as unamused as a man going to a German comedy club.

"Let me get this straight," he said, holding the incident report. "Ms. Harlow, you were smoking a cigarette inside a Santa sleigh on the roof of your family home."

"Yes."

"And Ms. Smile, you were keeping her company."

"Yes."

"Harlow, you dropped the cigarette and it started a fire."

"Yes."

"You tried to put out the fire, but you accidentally dislodged the sleigh from the roof."

"Uh-huh."

"It careened—that's the word in the official report, 'careened'—off the rooftop. In the process, it snagged the Christmas lights that were strung up on your house, and pulled them off."

"Yeah," Elizabeth agreed. "The front of the rails hooked that entire string—"

Byers held up a finger. "I'm not finished. The string of lights wrapped around the neck of a Santa Claus figure and pulled him off the rooftop as well."

"It almost hit me on the way over," Anne said. She held her hands inches apart. "Came this close."

"That's tragic," Byers said, ambiguous as to where he found tragedy. "So now the sleigh—on fire—careens off the rooftop, landing in the yard, still at speed, dragging an African-American holiday icon behind it by the neck."

"I really burned my finger bad," Anne said, raising her middle finger to show him. Elizabeth reached over and lowered her hand.

Byers ignored them. "The burning sleigh, which is also lynching this black Santa, now speeds toward a group of Christmas carolers from the Good Shepherd Northview Church who are singing out on the street."

"They all dodged," Anne pointed out. "That's the real story here. Baptists have great reflexes."

Elizabeth pressed her hands together and held them in front of her mouth. Realizing she looked like she was praying, she stopped.

Byers raised his voice. "The flaming lynch mobile proceeds to careen across your lawn and collide with the neighbors' nativity scene."

"Which totally absorbed the impact," Anne said. "Absolutely brought it to a halt. Really well built."

"The resulting blaze claims—" Byers consulted his report. "The Virgin Mary, Joseph of Nazarene, two out of three wise men, numerous farm animals, some of them infant, the already keelhauled St. Nick, and the King of Kings."

"We tried to put it out," Anne argued. "Used a fire extinguisher and everything, but whatever they made the Baby Jesus out of, I mean…damn."

Byers closed the incident report. "Are you aware that all of this could well be construed as a hate crime?"

Anne hemmed. "I prefer to think of it as a hate accident."

"Get out!"

Elizabeth grabbed Anne's hand and ran.

The moon was fat and whiter than white, making the undisturbed snow gleam like crystal when they left the police station.

It also made it seem like it should be easy for them to find their car, but…

"You know, it's not Christmas yet," Elizabeth reasoned. "It might unruffle a few feathers if you put up a new nativity scene and a new Santa. Away from the roof…"

"Yeah, but where are we going to find a black Santa at this short notice?" Anne asked. "Dad had to get the last one special order."

"You could always get a white Santa and paint him black."

Anne stopped and stared at her. "You want to put Santa in blackface?"

Elizabeth sighed. "Where the hell is Michelle?"

"Trying to kill Superman?" Anne suggested.

They walked around the corner of the police station and there she was, loitering under a humming lightbulb at the station's backdoor. Elizabeth could recognize a few curves of her outline and the roundness of her shorn scalp, but it was like she was looking at her from some new and alien angle, seeing her all wrong.

She was pressed against the wall with that McQuarrie deputy locked around her, the two of them moving like they were caught on each other and trying to get free, trying to find a new grip to push away. It was only their lips that seemed to continually snag and pull them back together. Their kiss never seemed to stop—some obsessed doctor trying over and over to resuscitate a corpse.

Anne grabbed Elizabeth and pulled her away, back behind the building. "Oh my God," she said. "I can't believe—Michelle would do that to you. I know she's...I mean, I knew she could be self-centered, but I never thought—especially after Will cheated on her, I didn't ever think... Oh God, Elizabeth, it's going to be okay. I swear, it's fine..."

Elizabeth couldn't pay any attention to her. All she could think about was what had transpired with Michelle. It didn't surprise her—why should it? Michelle had never pretended they were in love, never asked Elizabeth for that, not even for faithfulness. That was all her own doing, convincing herself and fooling herself and justifying to herself that eventually, someday, Michelle...

That Michelle would finally be hers. That all of this was some change that had started in college, *in college for God's sake*, and little by little Michelle was coming to her, and that if she just waited long enough then Michelle would finish changing and finally love her.

But she wouldn't.

Anne saw the elemental confusion on her face—the slow shifting of her mind to accommodate the truth—and mistook it for shock. "It's all right, Liz. She doesn't deserve you, that's all. She really doesn't. You'll find someone better. You're smart and funny and cute and there'll be someone who loves you. You'll find them so easy. Who wouldn't love you? Who wouldn't love you, Elizabeth Smile?"

She kissed Elizabeth's left cheek. Then the same cheek, only a little higher. Then, either bolder than before or totally lost in whatever delirium she felt, she moved her lips to Elizabeth's.

It happened so fast, it was like Anne was kissing someone Elizabeth hadn't become yet. And just as quickly, Elizabeth kissed her back, shutting out everything else and entering a world of Anne. There was the warm touch of her mouth inside the winter, the wet parting of her lips, the action of her tongue and the sharpness of her teeth. It felt like she'd been blind to them before, ignorant because she'd only looked at Anne from across the room or a few feet away. This collection of touches and sighs and wants that were now so easy to see, she had to have been willing herself not to see them.

Anne pulled away from her, from Elizabeth's hands on her face and the pressure of their lips together, and now it was an act of will for Elizabeth to stop herself from just wantonly devouring all she could get of that *feeling*, that need she hadn't known someone else could share. She opened her eyes and saw Anne standing there, so close it was like she wanted Elizabeth to kiss her again too, because everything about her was impossible not to kiss. The slight part of her lips, almost one of her insouciant grins, and the blush on her cheeks and the freckles on her nose and the snow in her eyelashes and her hair trickling into the wind. She was perfect. And she was Elizabeth's, in every way that seemed to matter.

"Elizabeth?" Michelle stepped around the corner. "There you are. Ready to go?"

It was an interesting ride home.

Michelle drove, and Elizabeth sat in the back, watching Anne. Mostly, she just looked straight ahead. It was snowing, only enough to speckle the windshield, not enough to make a sound or leave a drop of water on the glass.

"So, you lied," Anne said. "Both of you. All this lesbian stuff, just one big prank you pulled on us. On *your family*, Michelle."

"What other choice did I have?" Michelle protested. "Will was divorcing me. He was going to get half of everything!"

"Then, give him half!"

"No!" Michelle shouted. Elizabeth had never heard her so loud. "He doesn't get *half* for stringing me along, for cheating on me—he doesn't get to go off with *half* like we tied or something. No, he has to *lose!*"

"And the deputy? Deputy Steve McQuarrie of the Watson McQuarries?"

Michelle was quick to justify herself. "He's not like the others. He tried to get them to back off. Really, he did. Not that you guys would ever accept that someone's not buying into your idiotic family feud..."

"So you pretend to be a lesbian instead. 'Cause that's not... That's perfectly sane. Ever think he might be the spy you're so damn worried about? God, you'd think even a fake lesbian would be more suspicious of men." Elizabeth glanced up, in time for Anne's eyes to burn into hers. "And you." She rounded on Elizabeth next. "I suppose you're married with two kids?"

"She really is bi," Michelle said.

"Pan," Anne corrected.

"*Whatever.* I'm paying her. Which so far seems to be the most effective way to get someone to put up with this family for a week." Michelle squinted hard. "You can't tell anyone, Anne."

"Weak prediction," Anne said simply.

"You're my sister. My family. If you tell, it'll get back to Will. And I'm sure his lawyer will love catching Elizabeth and me in a lie."

"Hey," Elizabeth said, "don't—"

"Would you really do that to me?" Michelle persisted. "Your own flesh and blood. I could get nothing. *Elizabeth* could get nothing."

Elizabeth could feel the anger boiling off Anne. "How much is she paying you, anyway? Seems like a pretty easy job, just hanging around a big house all day. Really, the only work is lying, so how much does that go for? Minimum wage? Does sleeping in the same bed count toward your hours?"

"Twenty-five thousand dollars," Elizabeth said. It felt like she was talking with her tongue cut in half, every word hurting.

Anne thudded her head against the back of the seat. "Okay. I'm not greedy. I just want half."

"Half of twenty-five thou?" Michelle asked. "Twelve-point-five thousand dollars?"

"You can round it either way. I don't care. I just figure I should get paid *something* for not punching anyone in the face."

"Anne, c'mon, you're not being—"

"Pay her," Elizabeth said.

"What?"

Elizabeth tightened her fists and felt her own sweat under her fingers. "You can take it out of my cut. That's the terminology, right? 'My cut?'"

"Fine," Michelle said. "Half to Elizabeth, half to Anne. As long as no one talks."

Elizabeth felt Anne's gaze slide over her. She felt ashamed in a way she hadn't for a long time. She didn't feel shame over drinking or fucking or being queer, but this—this felt *wrong*.

"Not a problem," Anne said, and not a word was spoken the rest of the trip.

They got back to find the remains of a bonfire piled up on the curb by the trash, its soot smeared around the snowy lawn. Grady was waiting for them, tapping his watch as they pulled into the driveway.

"I know, I know," Anne muttered. She practically threw herself out of the car, and Elizabeth practically threw herself after her.

"Guys!" Michelle called, left behind. She snarled and closed the car door Elizabeth had left open.

Elizabeth slipped and slid through the mangled snow, churning it up with each kicking step. "Anne! Will you wait?"

"Go on ahead," Anne told Grady, then briefly looked back at Elizabeth. "I don't have time for this."

"I just want to talk."

"I think it's all been said."

"Could you wait up?"

Anne was climbing up the patio steps after Grady. "You've had your fun, you got me, I totally fell for it. I actually thought that..." Grady had stopped in front of her. She rammed the heel of her hand into his back.

"Go!" She turned back to Elizabeth. "Leave me alone. I feel like a big enough idiot as it is."

"I never meant to—"

Once she was inside the glass patio, Anne slammed the sliding door shut in Elizabeth's face, which sent a crack through the pane of glass. She saw it, growled, and stomped off after Grady, who needed another thumping on the back to keep moving.

Elizabeth turned around and sat on the patio steps, feeling like a monster. As if she should care what Anne thought. As if she should care about anyone in this family except Michelle, who she shouldn't care about at all, or at least not in the way she *did*—

Michelle ran her hand over Elizabeth's cheek as if following a familiar path. "Believe me, I know. Anne isn't the most understanding of women when you get right down to it."

"Should she be?" Elizabeth asked.

"It's none of her business," Michelle said dismissively, going up the steps and gingerly opening the cracked door. She went into the house, but that wasn't the turn Anne had taken. She'd gone into the garage, with its endearingly makeshift man-cave...

Sighing, Elizabeth went to the door and eased it open, heard sounds of an argument coming from the other side of the family car. Shane's voice. "I don't *need* the medicine, so of course I threw it out. I don't need it anymore."

Anne's voice had that edge in it that said she was trying exceedingly hard to be patient. "The doctor said you'd need it for the rest of your life—"

"No, *no*," Shane insisted pedantically. "He said I'd need to take the pills until I got better, and I feel better, I don't need them anymore. Grady, Grady, c'mon, would you tell her? You don't keep taking Advil after you stop having a headache."

Elizabeth poked her head around the car. She could see Shane sitting on the couch, Grady and Anne standing over him. Grady was in the spotlight, gesturing at Anne, saying he agreed with her.

"You know, you're a lot more adamant about this when you don't have to talk," Shane said. "What'd she say, you'd just have to stand there and point at her and then she'd stop nagging you?"

"I didn't nag him," Anne said calmly. "He was the one who found your pills. And if you want, we can call Dr. Sanjay. He'll tell you that you need to take your pills."

"I don't want to bother him. You're just going to bother him—" He caught sight of Elizabeth. "Liz! Liz! Would you tell them?" He jumped up from the couch and paced to Barry's Prius, slamming his hands on the cab. "You're a neutral party. The entire time you've been here, have you seen me acting crazy? I've been acting completely rationally. Completely. Tell them!"

Elizabeth's eyes flicked to the others, Grady breathing hard through his nostrils as he tried to stay stoic, Anne working her jaw in concern, eyes pleading. Elizabeth looked briefly downward. "Yes, Shane, you've seemed very rational the past few days."

"Thank you! Thank you!" Shane gesticulated to her like he was desperately trying to point something out to a blind person. "An unbiased opinion! Imagine!"

"But have you been taking your pills since you got here?" Elizabeth added.

Shane jutted his jaw out to the side, his eyes wheeling around, momentarily almost vacant... "I have, *have*, but I haven't needed them. It's like...you have a cold, you take medicine for it, you don't suddenly stop having a cold. It just makes the symptoms better. I haven't had any symptoms. I'm just taking cold medicine for no reason."

"So you don't think the pills are doing anything to help you?"

"Jesus," Anne muttered, but Grady put a hand on her arm. Elizabeth felt like she had about an inch of rope before she hanged herself.

"Of course they're not doing anything to help me," Shane said. "I'm not sick. I don't need pills."

"How about this?" Elizabeth suggested. "You've already paid for the bottle of pills, so, you finish taking the rest of them. And every day you take one, you write down how you're feeling. Then, when you stop taking them, you write down how you feel then. If you feel the same way, you can show that diary to Anne and prove to her you don't need the pills. Is that fair?"

Shane clenched his jaw tightly. "Do you think I need the pills?"

"I'm not sure," Elizabeth said, mostly honest. "I know you don't think you need the pills because you don't think you're sick."

"I'm not," Shane insisted. "I'm not!"

"So prove it."

Shane's lower lip flickered between his teeth as he thought furiously, almost feverishly.

"You're a man of your word, right Shane?" Anne asked. "You want people to know they can trust you."

"They *can* trust me…"

"And Elizabeth's suggested a way we can find out whether you need the pills or not. Does it not sound fair?"

"It's fair. I just don't need them."

Anne opened the pill bottle and looked inside. "Okay, you've got enough for about another week. Do you think you can take the pills for another week? For me? For Grady?"

"I don't need them." Shane shook his head fitfully. "I don't."

"This is how you show that to us. Otherwise we don't know what to believe. So can you do it? One week?"

Shane tapped his fingernails on the Prius's finish. "One week."

"Okay," Anne said, handing the bottle to Grady. "Why don't you go with Grady?"

Elizabeth got the immediate impression that Grady was in charge of making sure Shane followed through on his promise.

"Fine," Shane said, taking his hands off the Prius. "But I don't need them."

"We'll see," Anne said.

Elizabeth went to the left as the brothers came around on the right, then trudged across the porch and into the house. That left her alone with Anne, and even though Elizabeth was sighing with relief over the argument being decided, she felt suspicious about not being in the frying pan anymore.

"You're lucky," Anne said, flopping down on the couch. "If that hadn't worked, I would've had to use your head to get that dent out of Dad's bumper."

"I've had some experience in that department," Elizabeth said, sitting down on the Prius's hood. "The Shane business, not—bodywork."

Anne was lying down facing away from Elizabeth, her arms crossed. "Yeah, who?"

"My mother. She would, ah…" Elizabeth was surprised by how dry her throat felt as the words flowed out, easier and harder than she thought it would be. Easier because it was Anne. Harder because it was *her mother*. "Well, the last time, she thought I could work for the President of the United States if she took me to Mount Rushmore to show me to George Washington. My dad came home in the middle of the night and found the house empty."

Anne's head turned slightly to the side. "'The last time?'"

"There aren't a lot of things I wouldn't rather talk about than...the Michelle thing. But that's one of them."

Anne looked straight ahead. "So, what do you want to talk about? I figure Shane taking his pills, today at least, buys you *something*..."

"Just..." Elizabeth stood up from the car. "I don't expect you to understand what's going on with me and Michelle. But I didn't do it just for the money. She's my friend. I wanted to help her."

"Some friend," Anne said. "Getting you to lie to her family, over and over again."

Elizabeth bit her lip, wishing she could dispute that, but unable to. "I'd like to talk about the kiss, if that's all right with you."

"Oh my God!" Anne twisted on the couch, leaning an elbow on the armrest and finally looking at Elizabeth. "Are you just working your way through my entire DNA chain?"

"It's not like that. It's not about me and you; it's just about you. Can you scoot over? You're making my neck hurt just looking at you."

Anne heaved a sigh as she moved over, giving Elizabeth space to sit down beside her. Elizabeth felt like a weight was off her as soon as she was next to Anne.

She stared at their reflections in the mirror of an antique Victorian cheval glass. Anne was unusually quiet. She even looked away from her reflection. "You know what the bitch of it is? I'm twenty-five. Who doesn't realize this shit until they're twenty-five?"

"Well, there isn't a time limit or anything..." Elizabeth blew into her hands and rubbed them together. The concrete floors let a lot of cold seep into the room. "When I realized I was attracted to women, I didn't have anyone to talk to about it. People weren't, you know—they didn't seem like they hated it, but it was just like the Running of the Bulls or something. It happened out there, somewhere. It wasn't real. It wasn't really until I got to college that I found friends who were the same way, or who I felt comfortable talking to, or just who I could date, even. And so, if you need someone to talk to, about any of this, I could point you to some people I know, or I hope we could call a time-out on all this other stuff, because that really doesn't matter to me as much as what you're going through."

Anne's head fell back against the couch. "You know, it makes perfect sense. I've always thought I should be a bit more of a slut than I am. Thought I just couldn't find the guy who did it for me. Like that's how it works; you just find this one guy who's perfect for you and *then* it clicks. But there is no Prince Charming for me, is there?"

"I don't know," Elizabeth said. "Sometimes it's like two stereos playing in the same room. One's playing really loud and the other has its volume turned way down low. Then suddenly a track will come on one that's really quiet, or that's really loud… People can have lots of different stereos, playing at lots of different levels."

"Sounds confusing, having a bunch of stereos playing at once."

"It can be," Elizabeth said. "But you don't have to wait around for your stereo to play any one song, just because you think that's what should be playing. You can turn the radio on. Channel-surf. See what's on…"

"Okay, I think we've stretched that metaphor to the breaking point." Anne looked over at Elizabeth, pursing her lips together and blowing out her breath. "So what do you suggest? If I am gay?"

"Well, I could take you somewhere…" Elizabeth held up her hands. "Not a date! Just a wingman thing. Not even to meet someone, just to be somewhere where…there aren't as many expectations. You'd be surprised how freeing it can be."

As Anne thought about it, Elizabeth heard claws scrabbling on the concrete—Limey shimmied out from under the Prius and jumped up on the couch, resting his head on Anne's lap. She petted him softly, a small smile on her lips.

"Do I have to sit through another drag show?"

"I think we can do a little better than that." Elizabeth held out her hand. "We cool?"

"You're pretending to date my sister and you turned me gay." Anne reached out to reluctantly take Elizabeth's hand. "I think we're about as cool as we can get, but you're a very strange woman."

"Yeah, well, I'm cute, so people let me get away with it."

Chapter 9

December 23

ELIZABETH WOKE UP ALONE. SHE guessed Michelle was off "Supporting Her Local Sheriff," now that her secret was out. Elizabeth spent a moment wondering just how much had been real and what was for her benefit—had Michelle taken *some* comfort from their playacting, or was it all...method acting? Then she noticed Anne was sitting on the bottom step of the stairs. "Are you watching me sleep?"

"More like checking on the coma patient. Do you have narcolepsy or something?"

"I can't tell if you're genuinely concerned; I haven't had coffee."

"You've slept for about ten hours and you need coffee?" Anne knitted her fingers together. "What you said last night—how do we do that?"

Elizabeth tried to hold the covers over her body as she stretched. "I asked some friends and they told me about a pretty good lesbian bar over in Akron. It's a bit of a drive, but the place is clean, the music's good, servers are nice, girls are pretty..."

"Are any of your friends named Yelp?" Anne asked, and now Elizabeth wondered how much of her attitude was just bravado. Elizabeth remembered how nervous she'd been in college that first year, like just watching a movie about lesbians might've been a test. She also remembered how badly she'd wanted to be seen as cool and badass, a little like Gina Gershon in *Bound*, but with a nicer fashion sense.

"Oh, you've been gay five minutes, and already you're sarcastic about it?" Elizabeth teased.

"Set a new record, huh?" Anne's smile was almost at full strength. "What should I wear?"

Look at the fashion plate, asking her that... "Like I need to tell you."

"No, you do. I don't know what lesbians like."

"Well, if you are a lesbian, then whatever you like—"

"Not helping!"

"Anne, it's fine," Elizabeth assured her. "You're like the best-dressed woman I know. So, either I speak for most women and they'll like the way you always dress, or I'm just a freak and your lame fashion sense strangely only appeals to me."

Anne was silent for a moment. "The best-dressed woman you know? Really, New York girl?"

"Maybe I just have bad taste."

"No, you don't."

That afternoon, the girls went ice skating on a frozen pond that was a brisk walk from the house. All the guys but Barry begged off, and Anne said she wasn't feeling well, which Elizabeth didn't believe for a second. So it was just her, Michelle, Barry, and Patsy, along with some other random families. Adding small children learning to skate to the counterclockwise lap around the shoreline was like throwing a few drunk drivers onto the freeway. Patsy braved it, but Michelle and Elizabeth ended up sitting on a log, drinking hot cocoa from Barry's thermos. He stared at the pond as intently as an Eye in the Sky morning traffic report.

Michelle threw a snowball at his back and waved at him when he turned around.

"I think it's clearing up!" he called over to them, and went to take his chances.

"Do you want to talk about it?" Michelle asked.

"What's there to talk about?" Elizabeth asked back. "Don't tell me you want relationship advice. Clearly I'm not the person to come to."

"I don't want you to be hurt."

"I'm not hurt!" Elizabeth protested. "It's just an act we're putting on."

"It's a little more than that," Michelle said.

"Girls, come on!" Barry called. He was making good time around the pond, the kids who had started the traffic jam now flocking around their mother like baby geese.

Michelle gave a shrug and got up to trot to the ice. Elizabeth followed her. They wobbled on the ice together, Elizabeth staring at Michelle like there was some clue hidden on her—like if she looked hard enough, Michelle's heart really would be on her sleeve.

"You're a really good friend," Michelle said. She got her feet under her and took off at a good clip, forcing Elizabeth to keep up with her. Elizabeth hadn't even been to Rockefeller Center in years. She felt constantly on the verge of falling on her ass. "I need you. You have been so great and so nice and I just don't want you to feel unappreciated."

A kid went down again. Elizabeth put on the brakes, fearful of some *Final Destination*-style accident going down, but Michelle smoothly detoured around the accident and made a lap around the pond. When she got back, she skidded to a stop beside Elizabeth.

"I don't feel unappreciated," Elizabeth said, almost defensively.

"I'm not saying you're needy," Michelle told her as they both chuffed up to speed. "But however much you feel appreciated isn't enough. You should feel like a goddess with what you're doing for me. I just can't say enough how much you're helping me."

"It's cool," Elizabeth said. "We don't have to talk about it."

"You make me wish I were gay," Michelle said, "just so I could be with you and not have to put up with all these *boys*."

Elizabeth's skates got out from under her, chopping at the ice like Ginsu blades as she tried to regain her balance, and finally she fell, throwing her hands out for something to stop her fall, latching onto Michelle's arm, and pulling her down with her. The two fell side by side like they were making snow angels, still sliding over the ice. They came to a stop. Elizabeth groaned. Michelle gave a tinkling laugh and rolled onto her side. She put her gloved hand on Elizabeth's cheek like there was a place for it molded there. And she said "Kiss me. It'll help sell it."

Elizabeth touched her lips quickly to Michelle's, pulling away just as quickly, and the blush of heat through her felt like someone had rung Pavlov's bell, that it was all half-remembered feelings from that night in college and her own neurotic imaginings, but nothing *here*.

She got back up and kept skating.

With a lie about losing a bet to Elizabeth and owing her dinner, Anne got the two of them some alone time. She dressed in flared jeans, a sequin top with a gold luster, and a shearling coat. Heavy boots turned her walk into something of a stomp. "Next time I rethink my sexual identity," she told Elizabeth, "remind me to do it in spring."

"Well, if we could reschedule these things, I would've done it during the summer. Worrying about finals *and* homophobia?" Elizabeth shook her head.

Anne's knee rattled all through the drive, making Elizabeth glad she held the steering wheel.

"You don't have to be nervous," she said.

Anne slammed her heel down and ground it into the floor, like she was stomping on a cigarette. "Don't I? I know men want me, but women? I've never tried the women thing before. It's like being back in high school..."

"It's not that hard," Elizabeth said.

"What if I—" Anne began, virtually squeaking, then settled her voice. "What if I taste funny?"

"Taste funny?" Elizabeth repeated dully.

"Yeah, you know...that's the way women do it, right? Either the fingers or the...mouth. I'm pretty sure everything feels normal down there—"

"Yeah, I bet you are."

"I'm serious! I've been straight for twenty-five years. I have no idea how a woman tastes! Down there! I'm sure they taste, you know...they don't taste bad. I at least would've heard something if women tasted bad. Ellen would've told me. But what if *I* taste weird? What if every other girl tastes normal and I taste like Listerine or something? Like, maybe there's a special tampon thing I'm supposed to do..."

Elizabeth reached over and squeezed Anne's arm. "Okay, well, how does it smell?"

Anne looked at her dryly. "Like heaven."

"Then it probably tastes fine."

"You're sure I look good?" Anne hugged her coat tighter around herself. "They're lesbians. I'm not even wearing shorts; my legs are my best feature."

"No," Elizabeth said.

"*No?*"

"Your boobs. And I'm ninety-nine percent sure you're fishing for compliments right now. Relax. All you have to do is be yourself and keep looking like…"

"Like?" Anne prompted, a lilt in her voice.

"See? Fishing for compliments."

"Okay, tell me this. How do I tell the difference between a girl just being nice and telling me my hair is awesome," Anne flounced her hair, "which it is…and a girl who's trying to get into my pants?"

"Anne, if I knew that, I'd be a rich woman."

The Man in a Boathouse stood in a snowy field just off the highway. There was a marquee sign in a hollowed-out canoe on the turn-off, advertising drink specials, and a neon sign above the entrance with a mermaid sitting on a fishhook. Honkytonk music flowed out of the lit windows like water through a dam. The building was large, a juddering collection of planks and glass that looked like it could've been a colonial town hall in another life, seated on a checkerboard of salted parking spaces and snowy cars.

"I didn't know lesbians were such big fans of Willie Nelson," Anne said, getting out of the car.

"We are still in Ohio," Elizabeth reminded her. "And who doesn't like Willie Nelson?"

Inside, the music was loud but not omnipresent, billowing out from a jukebox in the corner. The large room that made up nearly all the interior of the building, save for a kitchen and restrooms, was a very traditional roadhouse, with wooden tables, oak beams slotting up to hold the ceiling, and nautical trinkets lining the walls. A fishnet, a ship's wheel, nothing too TGIFriday's, but still flavorful.

The crowd was a solid group of shitkickers: oil workers, roughnecks, and those who could keep up with them. Lots of flannel, lots of jeans, but an overall warm vibe. The room was dominated by five or six groups immersed in conversation, with some loners dancing at an open floor space in the back, or sidled up to the bar that ran the length of the wall nearest the door. It looked like a good prospect, so Elizabeth tapped Anne's arm and seated them there. The bartender came by fast. She gave them a sunny smile.

"Hi there, welcome to the Boathouse. What're you having?"

"What's your wine list?" Anne asked.

"Red and white."

"What beers do you have on tap?" Elizabeth asked, and got a Wikipedia article. She asked what was good, got recommended an IPA that was brewed not far away, and ordered that. Anne managed to finagle an off-the-menu martini and unbuttoned her coat.

Elizabeth followed suit, tying her jacket around her waist. She wasn't trying to glam up too much—Anne had to be the star of the show—but she thought the black cross-back top she'd gotten from Lululemon, which revealed the straps of the bra underneath and her toned back, was no embarrassment. Black twill pants graced her legs, showing off their svelteness. She wasn't trying to look too good, but after a certain point, it was out of her hands. Besides, everyone knew girls looked cuter in packs of good-looking. They were like kittens that way.

"So how's this work?" Anne asked, seemingly oblivious to the martini she'd just been given. "Do I fill out a form or something?"

Elizabeth tried her luck and picked up Anne's olive, spinning it around on its toothpick. "A form? Anne, it's a bar. You see someone who looks interesting and you talk to them. Even straight people can manage that."

"My sensors must not be calibrated right. You're the only one around who seems...interesting."

"Well, you can talk to me. Just don't push it."

Elizabeth dipped the olive into Anne's drink and stirred, which Anne finally noticed. She picked up her martini, but Elizabeth kept the olive.

"Okay," Anne said with a sip. "How does one end up catfishing herself?"

"Oh, you make it sound so trendy." Elizabeth bit into the olive. "Michelle's my friend. She needed help. Why not, right?"

"Yeah, but a girl like you? Why don't you have a real girlfriend? Or a real boyfriend? Or a real robot!"

Elizabeth tapped the toothpick against her lower lip as she watched Anne drink. "I don't do relationships."

"*Why?*" Anne asked innocently, playing at a grade schooler's curiosity. "You look cute, you dress nice, and you're good at lying. What else is there?"

Elizabeth laughed before sticking the toothpick in her mouth and circling it to the corner of her lips. "I told you about how my mom was bipolar. Not the cute kind either. The fucking Thorazine kind. Well, my dad…the guy who married her…he got pretty sick of dealing with her. He stuck her in an insane asylum. She died in there. I never saw her again. So that's my baseline of a relationship. It's there when it's convenient, but when it isn't—I don't think I'm very different from most people. I'm just honest. I'm not in a relationship for the long run, and no one else is either. They're there as long as it's easy. Why not just admit it?"

"That's one way of looking at it," Anne said. Her martini empty, she picked up Elizabeth's beer and took a swig.

Elizabeth stole it back. "Trust me, that's the only way of looking at it. Anyway, I don't really talk about it."

"Well, here we are while I come out of the closet, and you can't discuss childhood trauma? Man up."

"Seems like the wrong place for that. Anyway, it's not like I hate my parents or anything. I'm just not going to let their bullshit define me. They were supposed to be the perfect family, I was supposed to be the perfect little girl… Why keep going for that?"

"So, it doesn't define you? If they wanted a certain thing and you're defining yourself by not being that certain thing…"

"Being alone is what I want."

"Is it?"

"I know you're trying to sound wise, but you're really just repeating everything I say with a question mark at the end."

"Am I?"

The floorboards creaked behind them. They both turned at the same time, looking over their shoulders, Elizabeth feeling Anne's hair against her ear. Standing behind them was a woman of about six feet, taller, wearing jean overalls and a halter top shirt with the Jack Daniels logo on it. An American flag bandanna held down her auburn hair. She didn't look like she arranged flowers for a living. Her shoulders were broad and square, her arms clearly delineated with muscle from her bare biceps to the many rings she wore on her fingers, and her belly—visible from the sides of the overalls in her clinging tight shirt—was lean with abdominal muscles. She was a Valkyrie.

"Hi there," she said, her voice rich and husky and seemingly illegal, like bootleg liquor. "Haven't seen you around here before. I'm Hilda."

"Elizabeth," Elizabeth introduced herself. She looked to Anne to see if she would follow suit, but Anne seemed a little busy gawking. "This is my friend Anne."

"Just your friend?" Hilda asked. "You two looked pretty close."

"No, no, we're just having a night out. We're both, you know, so…"

Hilda nodded. "I get it. Two at a time can be fun, but I go one-on-one also."

"Oh God," Anne breathed, and turned back around to her martini. It wasn't until she picked it up that she realized it was empty.

When Hilda sat down beside her, she went a little rigid. "Hey, Charlene!" Hilda called. "Another of whatever she's having, on me. Her friend, too."

"I'm good," Elizabeth said, hoisting her beer. "I'm driving."

"And you're not?" Hilda purred to Anne. Her face was chafed and weather-beaten, with little make-up and no lipstick, but it had an odd kind of majesty to it that Elizabeth found very handsome. She wondered what Anne made of it.

"Well," Anne replied after a moment, "not if I go home with her."

"And if you don't?" Hilda pressed, seeming more gently amused than aggressive.

"I like to be in the driver's seat."

"If you can handle it."

"I can always handle it."

Elizabeth drained her glass like she was doing a kegstand. "I think I will take another drink after all."

Hilda glanced over at her. "The more the merrier. Charlene, another—"

Elizabeth thought a moment, trying to remember what she'd ordered. "Winter's Bone."

"Good taste," Hilda complimented.

Anne was vibrating like a polite person's phone in a movie theater.

"How about this?" Hilda said, focusing her attention all laser-y on Anne again. "I bet I can lift you off the ground with just my bicep."

"Are you complimenting how skinny I am?" Anne asked.

"If I can lift you with an arm curl, you buy me a drink." Hilda stretched out an arm. "Here. Get a grip."

She and Anne got up from the bar, then Anne wrapped her hands around Hilda's bicep. Hilda curled her arm up, an impressive musculature coming to the fore, and raised her arm. Without breaking a sweat, she lifted Anne off her feet.

Elizabeth had to admit, it was a power move.

"Whoa, you really did that," Anne breathed, back on the ground. "One arm. Yeah. Just one arm…"

"You should see what I can do with one finger."

"Oh!" Anne turned to Elizabeth, still seeming a little stunned. "She really is a lesbian!"

"Why else would I be hitting on you?" Hilda asked.

"Let's not get into that… Here." Anne took Hilda's hand. "I have my own little move, I just want to show it to you so you don't miss out."

Hilda grinned. "I'm all ears, darlin'."

Anne's cheeks colored. "Okay, so you take your hand, right, you just take it and…"

She held it against her top, dragging it over the sequins, and like magic, the touched beads changed color, going from gold to silver.

"Oh my word," Hilda said. She ran her fingers over Anne's stomach, writing on it with the change in color. "Trixie, get over here! You've gotta see this."

A crowd began to gather as Anne swept her hand over the trail Hilda had left, turning the sequins back to gold. Anne turned around, slipping off her coat so everyone could reach out and touch the fabric. "It's Sequin 2 Tone Flip Round Scale Fabric. Costs about twenty-five bucks a yard. I had to sew it myself, but—"

"You sewed it yourself?" one of the women asked, reaching out to gingerly change the color of Anne's side.

"Yeah, I'm kinda into all that stuff: make-up, fashion, whatever. It's a bit of a hobby."

"And it's just twenty-five dollars?" another woman asked, giving Anne a bit of a massage to see the color change.

"Uh-huh. Sometimes it's on sale. There are a few places that sell it. You just have to Google it."

"Well, I'll be damned," the bartender said, arriving with a round of drinks. "Does it have to be those colors?"

"I don't think so," Anne said. "They just have to turn around, you know, so I think you can do blue and green, blue and red, whatever. You want a bit of a dramatic change, of course…"

Looking at her, Elizabeth couldn't help but think of a kitten in a kindergarten class, getting petted by all the kids. She got up from the bar. "Well, I think you get the idea. I should go."

"You're leaving?" Anne asked, her top now looking like tie-dye.

"Yeah, I have an early day tomorrow. Last-minute Christmas shopping and whatnot. You gonna be able to find your way home?"

"Oh yeah," Anne said. "I'll call an Uber."

"Hey, don't call an Uber," one of the women said. She wore one of those shirts with a feminist slogan over her cleavage, which had always seemed counterintuitive to Elizabeth. "They underpay their drivers!"

Found the vegan, Elizabeth thought.

The drive back was long, the route easy enough that Elizabeth didn't really have to think. So she thought of other things. How pretty that top had been on Anne as its color changed, wondering what it felt like, thinking of leaving a handprint on Anne in silver like...

What?

She turned the radio on. Music played, but she didn't really hear it.

Did she not hope Anne and Hilda had a good time? No, she did hope that. She hoped Anne had twenty orgasms. She hoped they hit it off and went on another thirty dates. She hoped they got married and adopted forty Cambodian orphans.

She turned the music up louder. It shook her bones but bypassed her head entirely.

She wasn't jealous. You could only be jealous of something you wanted, and all she wanted for Anne was for her to be safe and have fun and be treated well.

Of course, the surest way to do that was to do it yourself—you want something done right and all that—but... impossible.

Anne didn't even like her like that.

The kiss had just been... Well, Elizabeth knew she looked good, but that was all it was. She and Anne were just friends.

And sure, *Anne* looked good, too, but just because two people were friends and they were sexually attracted to each other...

Not that she was sexually attracted to Anne. She just could appreciate some good facial symmetry when she saw it. She could see how someone could be into that even while not being into it herself. Like Libertarianism or that Steven Universe cartoon.

If Anne *were* into her and not just women in general, and she *did* try to kiss her again out of something other than misplaced sympathy, then… then…

Elizabeth twisted the wheel before she drifted completely out of her lane. Maybe she should just watch the road.

It was snowing when she got back.

Typhos leaned against the garage, his dark outline jarring against the mellow white of its paint. When Elizabeth got out of the car, he smiled at her.

"Got a minute?"

"All sixty seconds of it."

"Mind if I get a word, then?"

"About?" Elizabeth asked.

"I think you know what about." He nodded to himself. "Call Michelle to come outside. She'll want to hear this, too. I'd rather not say it twice."

With a sinking feeling, Elizabeth did as he asked. They met out back where they couldn't be seen from the street. Grady had been keeping his failed woodworking projects in the backyard, and with the snow covering them they were a little like the headstones of a cemetery, still and portentious.

Typhos sat down on one, biting off his gloves to rub his hands together. "Cold, ain't it? Don't worry, this won't take long. Just thought we shouldn't do it right in the living room, y'know?"

"Do what?" Michelle asked. Her innocent act was surprisingly… innocent.

Typhos pulled his gloves back on. "I know."

Elizabeth looked down. Michelle kept up her protests. "Know *what*? Seriously, you're creeping me out with this."

"Okay, Vic Mackey, let's do it," Typhos said, stuffing his hands in his pockets. "I was hired by Will Bridger a while ago to find out just what you were up to with this lesbian foolishness. He smelled a rat right from the beginning. Me, I figured you were too smart not to see me coming if I went head-on, so I came in from the side. I found Shane, befriended him, got myself an invitation to Christmas dinner."

"You're a detective," Elizabeth said. "Private eye."

"Yeah. I've been watching you, keeping my ears open, trying to figure out just what the hell was going on for a while now. See, at first, I couldn't figure it. Just couldn't put the pieces together. Michelle, I knew you were full of shit, no offense, but Elizabeth, you gave me pause. You seemed so sincere. I'm a pretty good judge of character—you have to be, in my line of work. So you can imagine how confusing it was to have a con where one of the grifters was real and one wasn't. Guess that's why they pay me the big bucks."

"We don't have to listen to this," Michelle said. "I *love* Elizabeth, and she loves me! Ask anyone!"

Elizabeth thought about how long she'd been waiting to hear those three words. God, it'd been years, hadn't it? Whole years...

"No to the first part, yes to the second. Mind if I smoke?" Typhos was already drawing out a pack of cigarettes and a book of matches. "Shane's a bit of a fitness nut. Hates the things, so I have to hate the things. He's a good guy—hate to do this to him. But if wishes were 401(k)s..."

He struck a match, lit a cigarette, and let the smoke spool out of his mouth. Neither Elizabeth nor Michelle said anything.

"I finally got it when I hacked Michelle's computer. You're a smart cookie, Michelle. Nothing incriminating, no PowerPoint presentation of your big smart plan. I had to go back and check the Internet history. Went back months and months—"

"You hacked my computer—"

"Hey!" Typhos snapped, pointing two conjoined fingers at Michelle, his cigarette smoldering between them. "Uncle Fester! Don't interrupt. Hate that shit. Fucking rude." He took a deep drag. More gray air. "Yes, I hacked your computer. Just said it, didn't I? And just a week or so before you went official on Facebook, I found Michelle going all over her old social media shit." He looked at Elizabeth. "MySpace. Remember that? Fucking MySpace. The Internet diary. Everything she'd ever written about you, Smile. What TV shows you used to watch, the songs you used to listen to, each and every detail of your friendship. Because, y'see, she didn't remember."

"Michelle," Elizabeth whispered. She wasn't trying to get Michelle's attention. It was more like she was saying a prayer.

The cigarette's glow seemed to turn Typhos's whole face orange, like war paint. "So I figure Walter White here turns up on your doorstep, taking you on a nostalgia trip. Remember this, remember that? And you fall for it. You think you feel the same way about her as she does about you. When she asks for a favor, well, shit…how could you say no to your old friend Michelle? You used to listen to Christina Aguilera with her. *Genie in a Bottle.*"

He stood up, finishing off the cigarette with a heaving breath. "I'm telling Will everything. I like you guys, all of your family. You're good people—some of you just did a stupid thing. But it's my job. So, you get a heads up. Tell the family yourself, cancel whatever vacation you had planned for that settlement money… I know, it sucks, but at least you get to spend Christmas with your family. I'm out here working a fucking case, aren't I?" He plucked the cigarette from his lips and tossed it down to fizzle in the snow. "That's my piece."

He walked between them and away, almost disappeared in the snow before Elizabeth caught a glimpse of him going inside the house. She didn't feel cold. Just numb.

"It's bullshit," Michelle said, her voice hoarse. "He's so full of shit. He's got no proof! So what if I looked you up online, Liz? So I was feeling nostalgic? So I wanted to relive some good memories for a change! Not like Will gave me any of those!"

"What *did* you remember?" Elizabeth asked.

"Liz, don't do this—"

"Don't call me Liz," Elizabeth said in one quick rush. "How much did you remember about me without some *website*?"

"He's playing you, Elizabeth. He's setting you up, setting both of us up because he's supposed to have proof and he has *nothing*."

"The first time we made love, you came into our room, you were a little drunk—"

"We can still pull this off! He's got nothing!"

"We watched a movie. What was it?"

"You're being ridiculous!"

"Did you kiss me first or did I kiss you?" Michelle was just staring at her. Elizabeth let out a shrill little laugh. "Do you remember anything about that night?"

Michelle threw her hands up. "I remember I was drunk and you were warm. God, you'd think you of all people wouldn't romanticize some fucking fling!"

"Why me of all people?"

Michelle just gave her a look. "Liz, Liz, I gave you a little push, I greased the wheels a little bit, but what did I lie about? I said we were friends, and we are! I told you I needed your help, and I did. So can we stop this *fucking Melrose Place* shit and *think*?"

Elizabeth tried to sit down on one of the snowy fixtures, as Typhos had, but she slipped and fell on her ass. She sat there, Michelle standing over her. Michelle was right. Even now, she was right. She hadn't offered anything or lied about anything, just hinted, just suggested, and that had been enough for Elizabeth. That'd always been enough for her. Because it wasn't real.

"You were never going to take a job in South America." She looked up at Michelle. "That was never the plan."

"No," Michelle said. She knelt down in front of Elizabeth. "The idea was, we would try this, and if it worked—"

"If people fell for it," Elizabeth corrected, not vindictively, but like she was fixing a misspelled word.

"If it worked," Michelle insisted, "then we could work out something on a more permanent basis. We could get married."

Elizabeth closed her eyes.

"Just hear me out!" Michelle said, her voice harsh. "It'd be an open relationship. You can go out whenever you want, have a one-night stand, have one every day of the week! It doesn't matter. After a while, we won't even have to live together. Lots of couples keep separate apartments. And it's not like anything serious is going to happen with you and someone else."

"Because I don't do relationships," Elizabeth said quietly. Her eyes were still closed. She thought she'd be able to picture marrying Michelle. She couldn't.

"Yes."

"And you and Deputy McQuarrie—"

"That can stay a secret. My family would never understand. And hell, even Typhos hasn't figured that out. Don't be jealous. It's nothing serious. I don't think I really like men that much. Can you blame me? But honestly, I doubt it'll be that hard to find someone young, dumb, and full of cum who *isn't* all about commitment. They're a dime a dozen in NYC. You know what I'm talking about."

"And your family?" Elizabeth asked. "They wouldn't know?"

"Why should they? They love you. We leave and they go on thinking we're just another happy couple. And people stop bugging me about having grandchildren, too. I think that alone makes the whole thing worth it."

"I need to think about it," Elizabeth said, though all she could think about was how she'd been right in trusting Anne. For once, she hadn't been let down, and Anne didn't even know she'd come through for her.

Why should that matter? Why *did it*?

Michelle squinted at her. "Sure. Go ahead. But I don't think you'll need that much time. This isn't a decision, Liz. It's just who you are."

Chapter 10

December 24

SOME EMOTIONS COULD BE AS exhausting as hard labor, and Elizabeth was feeling more than a few of them. Thinking of what an idiot she'd been. Going over and over Michelle's proposal in her mind with a fine-toothed comb—looking for the upside, trying to find the part that didn't hurt.

She kept trying to think of how it was kind of like what she wanted. She'd get to be with Michelle —in a way— but only on Michelle's terms. She could retain her independence, her freedom, like no other partner would let her. She could *have* Michelle, in some way, in some small way— hadn't she always told herself that was all she wanted? Michelle, any way they worked together, as long as it worked. It nestled into Elizabeth like a knife. She only had to say yes. Why shouldn't she say yes?

She missed Janet, and Wendy, but drew back from contacting them. And why? Because they were real people in a real relationship. Happy people. People who had that one-in-a-million thing that Michelle had blinked into life to raise Elizabeth's hopes and crush them all at the same time.

What she needed was a distraction. And what in America offered a better distraction than the holiday season?

So she tagged along when Shane said he was heading to the mall and lost herself in the crowd. Bustling shoppers, noisy kids, tired sales staff, none of them caring about her or each other. It didn't feel good. It didn't feel bad. It felt *nothing*, which was the best thing for her. She wanted this numbness.

She wanted to be alone, to be disembodied. To look at the lights, the toys, the clothes, the shows, and see nothing.

To try on a new outfit and feel nothing.

To listen to the din of the crowd and hear nothing.

To look into a sea of faces and see—a flash of red hair?

"Anne?"

Anne turned around and smiled. Once again, Elizabeth felt like she was the only person in the world. But this time it wasn't nothing.

"How much did you pack?" Anne asked immediately.

Elizabeth got the question. She was wearing a Spyder Eternity suit and some jewelry gifted to her by an attractive older man trying to get into the sugar daddy business. That had been a good week, but the ring and earrings were better. She looked like a Bond girl, if she did say so herself.

Not that Anne was any slouch. She wore the jeans and shearling coat of the other night, but her top was a red flannel shirt unbuttoned enough, and tied above the navel, to make up for being a size too big. Elizabeth figured if anyone would have a spare, it'd be Hilda.

"What are you doing here?" Anne asked, fighting her way through the barbarian hordes to get to Elizabeth. "Didn't you hear FEMA declared this place a disaster zone?"

"I'm, uh, shopping," Elizabeth said. She held up her shopping bag as proof.

"I can see that," Anne said. "I kinda assumed you were the sort who got her Christmas shopping done while she was still wearing a Halloween mask."

"I did!" Elizabeth protested. "I mean, I went online and bought stuff for everyone, it's just…it's you." She meant it in a way she wasn't sure Anne heard, and she didn't know if she wanted Anne to hear.

"Am I hard to shop for?" Anne teased. "*What* to get for the girl who has looks and talent?"

"I got you a gag gift, actually. Only that didn't quite feel right, so I got you a real gift, too."

"No fucking way."

"Yeah." Elizabeth nodded. "I got you a gag gift. Walk it off."

"I got you a gag gift, too," Anne said, incredulous. "And I'm here now—since you didn't ask—to get you something, you know, mildly nice."

"Oh?" Elizabeth asked. "I can't believe Saint Anne would *ever* do me wrong…"

"Why, what'd you get me? First draft?"

Elizabeth bit her lip. "You know that shirt of mine you stole?"

"Borrowed," Anne corrected.

"Yeah, I haven't gotten it back yet, thief. So I bought you ten more just like it."

Anne smiled like her face couldn't be wide enough. "Thoughtful, yet sarcastic. I like it!"

"And what'd you get me? Before you came up with the incredible Christmas gift I clearly deserve."

Anne licked her lips. "*RuPaul's Drag Race*: Season 6."

"Why the sixth season? Won't I not be able to follow the plot?"

Anne shrugged. "It was the cheapest. Tell you what I should've gotten you, breath mints."

"Oh, but then you remembered you weren't going to kiss me again."

Anne hoisted her shopping bag. "Well, you never know. I mean, about the gift. You don't know what the gift is. It's not RuPaul."

"Say no more, that's all the clues I need."

Anne spun the bag around, twining the plastic grips around her fingers. "So, I see you have something, I have something…" She held her bag out to Elizabeth. "Don't open until Christmas."

Elizabeth traded with her. "Likewise."

"So now what? You wanna sit in Santa's lap? Enjoy the food court's fine cuisine?"

"How about a ride home?" Elizabeth bargained. "Shane dropped me off. Now that Grady's on a liquid diet, he's determined to find some Hi-C Ecto Cooler for a Christmas present."

"That's not bad," Anne said. "I'll have to offer to go half and half with him on that."

The sun was low in the sky when they left, its light turning the sky a reedy pink. The road home passed by a river that flowed too fast to freeze over, but looked calm on the surface. Sunlight rippled in pastel shades on the water. All around, the trees were sleek and minimalist, powdered with white on sketched out branches. Riverbank bushes and reeds were frosted over totally white. Elizabeth looked out at all of it as Anne drove. It was a lovely day.

"So?" Elizabeth asked.

"*So?*" Anne imitated.

"C'mon, the last time I saw you, you were wearing your own clothes, surrounded by lesbian rednecks, about to go where no man had gone before with a Valkyrie. Let me hear the gory details!"

"Please don't tell me that fake-dating my sister has gotten you this horny—"

"No, no. In fact, I could use a distraction from all that."

"Want me to turn on the radio?" Anne asked. "You can choose the station. Top Forty hits or Top Forty hits."

Elizabeth smiled, reaching over to flick Anne's thigh. "I'm serious here. This stuff can be weird, complicated, intense. You should talk to someone about it."

Anne caught Elizabeth's smile. "It's not like anything happened. I got a taxi, must've gotten back home when you weren't paying attention. I was tired, so I went to bed early, and when I got up, I went to the mall. Must've missed you again."

Elizabeth's mouth hung open a little. "What about the shirt?"

"This old thing?" Anne looked down at it. "It's Shane's. Someone got it for his birthday a few years back, he didn't like it, so he let me have it. Cute, right?"

"Okay—Hilda? You weren't attracted to her? Because *God,* any woman who can make overalls look that good..."

"She was fine," Anne insisted. "Really nice. We talked, had a few drinks, made out a little, but...it just wasn't right."

"Wasn't right?" Elizabeth demanded. "Anne, that woman could've been Angie Harmon. She literally could've been Angie Harmon pulling a Hannah Montana. Not that I'm judging you or anything, but...c'moooooon."

"Hey, aren't you supposed to tell me how it's cool to go at my own speed and wait until I'm ready? I could've sworn that had something to do with sex."

"Well, yeah, but when Angelina Jolie's buff cousin shows up, *that's how you know you're ready.*"

"I was ready," Anne said firmly.

"Okay, so what's the problem? Did she say she thought the Earth was flat or something?"

Anne let out a strong exhale. "She was great. Absolutely great. She looked great and she kissed great and she felt great, but I couldn't do it."

"It wasn't that...you know...it felt sinful or something?"

"No!"

"Because a lot of people feel that way. It's not their fault; it's just something they've grown up with. It goes away."

"There was nothing wrong with me, there was nothing wrong with her, everything was perfect. I should've done it, I just didn't!"

Elizabeth winced at Anne's raised voice. "We don't have to talk about it right now. Even if you didn't go through with it, it took a lot of courage to admit to yourself that that's what you wanted—"

"Don't patronize me," Anne interrupted.

"I'm being serious. I might have a weird sense of humor, but I wouldn't joke about what you're going through."

"Yeah," Anne said. "You might tease me a little, but you'd never make fun of me. You'd just...be this person that's this way and then...while you're so understanding and so nice and so sweet, you're also... You're over there..."

"You're right," Elizabeth said. "You don't have to have sex. You don't have to go back to the club. Not now, not next week, not next month—not anytime you don't want to. I'm sorry if it feels like I'm pushing—"

"You're pushing?" Anne demanded. "You wanna know what was wrong with Hilda? You wanna know why I left and couldn't even look at her? Because she wasn't you, Elizabeth. She wasn't what I wanted because she wasn't *you*."

"Anne," Elizabeth said softly, "pull over."

"I don't want to."

"Anne..."

"You ever feel that way? Like you just wanna keep driving?"

"Please."

"Here," Anne said. She squeezed the brakes and cut across the empty road onto a small trail. It took them out of sight behind a billboard; the

'Hell Is Real' sign that was now outlined by snow, had icicles dangling under it.

She stopped the car and put it in park. They were as hidden as a cop car running a speed trap.

"I used to come here to get high," Anne said, looking up at the blank canvas behind the sign. The struts cast shadows across the white, making it look like an advertisement for Rorschach tests.

"Anne," Elizabeth said. "Still wanna know how you taste?"

Elizabeth could hear the grumbling of the engine and the blood pounding in her ears and the stillness of Anne's held breath. She saw Anne's lips part and thought very clearly, *I need that.* She clambered out of her seat and onto Anne at the same moment Anne slammed her seat back as far as it would go. Anne pulled her in. Her lips, her kiss—she felt the wonderful curiosity of Anne kissing her, Anne's tongue seeking hers. Her hands were trailing over Elizabeth's body, enjoying her—Elizabeth loved being enjoyed. She felt stripped before Anne had taken off a stitch.

Elizabeth reached between Anne's legs and touched her thigh. The fabric was so thin she could feel the warmth of Anne's skin through it. And still Anne was kissing her.

God, Anne was good at kissing her. Her hands spilled through Elizabeth's hair, tilting her head back, baring her throat. Elizabeth felt little touches of heat under her chin and down her throat to the rise of her breasts, each warm bloom bursting with the promise in Anne's lips. Promising that the next kiss would feel even better. And the next. And the next.

"Oh fuck," Elizabeth muttered. Her free hand rested on the nape of Anne's neck, and it felt *very* good to know Anne would be staying tucked between her breasts for as long as she could hold her there. Except Anne had other ideas. She pried away, grabbed the hem of Elizabeth's blouse, and pulled it loose.

Anne stopped and stared for a moment. Elizabeth actually felt bashful. People were always in such a hurry to touch her, to be touched, that it was hard to remember the last time someone had really looked at her. The last time she'd been seen. "La Perla plumetis bra," Anne breathed. "In pink. *Fuck*, that is adorable."

She looked up at Elizabeth, and suddenly it was almost a struggle in their aggression, Anne's body up against Elizabeth's and Elizabeth's pulled down to Anne's, Anne kissing her as Elizabeth tried to get her left hand back on Anne's head, her hair, her neck, *something* to keep her there. Her right hand was between Anne's legs now, rubbing hard on the seam of her jeans, into the subtle swell of her crotch, the tingle of wetness she felt there, the buried heat. She could *feel* Anne groan, rumbling in her own chest where she pressed against Anne's. An echo so deep, so intense she didn't know where her body stopped and Anne's started, and she didn't care because it felt good either way.

"Fair warning," Anne said. "If you let me get you naked, I'm stealing that bra."

"This is why I'm pan. At least men like my boobs more than what's covering them."

"You could just not wear a bra. I won't say anything."

She gave a ragged, smart-assed smile, and Elizabeth was forced to swoop and obliterate it with another kiss. "I wouldn't believe you not saying anything if Nate Silver predicted it," Elizabeth said.

Anne bit her nipple.

"Oh shit, can we just agree you're the wittiest and—"

Elizabeth's breath left her as Anne's hands began tugging on her belt. Unbuckling it, unzipping her slacks, drawing her fly open.

"I *am* the wittiest," Anne agreed, skirting her pants and bottoms halfway down her hips.

There was a tattoo on Anne's pubic bone: *You Just Hit the Jackpot.*

"Jesus, you're insufferable," she said as she slipped her fingers into Anne's panties and down over her slick labia, felt the soft bloom of her sex, soaking wet.

"You must have shitty taste in women then," Anne replied, though it was gratifyingly broken by a moan. "Oh, I forgot, you used to lust after my sister."

"The worst," Elizabeth confirmed, tracing her fingers from Anne's clitoris, up over the downy softness of her mons, and back again to the glossy slickness. Anne's eyes widened as Elizabeth's fingers slowly explored. Her lips trembled, and a whimper hung on each breath. Elizabeth knew exactly what Anne was thinking: *How can it feel so good when it's another woman doing it?*

Elizabeth took her hand away and licked her gleaming fingers.

"So?" Anne asked, with a hitch in her voice that made Elizabeth *throb.* "How's my taste?"

"Sweet," Elizabeth told her.

"No, it isn't. But you're nice for saying so."

"It tastes sweet to me," Elizabeth said, reaching for her, pulling Anne's jeans further down—

A searchlight shone into the car. It grew brighter as Elizabeth threw herself back into the passenger seat, pulling her shirt down. Anne was shimmying her pants back up her hips—when her foot slapped the gas pedal, and the engine revved through the parking brake.

Byers's shadow fell across them as he stood in front of the searchlight on his squad car. "Ah, peaches and cream!" he cried. "I thought you'd run yourselves off the road. I was worried."

"Sorry!" Elizabeth said loudly, pulling her seatbelt back on. "Really sorry, we just, we were…"

Anne was trying to get her belt through its buckle. Her fly was still undone. "We were!" she agreed, half-listening.

Byers flicked his wrist dismissively. "Would you two just get home or get to a hotel room or something? That's horrible on your engine, especially in this weather. You're gonna need a tow truck if you do that much more."

"Yes, sir," Elizabeth replied, as Anne zipped herself up.

"At least tell me you have a cell phone with you."

"We do," Anne chimed.

"Okay then. And you should visit the department's website. We have a comprehensive list of things that could come in handy, if this had been an emergency. Road flares, a first aid kit, all sorts of things. You just put them in your trunk, then you don't have to worry about it."

"I have those," Anne said.

"Okay. Good. You get going. I'll just hang back, make sure you don't need the winch."

Anne put the car into drive and backed them out from behind the billboard. They didn't need the winch.

Elizabeth closed her eyes for a long moment. All she could think about was that kiss. Those kisses, plural. Those kisses and *other things.*

Her heart was racing. She could barely breathe. Her smile felt extremely stupid. She wanted to touch Anne. Not sexually—not *just* sexually—but to convey something. To feel the energy throbbing in her body and know that it was the same as her own.

She wanted to kiss Anne again. She really, really wanted to kiss Anne again.

"So," Anne said, her fingers drumming on the wheel. "I've been thinking about that for a while."

"I doubt much thinking was involved." Elizabeth felt chipper. It was like finding a candy bar in her purse. Hearing her favorite song on the radio. Seeing a celebrity at a restaurant. Kissing someone who really needed to be kissed.

She could still taste Anne, and smell Anne, and remember Anne's warmth. It wasn't nearly enough.

"How do you feel about going downstairs, locking the door, and not thinking some more?"

Anne smiled. "I don't know. I really like that outfit. It'd be a shame to take you out of it."

"I could put it back on later, if you're really good."

"You've talked me into it."

Elizabeth's head drifted back against the headrest as she luxuriated in this experience of Anne. She felt like kissing her for days. "It doesn't have to be a one-time thing, either. Maybe it could be our regular Saturday night thing."

"Sounds serious," Anne quipped.

"No," Elizabeth said. "Fun. It's just fun. We won't get married or anything."

"How do you know?"

"We just won't."

"So how will it end up? I get bored of you and move on? You get bored of me and move on?"

"I don't know. I just know we won't get married."

"You won't get bored of me," Anne promised. She reached over to pet Elizabeth's thigh. Elizabeth put her hand on top of Anne's. "Tell me this, though. What's going on with you and Michelle?"

"I'm not sure. Nothing serious—nothing fun. I guess we're just keeping up appearances. She wants us to get married to really throw Will off our track."

Anne took her hand back, although maybe she just had to work the turn signal. "And are you going to?" Her voice cooled slightly.

"I don't know."

"For such a self-assured woman, you're very unsure and unknowing suddenly."

Elizabeth glanced over at her. Anne still looked casual, cool. "What's it matter? There's nothing going on between me and her. In fact, I think just about the only thing all three of us have in common is that none of us wants a relationship. So this works out great. I have the fake marriage with her, then you and I can enjoy ourselves. No stress, no judgment, no responsibility—"

"Maybe I want those things," Anne said. "Elizabeth, last night at the Boathouse—maybe I didn't go home with Hilda, but I did like it there. I liked being open about myself, being able to say what I was, who I was. I don't want to go back to pretending to be something I'm not just because it's easy."

"What are you saying?" Elizabeth asked. "You want a real relationship?"

"I want you," Anne said. "Not just fun. *You.*"

"Well, all I have to give is fun. That's all I'm offering. Maybe there's someone out there with more to offer, but I'm not her. You want a commitment, I can't give you one." Elizabeth saw the house coming up on the right. "We're here," she said flatly.

"You want to keep going?" Anne asked. "Because to tell the truth, I just want to go on driving."

Elizabeth didn't say anything. Anne took that rightly as a no.

Christmas Eve, and contrary to the cultural ad blitz that started at midnight on Halloween and bulldozed through Thanksgiving, *now* it felt like Christmas. Patsy hummed carols under her breath, while Grady carved an outline of reindeer and Santa's sleigh out of plywood. When he put it up in the lit windows of the second story, it became a tasteful little Christmas decoration. Elizabeth felt compelled to compliment him on the work. He brushed off her praise with pleased aplomb.

The Christmas tree in the living room was now fully decorated and lit, last-minute gifts crowding under it. A roaring fire in the fireplace shot out flicking shadows of the stockings hanging from the mantelpiece. Elizabeth saw one with her name on it as she snitched a candy cane from the tree and felt oddly choked up.

They watched a DVD of *A Muppet Christmas Carol* that played like the disc had been dipped in antifreeze. Elizabeth tried to think of a better Christmas movie they could put on and couldn't come up with anything. And one by one, the Harlows gravitated to the living room, kicking back and watching the show with the relaxed pleasure of people who had seen a movie before and knew that it would entertain them again. All except for Patsy, who was on her phone like it was hiding the secrets of the universe from her.

Anne stopped in the doorway, lingered, moved on. She was wearing her flannel unbuttoned, layered over a ripped white T-shirt that hung down to show her bra in a slack, rock-star sort of way. It was a good look. Elizabeth could imagine cleaning up the apartment with Anne dressed like that, jean shorts, knee socks. She herself was wearing the Spider-Man top. Anne had returned it.

Michelle sat down beside Elizabeth, an arm around her, a kiss on her cheek. It felt awful. All she could think of was Anne, and how it had felt to be with someone who needed her, who savored her in every iota of her being. With Michelle, she felt like a dummy sitting on a ventriloquist's knee and telling jokes before she went back in the case at the end of the night.

She got up. "Excuse me a minute," she said. "There's a phone call I've just got to make."

Downstairs, she booted up her laptop, started up Skype, and called Janet and Wendy. Like a high school couple, at this point they were their own portmanteau. And indeed, it was Wendy who picked up, with Janet in the background.

"Merry Christmas!" Wendy chimed, then shuffled the laptop to aim at Janet.

"Happy New Year," Janet added, immersed in a book.

They were arranged peculiarly to each other, and it took a moment for Elizabeth to realize what was going on. Wendy and the laptop were on the floor, Wendy on all fours, while Janet sat on a couch off to the side. Janet had her feet up, but instead of resting on a coffee table, they were propped up by Wendy's back.

"Is this a bad time?" Elizabeth asked.

"Well, that's debatable," Wendy said. "It is Christmas, but then there's that seasonal depression stuff. More people commit suicide on Christmas than any other day of the year."

"That's actually an urban myth," Janet said, turning a page. "It's in spring."

"Of course you would know that," Wendy said.

"I mean why do you two look like you're acting out an editorial cartoon?"

"Oh," Wendy said, "I was a bad girl, so now I have to be a human footstool for Janet."

"It's the only way she'll learn," Janet said disinterestedly.

Elizabeth paused for a long moment. "You're fucking with me."

Janet put her feet down. "Of course we're fucking with you. Do you really think I'd use Wendy as a human footstool? It's not even that hot."

"It's kinda hot," Wendy said.

"This isn't just a courtesy call!" Elizabeth cried. "I actually need to talk to my friends!"

Janet got down from the couch and laid down next to Wendy, letting the younger woman cuddle up against her like a patient cat with an excited dog. "You know you can tell me anything," Janet said.

"Yeah," Wendy added. "Dish."

It all poured out. Everything that had happened since she'd gotten to Ohio. Not just with Michelle, but with Anne, with Shane, with Grady, with Patsy and Typhos and Barry, the McQuarries, everything piling up and piling up until it seemed impossible that the wobbling tower was still standing, but equally impossible that it would ever fall.

"And I know what you're going to say!" Elizabeth finished, feeling not on the verge of tears but *drained*, like she'd just sobbed for hours and hours. "Because I told you to go after Wendy, you're going to tell me to go after Anne. But how am I just supposed to…start believing in true love? That she wouldn't give up on me, for anything, when I'm so used to being alone? I've always believed that everyone was alone, they just don't know it. This…this feels like I'm willfully denying everything I've ever thought."

"Wow, your love life is even weirder than mine," Wendy said. "That feels very strange at this end. Like I'm not the hero of my own story anymore…"

"Wendy," Janet chided.

"I'm thinking, I'm thinking! It's complicated. I was really pulling for you and Zordon."

"Elizabeth," Janet said, shouldering Wendy over a little. "Can I be blunt?"

"I think that's been well-established at this point."

Janet smiled slightly. "It sounds like what you want is to go after Anne, but you're trying to talk yourself out of it because you're afraid you won't get married and live happily ever after."

"Or trying to talk yourself into it," Wendy added, "because you're hoping you can."

Janet continued, "I hope you realize that there's no guarantee of a long, happy life, not with anyone. The trick is just to find someone who's worth the risk."

"Do you mean me?" Wendy asked.

"Yes."

"Just checking. I like validation."

"Anne's worth the risk," Elizabeth said confidently. "But how am I supposed to stop thinking...that she'll leave me if things get hard? Or that I'll leave her? I've spent my whole life believing nothing could last if things got really hard. It's like I grew up in the Soviet Union and you're asking me to just start believing in God."

"I believe in God," Wendy said.

Janet said, "I'm Catholic, so I believe in God with a little God on top of it."

"You're Catholic?" Wendy asked.

"What did you think was with the rosary beads?"

"Oh, those were *rosary beads*! I was wondering when you were going to—" Wendy coughed.

"And what's so wrong with being single anyway?" Elizabeth asked. "One-night stands and casual sex? Am I supposed to apologize for enjoying that? Shouldn't that be enough for Anne? I never heard anything about *her* hating hook-ups."

"It sounds like she doesn't want that anymore," Janet said.

"Oh, so she just stops wanting it? How does that work? Because she wants something, I'm suddenly supposed to want it, too?"

"That is kinda how relationships work," Wendy said. "I mean, Janet and I want the same things, mostly."

"So she wants me to change," Elizabeth said bitterly.

"Or you want to change," Janet put in. "I somewhat doubt we'd be discussing this if you weren't at least a little interested in this woman."

"Change," Elizabeth muttered. "Going back on everything I believe, wanting what everyone else wants, having what everyone else has. Are you really telling me she's worth that? You've never even met her."

"Elizabeth," Wendy said. "Can I do like story time here for a moment?"

"What?"

"When I was a kid," Wendy began, "I hated Brussels sprouts. I'd never even tried them, but I heard all the jokes and they looked weird, so I hated them. Just 'cause I was supposed to. And then…and this is a real feat of will on the part of my mom, so I don't want to understate it…I tried them. And I actually liked them! They tasted great to me."

"Is she high?" Elizabeth asked Janet.

"Yes, but it's a natural high. You get to find it charming."

"If I can finish?" Wendy asked. "So there I am, loving the taste of Brussels sprouts. But I still don't eat them! Just because I don't want to eat something that's good for me, that my parents are pushing on me. I'm a rebel, after all. And it takes me months to realize this, but—*not* wanting something because everyone else wants it can be just as silly as wanting something because everyone else wants it. Now Janet here, she hates Brussels sprouts—"

"I'm normal that way," Janet interjected.

"So I'm not saying the moral of the story is that Brussels sprouts are great. Or that they're awful! Just that you can't judge something based on what everyone else thinks, whether it's positive or negative. You have to decide what *you* want." She glanced over at Janet. "You and the Pope in Rome. *In Rome*, Janet."

"Is this really that weird?" Janet asked. "You know there's 1.3 billion of us in the world. You like those *Chronicles of Riddick* movies. I'm sure there's a lot less of you."

"It's not weird, but it's weird I'm just finding out now. We watched *The Da Vinci Code*. That would've been a great time to bring this up."

"I don't think *The Da Vinci Code* counts as a 'great time' in any capacity."

Elizabeth cleared her throat. "Don't ask me how, but I think you've actually given me an idea about what to do."

"Must've been an accident," Janet said. "Good luck with *Star Trek: The Motion Picture*."

"Janet, what do you do in *The Young Pope* situation?" Wendy asked. "Have you even thought about it?"

Elizabeth closed the laptop screen.

Upstairs, eggnog was being served and *A Muppet Christmas Carol* was wrapping up. Patsy had put her phone away, but looked lost in thought. There was an empty space to sit next to Michelle. And Anne was lying on the ground, just right for someone to lie down behind her and cuddle by the fire.

Elizabeth stood in the doorway, sipping her eggnog.

She knew what to do. She just had to do it.

Limey marched up to her, holding a fresh chew toy in his mouth. He dropped it at her feet.

"Aw," Elizabeth said. "That for me?"

She reached down for it and Limey growled her into standing up straight, then dropped at her feet and chewed on the toy.

This had to be why lesbians got cats.

"Don't any of you get up," Barry said, heaving himself out of a chair that he made seem like the most comfortable thing in the world. "I think I have a copy of *Scrooged* around here somewhere…"

"You guys just watch *A Christmas Carol* adaptations?" Typhos asked. "Thatta theme?"

"We have the Patrick Stewart one," Michelle replied.

Patsy got up and stretched as Barry kept looking for the tape, muttering that he had gotten it out of storage earlier just to be sure where it was. "Hey, Typhos, weird question, but what did you say you did again?"

"Real estate," Typhos answered.

"So like a realtor?"

"Uh-huh," Typhos said slowly, his hackles up.

"That's funny, because I checked online and you don't have a realtor's license. At least, not in the continental US."

Barry stopped looking for the tape. He pressed stop on the DVD player, muting the soundtrack and sending the TV to a blue screen. "Patsy, are you sure you want to be—"

"In fact," Patsy said, "the only thing I can find on you is a private investigator's license, right here in Ohio. Shane, where'd you say you met Typhos?"

Shane sat up straighter. "Back in Jersey. We practiced fencing at the same club."

"Sorta begs the questions," Patsy continued, "what are the odds that a guy from Ohio meets another guy from Ohio, in Jersey, *fencing*?"

Typhos got up from the couch and went to the pitcher of eggnog that had come off the blender. He filled his red cup again. "William Bridger hired me to find out what was going on with his wife looking like Dr. Evil."

"What was going on?" Barry asked. "She was dating Elizabeth. It's all over their Facebooks."

"Yeah…yeah…" Typhos replied. "Will said Shane would be the easiest one to get close to, so I headed to Jersey, took up an interest in fencing, chatted him up—when he heard I didn't have anywhere to go for Christmas, he invited me to his place for the holidays. That was my way in."

"I knew you weren't who you said you were. Why else would Will know who you were when he came over?" Patsy said. Then she looked around. "Was I the only one who picked up on that?"

Shane jumped up. "So, wait, all this time—you were just pretending to be my friend? You were only using me to check out *my sister*?"

"No!" Typhos protested, holding out his hand. "That's not it. Maybe it started out that way, but you've been a real friend these past few months. The first friend I've had in a long time."

"If I'm such a good friend, how could you lie to me?"

Typhos shrugged helplessly. "It's my job." He made a weak gesture at Elizabeth. "The lesbian thing is all bullshit. Or…mostly bullshit. Elizabeth had a crush on Michelle since college—Michelle never really returned it, but she knew she could dangle it like a carrot in front of Elizabeth to get her to go along with this fake relationship. And if the judge buys it, then Michelle comes out of her divorce with millions. Will doesn't get a dime."

"That's not true!" Michelle shouted. "I love Elizabeth! I've always loved her, I've always been a lesbian, I just never knew it until *his boss* treated me so…so badly… We're getting married. Do you think that's fake? Tell them, Liz. Tell them you're going to be my wife."

Suddenly all eyes were on Elizabeth. She thought she'd moved past their uncertainty, their suspicion, the question of whether Michelle's transformation was for real—but now it was all rushing back, all at once, and she *had* to say something. She couldn't just keep going…couldn't nod and play along… She just had to open her mouth and—

"I can't marry you," Elizabeth said. "I don't love you. I'm in love with your sister."

The pit fell out of her stomach. She could taste bile at the back of her throat. And she felt like a weight had come off her back so heavily it was a wonder no one had heard it fall.

"You—" Michelle exploded.

"Oh my God!" Patsy cried. "This is all—all so sudden…"

"Not *you*, you twit," Anne said. "She means me."

"No, she doesn't!" Michelle said.

"Holy Christ!" Barry screamed. "How many of my daughters have you slept with?"

After that, there was no small amount of pandemonium. Grady was furiously scrawling down whatever he wanted to say, though no one took the time to read it. Typhos was insisting that he *was* Shane's friend, while Shane angrily denied it. Michelle was demanding that Elizabeth keep up the charade, even if the entire family was in on it now. And Patsy was trying to comfort Barry.

Anne just stood there, such a stricken expression on her face that Elizabeth feared getting closer, feared seeing her emotions in any greater detail. Still she couldn't look away, she strained to see every nuance Anne was feeling and to hear any whisper she might make in the roar of the family squabble. But all too soon, Anne turned her head. Like she just couldn't look at Elizabeth.

It was almost a wonder they heard the doorbell ring.

"I'll get it," Barry said, casting a glance at Patsy as if worried she'd be bicurious when he returned. He was gone for a solid minute, an awkward silence reigning as everyone realized there was absolutely nothing to say. Anne looked at Elizabeth, but it was as if she couldn't process what had been said. Everything had been too loud before, and now it was too quiet.

"I just..." Anne started, a frog in her throat. "I need a minute."

She pushed her way to the hallway and out through the dining room. Elizabeth followed her as the front door slammed, but Grady stuck out his leg and blocked the doorway. Elizabeth looked at him.

"You're not doing so hot on intact bones already this week."

"Give her a ten-count, at least," Shane called. "Goddamn..."

That freeing sensation of having her stomach pitched between her feet hadn't gone away. But now it was feeling less like a jolt of adrenaline and more like she'd walked off a plane in mid-flight. Maybe this was how gamblers felt when they put it all on red and the little ball was just starting to slow down.

It felt like there should be a lot more hugging and cheering. She'd finally admitted the truth, she'd come out and said what Anne meant to her, it should've been like she'd taken her finger out of a dike. All the love and affection she'd been denying herself should come sweeping in like a promise; there shouldn't be this goddamn *suspense*. And she shouldn't be so fucking worried about Anne, who she'd done all this for in the first place, and now... *What* now? Had she mangled it all, gotten it wrong somehow, been so inexperienced at actual factual relationships that she'd bungled one right out of the gate. She wanted Anne to be happy, she'd put herself out there just for Anne to be happy and now, more than being alone, she feared she'd hurt Anne in some clumsy, thoughtless way. She hadn't meant to, but more and more it seemed like what she intended didn't matter at all.

Barry came back holding a bouquet of flowers. He stood in the hallway. "Not all of you know this...but before my Margaret died, she opened an account with a flower shop. She set it up so there was a trust fund that would pay for sending flowers to me—to all of us—every Christmas. She's gone now... I'm sure to some of you it seems like she was gone forever, it's been so long and you were so young. But a love like that doesn't die, even if you can't touch it anymore. It's still there, just under the surface. Waiting for when you need it."

He took a sniff of the bundle. "And it's as sweet as... I know you think it's a bit silly, me going on about black Santa Claus and drag shows and everything. And it is a little silly. But all I want is for everyone to feel loved and accepted. That's what Christmas is all about, to me. The one time of the year when nothing else should matter but that, because you're with your family, whatever your family is…that's what family is about. And I'm sorry if I haven't been the best father, but as far as I'm concerned, if I have kids like you, I must have done something right. Because you're the best kids a man could want. Even if you're going through some changes." He looked at Michelle. "Even if you make mistakes sometimes." He looked at Shane. "Even if you need support." He looked at Patsy. "You, you're doing just fine. I haven't forgotten you." He looked at Grady. "Grady, I like your woodworking. I think you have a real future in it."

Grady thumped his chest manfully.

Out on the porch, the wind was howling, the cold only kept somewhat at bay by the closed door. The crack in the glass let in a hiss of wind and snow that stirred around at their ankles as Elizabeth stopped in the doorway.

Anne was pacing in front of the garage, hugging herself. "So," she said. "I guess that handles the coming out."

"Sorry," Elizabeth said, following her. "I'm an idiot. I'm a complete idiot."

"It's fine. I probably just would've told a joke."

"'Once you heat this spaghetti up, it's as straight as I am,'" Elizabeth said.

At that moment, Shane and Typhos came barreling through the house door. Elizabeth quickly moved out of their way.

"I am your friend, Shane!" Typhos was saying. "I know I haven't been a good one. I know I've lied to you. But that was all just a job… You're my brother."

"How am I supposed to believe you?" Shane asked, tears in his eyes. "All you've ever done is lie to me."

"Because I didn't tell Will anything," Typhos said. "And I'm not going to. As far as he's concerned, Michelle really is gay. Things just didn't work out with her girlfriend."

"Guys!" Elizabeth said. "Anne and I are kinda settling some stuff here…"

"Well, we have stuff to settle, too," Shane said.

"Yeah!" Typhos added.

"We were here first," Anne said.

"My best friend betrayed me!" Shane said.

"I'm in love with her!" Elizabeth cried.

"And I love him!" Shane cried. "In a way, way less physical way..."

"I love you, too, man," Typhos said.

Shane nodded manfully. "Let's just talk this out in the garage, bro."

Typhos nodded. "Bro."

Elizabeth and Anne went out into the yard.

"Your brother, he..." Elizabeth asked, making her wrist limp.

"Broke his wrist?" Anne replied. "Yeah. Freak arm-wrestling accident. Well, okay, pretty normal arm-wrestling accident."

Elizabeth shrugged. Suddenly there didn't seem like a lot to say.

She'd always thought a kiss was a good way to end a conversation when there was nothing left to say.

She really wanted to kiss Anne.

She didn't think she'd ever want anything else.

"I want to believe you," Anne said. "But you were so certain about your freedom and your independence... How long are you going to give that up to be with me?"

"When my mom got sick, I put myself in my dad's shoes. I thought that there was no way I'd be strong enough to stay with someone who was just...burning. And I thought no one else would do that for me either. They'd either be lying or crazy if they said so. But you, you mean it. These people, you take care of them, you give to them, you protect them. And if I were ever in trouble, if I were ever a burden, you'd stay with me. You're that person. And I think I can be that person for you too. I do want to be free. And I do want to be independent. But what I want—even more than that—is to be part of a family. To be part of your family, Anne. Even though they are all crazy."

"Good, you noticed that. I was afraid I'd have to point it out." Anne smiled at her. "So, are you *ever* going to kiss me? We've been alone a whole thirty seconds and you're *supposed* to be in love with—"

It was amazing how gentle the kiss was, considering how quickly Elizabeth went to her and how roughly she brought their lips together. There was the heat of passion, a deep-down need that made Elizabeth want to tear apart clothing and do things anywhere but in bed. But there was also this melting that persisted after that first plume of heat, when she and Anne were holding their lips together just because they couldn't think of anything else they'd rather be doing and they didn't want anything but this moment. Then, slowly, as if she were waking up, Elizabeth could feel Anne's body against hers, taste her breath, smell her perfume, and started thinking of all sorts of things that would be romantic and passionate and, if they weren't done in a bed, would probably require some Lysol spray afterward.

She decided to start by dropping a handful of snow down the back of Anne's shirt.

"Agh!" Anne cried, with an excess of volume and a minimum of dignity. She danced around crazily.

Elizabeth said, "You got me with a snowball to the face. Told you I'd get you back."

"You sultry minx," Anne said, awe in her voice. "I fucking love you."

"That'll make things easier. I plan on taking you on quite a few dates before my vacation is over. And who knows? Maybe I can introduce you to the glorious lesbian tradition of the U-Haul."

Epilogue

New Year's Day, 2019

IT WAS THE FIRST HOUR of the first day of the new year. Part of Elizabeth felt it was far too early to be going home. But she *was* tired, and she owed Janet enough to have volunteered herself for a special project first thing in the morning. And if those reasons sounded lame, then there was always the fact that being back in their apartment meant she had Anne all to herself. *I'm not getting old*, she thought. *I'm just getting older.*

Outside, fireworks were still going off, so frequently as to set a bassline over the city. Through it she could hear the thump of a million parties. If she wandered, meandering after any particular beat, she would find one, and with it, mystery, wine, adventure. Elizabeth still loved those things. Just not as much as she used to. There were other things she loved more, and in different ways. And far more permanently.

It was 2019, and everyone was certain, or trying to be certain, that this latest orbit around the sun had changed everything. That this year would be different, that they would be different, that they *could* be different. Once that would've brought out the cynic in Elizabeth. Now she couldn't fault them. The last year *had* been different.

And not all good. The rest of winter had been, to turn a pun, frosty. If faking a relationship with Michelle hadn't ingratiated her to the Harlow clan, picking up with Anne had outright alienated them. Then there'd been the simple logistics. She lived in New York, Anne lived in Boston, so whenever she wanted to see her girlfriend, it was either a four-hour bus ride—an estimate that didn't take into account either traffic or New York drivers—or a flight that feasted on her wallet. And call her old-fashioned, but Elizabeth liked to do a little more for her dates than order pizza and cue up Netflix.

So for half the year, she'd spent her workdays feeling painfully millennial as she communicated with Anne over phone lines and Wi-Fi, and spent her weekends riding the bus up into Massachusetts and back again. She did, however, get a lot of reading done.

Eventually, Anne had managed to drag her back into the Harlow fold. Maybe it was that Michelle had made things right somehow. Maybe it was the springtime being too damn thematic for things not to thaw out. Or maybe Barry didn't want to wait for another holiday to sort it all out. But, starting with Grady—slightly more talkative now that his jaw had healed— she and Anne began to return for birthdays. By summer, Anne had agreed to move in. Even if, as she loved to point out, paying half the rent in New York cost more than all of her studio apartment in Boston.

It felt insane, contrasting that vague, ineffable time she'd cohabited with Michelle to living with Anne. Michelle was, at best, a roommate, and Anne was a *sun*. So much of the time, she was just light, and she never seemed to set before she was rising again. A summer day, that was Anne. Even when they argued, Anne was almost ridiculously passionate, launching her words with kung-fu gestures and a sense of drama that was almost operatic. But she was equally quick to forgive, touching Elizabeth like the mere thought of not doing so had been frightening for her. She'd make up with small, reassuring gestures. Like hanging off Elizabeth, pulling them back together. Even just scratching Elizabeth's back while she read. Reassuring herself that Elizabeth was still hers, no matter how angry either one of them got. Elizabeth knew because she liked to be held for the same reason.

For something that felt so indescribable, love was maddeningly, howlingly simple. They had a buddy system. With Anne, Elizabeth knew she had someone who would be there for her and understand her in a way that no one—not her family, not even Janet—ever had. There was someone when she came home from work. There was someone when she woke up. Whatever she was going through or doing or just *feeling*: there was Anne. That was all it was. A fucking amazing buddy system. A connection. A little family of two. It was there, in the tiniest looks, the smallest touches, and now she couldn't imagine her life without Anne.

Getting older, not getting old.

Anne took to New York like a duck to water, even if she missed the driving. Sometimes she got so zealous that Elizabeth felt like she was holding onto an overexcited dog, straining at the leash to pull her to the next new thing. A thought she was careful not to share with Wendy and Janet.

Anne found a part-time job at the make-up department in Macy's Herald Square to keep busy, and also managed a publishing deal for a book of make-up tips. Elizabeth made so many appearances on her YouTube channel, a willing victim for any new look Anne wanted to show off, that Anne's coming out became a simple matter of an impromptu recording session kiss that she couldn't bear to edit out.

Through Anne, Elizabeth became a sort of relief pitcher for the Harlow family. Things were still awkward with Michelle—Elizabeth thought they would always be awkward—but she supposed that was family for you. Whatever their misgivings, the course of the year had found the Harlows far too busy to keep her on the outside looking in. With the wonderful convenience of unspoken words, they'd slowly started treating her as if she had always been there.

Shane went on and off his meds a few more times, meeting with a therapist this week and vowing he didn't need one the next. Elizabeth could always tell when there'd been a blow-up with him, even if Anne sometimes didn't or couldn't talk about it. She'd come to bed all knotted up and *need* Elizabeth in a quiet, yearning way that broke Elizabeth's heart no matter how much she appreciated being the woman Anne went to.

By December, it had settled as much as Elizabeth thought it ever could. Shane was taking his pills, going to therapy, and had started a small detective agency with Typhos. The way he told it, there was nothing more to it than waiting for someone to do something stupid than taking pictures of it. Elizabeth privately thought it sounded like the setup for one hell of a buddy movie.

Grady still lived at home, making a modest wage from his woodworking, which he continued to enjoy. When Barry's health troubles grew into a heart scare, Grady took over as something of a nurse to his father—putting plans to get an apartment on hold and doing exercises with him. Anne was trying to get him to start a fitness vlog. With Shane on the mend, her latest project seemed to be taking Grady's Scrabble-champion vocabulary and putting it to work at actual social interaction.

Michelle's relationship with Deputy McQuarrie lasted no longer than her Buddhist monk look, but her divorce with Will dragged on and on. Typhos had been as good as his word and refused to come through with a smoking gun for Will, so Michelle just kept at it. She'd just about managed to convince the courts that she really was a lesbian whose ex-girlfriend had just happened to start dating her sister. Her latest attempt was holding a lesbian film festival on the cheap. She'd booked *Showgirls* as a depiction of some trope or another. It all made Elizabeth think that for some people, karma was its own reward. Mostly, she felt sorry for the lawyers.

Patsy graduated college with flying colors and a Marxist boyfriend no one could stand.

It was all a bit boring, stretched out over the months and then summed up in so many words. Her lasting impressions of family was that they were much like life as a soldier—months of boredom, followed by moments of sheer panic. And absolutely bearable so long as you had the right person at your side. Anne was most definitely the right person.

"I'm the rock girl. I know this stuff, okay?" She was hanging off Elizabeth's arm, as she had been since the Ball had dropped—before that, since Janet's party. As touristy as it was, Elizabeth couldn't deny her girl Times Square on New Year's. "The best rock and roll movie of all time is *Wild Zero*, because no other band...no other band fights zombies in their movie. If I get around to watching *A Hard Day's Night* and the Beatles fight zombies, I'll reevaluate it, but...the members of the band are named Guitar Wolf, Bass Wolf, and Drum Wolf. *Drum Wolf.* That's like the one drummer a girl would sleep with."

Anne was fantastically drunk, with a champagne bottle in her hand and 2019 sunglasses somewhere in the vicinity of her eyes, if not actually covering them. She had a hollow leg, but Elizabeth still kept a steadying hand on the small of her back as they went inside the apartment. Anne took advantage of the helping hand. She carefully missed Elizabeth's head with the bottle—if not her hair with sloshed champagne—as she threw an arm around Elizabeth's shoulders.

"Did you know there's a guitar..." Anne took a deep breath, contorting the letters on the Lifeguard shirt she was wearing. "*A guitar...with a sword inside?*"

"I may have to watch that with you. If there isn't, this is a fascinating look at how you think when you're drunk." Leaning Anne against the wall, Elizabeth stooped down to undo the straps on Anne's heels. It was a little like solving the Gordian Knot, if the Gordian Knot was below a cute dress and a very cute set of panties, but Elizabeth was too damn fashionable not to be able to figure it out.

In her other hand, Anne still held two champagne flutes looped through her fingers. She tried with the excessive care of the insufficiently sober to fill them. "Are you going to take my clothes off? Are you going to take me to bed? Are you going to ravish me?"

"Yes, yes, and maybe."

"Just so long as it's me you're ravishing. I don't want you ravishing anyone else. I'm the official person that you ravish."

"I think you've just shown how marriage was invented."

"Well, yeah," Anne said. "You can ravish me and only me forever. Just don't ravish anyone else. I'd have to move, you know. I live here."

Elizabeth rose and took Anne by the waist. "If you're asking me to marry you, you should sober up by at least fifty percent and give it three months after Janet and Wendy set a date. We don't want to look like we're copying them."

"Hey, I know there's a new Pope and everything. Still, I'm Catholic. I can be as gay as I want, but I need to get married. Which is why it's a good thing that you're an atheist, because it means you're not a Protestant. And you're probably going to spend some time with unbaptized babies when you die."

"Well, I worked in a daycare once. Not as bad as you might think." Elizabeth got up, took the glasses from Anne, and set them aside. "But still, maybe you could teach me a few Hail Marys."

Anne consented to being undressed as long as she was part of the same tangle of limbs as Elizabeth. Elizabeth got her bottoms off easily—experience—then ran into trouble getting the bottle away, but finally disarmed Anne and got her top off as well.

Anne was left more or less naked, bottomless but with her bra on, which Elizabeth couldn't consider sexual so much as…domestic. Anne had walked around the apartment like that more than once. She didn't need pants, but her breasts needed a bra. It made her grin. *I'm used to having this woman half-naked around me. Awesome.*

Anne looked out the window. The streets were still packed, the fireworks were still going off, and Anne still looked beautiful. Like she was one of those pale stars in the night sky, but only shining for Elizabeth.

Elizabeth went over to her and wrapped her arms around her and held her like she could *squeeze* just how much she loved her into Anne. "You know what?"

"My boobs are awesome?" Anne asked, admiring her reflection in the glass.

"Well, yeah. But I used to never know where I would ring in the New Year. At a ski lodge or on a yacht, or I'd just sleep through it with someone because I was, ah, retroactively making you jealous."

"I'm not the jealous type," Anne slurred. "But you've never done anything with your hot boss and her lady friend who wants to try everything she read in *Fifty Shades of Grey*, right?"

Elizabeth patted her. "No. But I was just thinking that for the first time, I'm going to end this year the exact same way I started it."

"Yeah?"

"Going to bed with you."

Anne's jaw dropped. "Are you asking me out?"

"Anne, we live together."

"Okay, but let me check my schedule…"

Elizabeth started dragging her toward the bedroom.

"I may have a pole-dancing class that day, for fitness, and also if Trump gets reelected and I need a job," Anne continued.

"I could always be your sugar daddy," Elizabeth said, giving her a shove through the door.

Anne pointed at her. "That's true. I'm going to practice calling you Daddy."

"I'm surprisingly okay with that."

Anne collapsed on the bed, upsetting a small furry lump. "And you remember how we agreed to dog-sit Limey?"

"Yeah," Elizabeth said. "I seem to recall a third living creature in this apartment."

"When we left he was sleeping in our bed and I think he's still here, and also I'm going to pass out. You can still ravish me if you want. I know you have needs."

Elizabeth tried not to feel jealous of the bull terrier licking Anne's face. "I think I'll just wait until we shower tomorrow morning. And my long lunch break at noon."

"Another date!" Anne clutched her heart. "I'm such a popular girl!"

"Yeah, everyone here's trying to steal you away from the dog." Elizabeth clapped her hands and gestured Limey off the bed. He jumped down.

"Lizzie, please. Dogs are like dry runs for having kids. Is this how you're going to treat our adopted Cambodian kids?"

"Fine," Elizabeth said, wiping Anne's face off with her sleeve as she climbed into bed beside her. "But if he starts humping your leg, tell him that's my job."

"So then we *are* engaged to be engaged to be…something."

Elizabeth fit herself to Anne's body and Anne fit herself to her, big spoon and little spoon, and a dog at the foot of the bed. And she would rather have cuddled half-drunk with Anne than ravish anyone else.

Maybe I am getting old, she thought. *But at least I'm getting old with her.*

"That's three dates you've got me down for," Elizabeth said, kissing Anne's hair where it was safely clear of doggy licks. "You really are a popular girl."

"Face it, Elizabeth. You won the lottery."

"Uh-huh. And what about you?"

"Me?" Anne went quiet, and Elizabeth leaned over to see her wearing a thoughtful expression. "I paid for one candy bar from a snack machine and it gave me two."

Elizabeth laughed, then proceeded to demonstrate why there were some things you just shouldn't say when there was a pillow within arm's reach.

About Georgette Kaplan

It was never easy for Georgette Kaplan. She was born a poor child in Mississippi, where she still remembers sitting on the porch with her family, singing and dancing around her. After learning she was adopted, at the age of 21 she hitchhiked to St. Louis, where she worked at a gas station and in a traveling carnival. After a shooting incident at the gas station, she decided to quit and pursue her lifelong dream of a career in writing. She now lives back in Mississippi with her life partner Marie.

CONNECT WITH GEORGETTE
Tumblr: georgettekaplan.tumblr.com
E-Mail: kaplangeorgette@gmail.com

Other Books from Ylva Publishing

www.ylva-publishing.com

Scissor Link
(The Scissor Link Series – Book 1)

Georgette Kaplan

ISBN: 978-3-95533-678-3
Length: 197 pages (72,000 words)

Wendy is in love with Janet Lace. Janet is beautiful, she's intelligent, and she is also Wendy's boss.

Still, a little fantasy never hurt anyone. Or so Wendy thought until Janet got a look at the e-mail she sent. The one about exactly what Wendy would like to do to Janet.

But when Wendy gets called into the boss's office, it might just be her fantasy coming true. If it doesn't get her fired first.

You're Fired

Shaya Crabtree

ISBN: 978-3-95533-754-4
Length: 193 pages (61,000 words)

When an inappropriate Secret Santa gift backfires, Rose needs her smarts to save her job, while Vivian, her sexy boss, needs her smarts to save the business. Can they stop bickering long enough to do a deal?

Who'd Have Thought

G Benson

ISBN: 978-3-95533-874-9
Length: 339 pages (122,000 words)

When Hayden Pérez stumbles across an offer to marry Samantha Thomson—a cold, rude, and complicated neurosurgeon—for $200,000, what's a cash-strapped ER nurse to do? Sure, Hayden has to convince everyone around them they're madly in love, but it's only for a year, right? What could possibly go wrong?

The Brutal Truth

Lee Winter

ISBN: 978-3-95533-898-5
Length: 339 pages (108,000 words)

Aussie crime reporter Maddie Grey is out of her depth in New York and secretly drawn to her twice-married, powerful media mogul boss, Elena Bartell, who eats failing newspapers for breakfast. As work takes them to Australia, Maddie is goaded into a brief bet—that they will say only the truth to each other. It backfires catastrophically. A lesbian romance about the lies we tell ourselves.

Coming from Ylva Publishing

www.ylva-publishing.com

Up on the Roof

A.L. Brooks

When a storm wreaks havoc on bookish Lena's well-ordered world, her laid-back new neighbor, Megan, offers her a room. The trouble is they've been clashing since the day they met. How can they now live under the same roof? Making it worse is the inexplicable pull between them that seems hard to resist. A fun, awkward, and sweet British romance about the power of opposites attracting.

Chasing Stars

Alex K. Thorne

For superhero Swiftwing, crime fighting isn't her biggest battle. Nor is it having to meet the whims of Hollywood star Gwen Knight as her mild-mannered assistant, Ava. It's doing all that, while tracking a giant alien bug, being asked to fake date her famous boss, and realizing that she might be coming down with a pesky case of feelings. A fun, sweet, sexy lesbian romance about the masks we wear.

Face It
© 2018 by Georgette Kaplan

ISBN: 978-3-95533-976-0

Also available as e-book.

Published by Ylva Publishing, legal entity of Ylva Verlag, e.Kfr.

Ylva Verlag, e.Kfr.
Owner: Astrid Ohletz
Am Kirschgarten 2
65830 Kriftel
Germany

www.ylva-publishing.com

First edition: 2018

Credits
Edited by Gill McKnight, Allissa McGowan, and Amanda Jean
Proofread by Paulette Callen
Cover Design and Print Layout by Streetlight Graphics

www.ingramcontent.com/pod-product-compliance
Lightning Source LLC
Chambersburg PA
CBHW030324020726
47493CB00004B/1146